THE CAREER OF DAVID NOBLE

Novels by
Frances Parkinson Keyes

THE ROYAL BOX
LARRY VINCENT
STEAMBOAT GOTHIC
JOY STREET
DINNER AT ANTOINE'S
VAIL D'ALVERY
THE RIVER ROAD
ALSO THE HILLS
IF EVER I CEASE TO LOVE
ALL THAT GLITTERS
FIELDING'S FOLLY
THE GREAT TRADITION
THE AMBASSADRESS
HONOR BRIGHT
THE SAFE BRIDGE
CHRISTIAN MARLOWE'S DAUGHTER
LADY BLANCHE FARM
QUEEN ANNE'S LACE
THE CAREER OF DAVID NOBLE

FRANCES PARKINSON KEYES

The Career of
David Noble

EYRE & SPOTTISWOODE

LONDON

First impression 1941
Second impression 1941
Third impression 1942
Fourth impression 1955

To

HENRY WILDER KEYES

whose career, from Selectman of Haverhill, New Hampshire, to United States Senator from New Hampshire, has been a source of great pride and deep joy to those who know him, but most of all to his wife, this story of a New England boy is dedicated with much love.

This book is printed in Great Britain for Eyre & Spottiswoode (Publishers) Limited, 15 Bedford Street, London, W.C.2, by Billing and Sons Ltd., Guildford and London
G8394

Contents

PART ONE

PART TWO

PART THREE

PART ONE

CHAPTER I

IN WHICH TWO FAMILIES DECIDE TO MOVE TO HAMSTEAD

It was a raw, cold night, as March nights are apt to be in Vermont, the snow piled in great drifts about the house and along the silent road, the wind blowing fiercely from the south—that cold south wind which portends to any intelligent Vermonter at that time of year a thaw, followed, if the Fates are propitious, by " a sugar snow," and then by " mud-time." The kind of night, in short, which makes you glad that winter is almost over, and at the same time gives you a feeling of dread for the disagreeable season that still lies between you and real spring weather.

Hiram Noble, who had driven ten miles over the hills to Hamstead that afternoon, banged the kitchen door behind him with a sense of weary satisfaction, and threw a number of packages done up in pink paper on the table that stood near it. The kitchen was not cold. On the contrary, the thermometer, had there been such an unnecessary luxury in the Noble establishment, would certainly have registered eighty-five. On the whole, the scene was one of comfort and good cheer. Mrs. Noble, dressed in a grey calico overall, partially covered by an apron of brown print, stood by the red-hot stove, frying potatoes and salt pork, which gave forth sharp, hissing sounds, and smelled most fragrantly. The larger kitchen table, covered, like the one near the door, with a red tablecloth, was already set with the remainder of the evening meal—a great plate of bread, a smaller one of cake, a dish of maple syrup and another of pickles. In the further corner of the room, around a lamp with a purple shade set upon an old-fashioned desk, sat four boys, the eldest apparently about fourteen, the youngest seven or eight, who were alternately studying and quarrelling; while near the stove, her attention about equally divided between a doughnut and a rubber comforter, was a baby girl in a high-chair.

Mrs. Noble shoved back her frying-pan, and turned to greet her husband with characteristic New England demonstration.

"Wal, here ye be at last," she said, wiping her hands on her apron. "I'd about decided you wuz a-goin' to spend the night in the pool-room, or some sech den of iniquity. Did you get all them things I told ye to? I s'pose likely you forgot more'n half! Leon, don't you touch them pickles! You wait for the rest to git to the table, and then take your proper share. There now! You've et up most of what I had laid out already! Sam, pull up the baby. I don't s'pose David wants any supper—he can go right on readin'—he won't be missed none."

The various individuals thus pleasantly addressed responded promptly. Leon, the boy of eight, swallowed the last offending pickle hurriedly, and without answering. Sam shoved his slate aside, walked over to the baby, and, removing the comforter and doughnut stub with a tactfulness which plainly showed that he was used to much dealing with infants, put her at her proper place at the family board. David, the eldest boy, glanced up, and still holding his finger in his book, reluctantly moved towards the table; while Mr. Noble, deep in ablutions from the tin basin in the sink, was the only one that replied.

"Left Hamstead at four o'clock," he said, "an' the pool-room ain't open until seven. I wouldn't ha' been so long if you hadn't given me so many fool errands to do. Land! When do you think Susie's goin' to wear out all them clothes? I notice you didn't send for nothin' for the boys."

"The boys didn't need nothin'," said his wife, sharply. "Here, Harry, wake up! Is that the way you do your sums? You won't get through grammar school at this rate."

"There you go again," said Hiram good-naturedly, "always scoldin' Harry because book-learnin' don't seem to come just natural to him, good boy as he is at his chores and around the farm. And forever lightin' into David because he won't do nothin' much *but* read and study, when he's at the head of his class, and always has ben. What you got there now, David?"

"It's some plays," replied the boy, looking up with glow-

8

ing eyes, "written by a man named Shakespeare. There's a story of his life in the front of the book. He lived in England ever so long ago, in a little place no bigger than Wallacetown, but he went away from there to London, and—Oh, they're great! Do you suppose they're ever acted at any of the entertainments down in Hamstead? I wish——"

"And I wish," interrupted his mother, "that you'd fill the wood-box a little more regular, and not waste your time on such trash. Plays! I don't see where you ever got such notions! I'm sure all my family is respectable, God-fearin' people, that has nothin' to do with Shakespeare and sech. You must get your taste from your father's folks. Them plays is immoral as can be, like as not!"

"They're ever so much more respectable than the Old Testament," retorted the boy, "and you don't mind hear-in' that read, right out in meetin', if you don't ever read a word of anything yourself. No, Susie, you can't have that book to tear up."

"'Twould be the best use 'twas ever put to if she did," said his mother, "but then you don't care nothin' about pleasin' her, and never did—and she the only girl I've got left, out of three, with all you boys livin' right on and thrivin' and eatin' your heads off, let alone bein' pert and lazy."

"There, there," interposed Hiram again, soothingly, "don't sass your ma, David, and don't rub the boy the wrong way all the time, Lizzie. I heard a great piece of news down to Hamstead to-day. What do you s'pose it was?"

"Nothin' good, I'll be bound," said Mrs. Noble. "I knew perfectly well you wasn't doin' errands all that time. Standin' around the air-tight in the post-office gossipin'! No, Leon, you can't have any more syrup—you are the greediest boy I ever see."

"Well, 'tain't bad news, anyway," went on her husband. "Do you remember the Huntington family, Lizzie?"

"Do I? Do I remember that gamblin', drinkin', young reprobate and his high and mighty old pa that treated every one as if they wasn't good enough to lick the blackin' off his boots? I should say I do!"

"Come, Lizzie, they wasn't so bad as all that. Hal Huntington was what you might call a little lively, but he was always awfully generous and good-hearted, and I liked him. We was about the same age, you know, and I used to see quite a lot of him, when he used to come up here summers from Boston. There warn't nothin' high and mighty about *him*. He was friends with everybody, even if he did get all the boys in the village into scrapes. You wouldn't remember that as well as I do, bein' a little older."

"All the *boys*! How about all the *girls*!" cried Mrs. Noble with unmistakable meaning, wiping the baby's mouth and taking her in her lap. "Lucky for me I *was* older. You needn't always be flingin' that in my face, neither. There ain't but four years difference between us, and I don't know where you'd ha' been to-day, if you hadn't had a good prudent wife to look after you, shiftless like you've always ben. Wal, whatever become of Hal Huntington? Nothin' good, I'll warrant."

"Wal, you know old Huntington allus thought the sun rose and set on Hal's head," went on Hiram. "'Twarn't but natural, being all he had in the world. Hal went to Harvard College, down to Cambridge, Mass., and wuz invited to leave before he wuz really quite due to be through. So he and his father went to Europe, and I never heard from that day to this what happened to 'em after that."

"What did?" asked Mrs. Noble, trying to suppress the eagerness in her voice, and wondering how she would ever be able to wait until the next meeting of the Ladies' Aid to pass along this thrilling story.

"They went to Paris," said her husband, in much the same tone that a clergyman of the old school used in speaking of the infernal regions, "and Hal fooled 'round for a spell, enjoyin' himself like he always did. Then he took-up kinder pointed with a French actress, the kind that's called a *ballet* dancer, that wears pink tights, and awful short petticoats."

"Don' speak of such things too loud before the boys," admonished his wife. "I told you nothin' good would ever come of him. What next?"

"He took sick with typhoid fever, and when the doctor

told him right out plain there warn't any hope for him, he sent for the girl and married her. His father came into Hal's room and found her settin' by the bed, dressed jest like any other woman, and Hal says, ' This is my wife.' "

"Hiram Noble! You're makin' this up!"

"Land! You don't suppose I've got brains enough to make up an unlikely story like this, do you? Wal, the old man swore something awful, and vowed there weren't a word of truth in it and all that. But Hal told his father he was dying and that they wuz married fast enough by the American minister, but the girl bein' a Catholic, wanted to get his consent, so they could be married over again by a priest, and accordin' to French law—it seems you can't do that way without the parents is willin'. Then he told the old man why they'd got to be good to her—Hal warn't all bad, Lizzie. And Mr. Huntington see that he wuz dying sure enough, and he promised to see that she was looked after all right, finally, and give in about them havin' another ceremony, too.

"He didn't see her again for some months after the funeral. Then she sent for him. She wuz livin' in a place called Fontainebleau that ain't far from Paris. He'd kept track of her actions, and had had his lawyer send her enough money to live on. Well, he went, when he got her message and wuz met at the door by one of them Catholic women called nuns, or sisters, or somethin' of the sort, and she told him that Hal's widow couldn't live 'til mornin', and that there was a baby girl a few days old. I guess there must have ben some good in the girl, and she was pretty, and she was dyin', and Mr. Huntington promised her he would take the baby, and bring her up a lady.

"He never felt much like going back to Boston; so he's ben wanderin' around Europe all these years. Now he's gettin' old, and he's tired of that—wants to settle down, so he's comin' to Hamstead to live—not just summers, but all the year round. The old house is bein' fixed up for him —land, you never see such goin's on!"

"What they doin' to it? I should think 'twas good enough for any one, the way 'twas—the best in the country, now that the old Gray place has got so awful run down."

"Wal, 'twarn't good enough for him. I went all over it this afternoon with his confidential agent—the same as told me this yarn," said Hiram with a chuckle. "Sunday I'm a-going to get out the carry-all and hitch up, and take you in to see it, too, Lizzie. My, but it's tasty! There's a steam-heat furnace, and hard-wood floors everywhere, and four bath-rooms. Sol Daniels is paintin' with three men to help him, and Tony Smith is buildin' a new piazza for the help. It's rumoured 'round some that they're going to have one of them new machines called an otter*mobile, but I guess there ain't no truth in that. The stable's bein' fixed up for three horses, though, and there's a pony for the little girl, too. She's most twelve years old now, and pretty as a picture, they say, with a heathenish foreign name that nobody can't pronounce."

"She'll grow up a lost creature, like as not, with such a father and mother," said his wife cheerfully, rising from the table with Susie, who had gone to sleep with her thumb in her mouth. "Boys, clear off the table and wash up the dishes, while I put the baby to bed."

"'Twon't take you long to lay her in her cradle—she's asleep already," muttered David. "Father, are they awful rich?"

"Who, the Huntingtons? Lord, yes, I s'pose there wouldn't be no countin' their money, there's so much of it!"

"I s'pose the little girl has all the books she wants to read, don't you? I s'pose she can go to High School in Hamstead, and to the University of Vermont afterwards, don't you?"

"Like as not. I did hear she had a French woman called a governor—no, that warn't just the word, but 'twas something like that—to teach her, but of course it ain't to be expected that she gets much of an education that way."

Mr. Noble lighted his pipe, put his feet in the oven, and unfolded his favourite periodical, the *Rural Outlook*. Mrs. Noble remained in the bedroom that led out of the kitchen with the baby. David buried himself in his book again, and the three younger boys, after remarking scornfully that they would rather get along without his help than having him "bossin' round," washed and wiped the dishes,

12

set the table for breakfast and swept up the kitchen, then went upstairs to bed. He read on, undisturbed, his cheeks growing brighter, his lips parted with excitement, until finally, conscious that some one was watching him, he started up, to see his father standing beside him with an unusual expression on his face.

"Dave," he began haltingly, and stopped, visibly embarrassed. "Dave——"

"Yes, Dad—I forgot about the wood—honest, I did—I didn't leave it a-purpose. I'll get it now."

"I warn't thinkin' about the wood," said Hiram Noble. "Set where you be a minute. You're a good boy, and I hate to see your ma so down on you. You ain't as handy about the farm as some, but once you make up your mind to a thing, you hang to it like grim death, and you work real hard—and I swear you're awful smart at your books. What you want to be when you're grown up—a farmer?"

"I s'pose of course I have to be," the boy muttered sullenly. Then without warning, the smothered resentment of years broke out. "But I hate it! Loathe it! Maybe if we'd had one of them nice valley farms down by the river, it wouldn't be so bad. That's good fertile land, and there's schools around, and—and shows once in a while; but here, out back—what's a fellow got ahead of him but ploughin' up rocks all his life, and tryin' to get a livin' off 'em? What chance has he ever got to *learn* anything?"

"Now, Dave, it ain't fitten to speak ill of your own home——"

"You asked me. I've *tried* to like it, honest, I have, Dad, and the other boys do; but if I could only get away——"

The boy drew a long breath. Looking at him, his father was surprised to see that his eyes were full of rebellious and angry tears.

"Well, s'posin' you could?" he said, hardly less excited than David himself.

"I'd clear out so quick you couldn't see me for the dust. And I'd learn to be a doctor—the kind that cuts people up and sews 'em up again—a surgeon. And I'd have an otter-*mo*bile—I've bin readin' about 'em in a magazine that I picked up in the road—some one must have dropped it out

13

of a team. And a whole houseful of books. And—and everything," he ended weakly.

"Wal——" said his father slowly, "I don't know but what you would, give you half a chance. What do you think would be the first step to take to get all them little fixin's?"

"To go to High School in Hamstead," replied the boy promptly.

"Wal, Dave," Mr. Noble spoke slowly, but his voice quivered with emotion. "Wal, Dave—set down and listen to me. The Huntington family ain't the only one that's a-goin' to move into Hamstead. The Noble family's a-goin' too, and you kin go to High School."

Shakespeare slid to the floor, and lay there, disregarded. David fairly sprang at his father.

"You're joking," he gasped. "Oh, what'll mother say?"

Hiram cast an uneasy glance in the direction of the bedroom, and lowered his voice, but he spoke none the less firmly for all that. "She won't say nothing about it," he declared softly, but decisively. "Your ma's a good woman, but she's ben sayin' for a spell of about sixteen years, and I reckon it's time for me to do a little talkin' myself. Anyway, it won't do her no good if she does make a fuss now. I've sold my farm to a fool from New York who wants to come into the country to lead the simple life, and I've bought Daniel's house right next to the post-office. I've ben savin' quite a little money sence you boys got big enough to help me, and I ain't had to have no hired man; and I've got about three times what this place is worth from that crazy dude, on account of the view. I guess he'll find views ain't real nourishin', if he ever gets down to hard tacks. I've taken my turn ploughin' up stones, just as you say, and my father and grandfather before me—now I want you should do somethin' else if you kin, and I kinder think you kin. You kin go to High School anyway, and the other boys too, when they get big enough. I'm kinder hopin' to get an appointment for postmaster. That would tickle your ma—she could help out there and get a chance to see what mail every one in town had. Jake French don't care to have it again on account of his liver trouble, and he

14

said he'd like real well to have me get it, so I know he'll use his influence for me, and he's got considerable. And maybe, if you're smart and hire out regular for chores round, in school time, and work out at something summers, I wouldn't be a mite surprised if you could lay by enough to go to the University of Vermont by and by and learn to be a doctor."

CHAPTER II

JACQUELINE DÉSIRÉE

It was a stifling hot afternoon in mid-July, but a slight breeze stirred the leaves of the willow-trees along the river bank, the swift current made cool rushing sounds, and the shadows grew long in the late afternoon sun. David Noble, stretched at full length in the shade, threw his arms over his head and shut his eyes. His hair was wet from a swim in the river, and lay close and thick about his thin tanned face; his bare feet and legs shone golden brown; as to his costume, few words suffice to describe it, for it consisted solely of a calico shirt, and a pair of shabby trousers.

He had been to church that morning, not because he wanted to—for indeed, there was nothing in the bare, close building or the gaunt unloving minister which could possibly attract the boy—but after the manner of New England children, because he was expected or forced to go. The minister and his wife had come to dinner afterwards. It was the first time the Nobles had had company since they moved to Hamstead, six weeks earlier, for Mrs. Noble entertained, after the manner of the New England housewife of her time and station, seldom and profusely. In fact, the dinner left nothing to be desired. There were fricasseed chicken and mashed potatoes, and the first green peas from the garden, there were currant jelly, and sweet pickles and hot biscuit; there were custard pie and vanilla ice-cream and three kinds of cake; there were coffee and molasses candy. But afterwards, when they had sat in the parlour—which had been opened for the occasion, but still suggested funerals rather than sociability—in uncomfortable state for over an hour, David watched his chance and slipped from the room, beckoning Sam after him.

"If you'll do my chores tonight," he whispered, "I'll give you a dime. I'm goin' down to the river—goin' in swimmin'."

"But it's Sunday," Sam whispered back in amazement.

"I don't care if 'tis—I'm just as hot as if 'twas Monday. I'm going to change my clothes, and take that book I got outter the liberry yesterday, and skin outter the back door. Don't you tell until it's too late to get holt to me, and I'll give you the dime tomorrow mornin'. See?" And Sam saw.

David had been by the river now for almost two hours, reading in undisturbed bliss, and swimming to his heart's content. He was growing drowsy. In another five minutes he would have been fast asleep, when suddenly the sound of a singing voice, growing nearer and nearer, made him sit up, rubbing his eyes and listening intently.

It was a child's voice, very sweet and clear, but he was greatly puzzled by the fact that distinctly as each syllable seemed to be pronounced, he could not understand a single word of it; neither did it sound in the least like a hymn, the only kind of song he had ever heard on Sunday. It was half gay and half sad and altogether teasing. He jumped to his feet and looked around him, then stood staring with his mouth wide open, first in surprise and then in reluctant fascination.

Half a dozen rods away was a little girl, coming nearer and nearer, singing, and dancing as she sang. She was so light, so exquisitely rapid and graceful in every movement, that she seemed hardly to touch the ground. David had never seen anything like her before. She had on a very full white dress, which reached scarcely to her knees, leaving her legs quite bare except for short white socks and bronze ankle-ties. There was a great pink bow on the top of her head, and her hair, shining in the sun, fell around her rosy face in a mass of brown curls. He held his breath, involuntarily taking a step nearer her. This was the first vision of loveliness and charm which his barren life had held. Suddenly she caught sight of the boy, waved her hand as if in welcome, and when she was quite close to him stopped dancing and singing, and gave him a friendly smile.

"Hello," she said pleasantly.

"Hello," muttered David, watching her furtively. Now that she no longer danced and sang, the spell was broken; he was ashamed of having been so swayed by something he did not understand, and was not at all sure that he admired her, after all.

"It's a nice day, isn't it?" she went on with persistent amiability.

"Kinder hot," vouchsafed David grudgingly.

"Yes, but it's lovely here. Grandfather went to sleep after dinner, and Mademoiselle was in her room, so I ran away. I came down a lane that leads right back of our house. I think I'll come quite often after this, it's so cool and pleasant."

David made no answer. If the child beside him felt no embarrassment, as was quite evident, he was shy enough for two. Never had he seen a little girl who talked and acted like this one. He stood twisting his bare toe until it made a hole in the ground, regarding her sidewise, suspiciously. Apparently oblivious of his lack of cordiality, she sat down on the grass near him, her white skirts spreading out like a fan around her, and picked up the book he had been reading.

"'The Last of the Mohicans,'" she exclaimed. "Oh, isn't it splendid? Grandfather's just finished reading it to me. How far are you?"

"Not very far."

"You're rather hard to talk to, aren't you?" said the little girl cheerfully. "Are you always this way? If you are, you ought to practise, by yourself, I mean, and look straight at any one, too, when you're speaking—grandfather says that's very important. Where do you live? How old are you? What's your name?"

David, crimson with bashfulness and resentment, but stung by her remark about practising, sat down beside her.

"I've always lived out back——"

"Out——? Excuse me."

"Back—over the hills. West Hamstead, you know. But now I live in Hamstead. My name's David Noble, and I'm fourteen."

"I live in Hamstead too, now. I've always lived in Paris before this. Except sometimes, this last year or two, grandfather's taken me on trips to Italy and Switzerland in the summer-time. I'm eleven. I just had a birthday. This locket was my birthday present. It has pictures of my father and mother inside. My name's Jacqueline Désirée Huntington—why, what's the matter?"

A sudden light broke upon David. He looked her full in the face at last, overcome with excitement.

"Are you the little girl who lives in the Big House with dozens of servants and hundreds of books?" he cried, "whose father——" he stopped, abruptly.

"What about my father?" she asked quickly, as if thirsty for information. "He died ever so long ago—before I was born."

David's training along lines of tactfulness had been limited, to say the least. He had no wish to hurt the friendly child's feelings, and he knew that he had made a stupid break, that there was little good that he could say of either of her parents.

"My father used to know him when they was both boys," he said, awkwardly. "He used to come up here in the summer-time. They went fishin' and swimmin' together. And dad says he was—real kind and generous."

Désirée's eyes shone with pleasure. "I'm awfully glad I found you," she said. "It's hard to get any one to talk about him. Grandfather doesn't like to, he still feels so badly because he died. This is the first time I've ever had a picture of him—or my mother. It's lonely here, after Paris. I haven't had a soul—a young soul, I mean—to speak to since I left the convent."

"The what?"

"The convent—where I went to school, you know."

"Are you a Catholic?"

If he had asked her if she were a leper, his tone could hardly have conveyed more horror. He drew his clean bare legs further away from possible contact with her frilly skirts.

"Do you—mind?" she asked wistfully. Her voice sank, the fresh gaiety gone from it. "Grandfather minds too, but he tries not to let me see. He promised my mother, before she died, that I should be one, you see. She wanted me to be. I don't understand why any one should—think it's queer. I was awfully happy with the Sisters, and I miss it all so much—the incense and the music and the stained-glass windows, and that feeling of being all good and happy, the minute you get inside the chapel and hear the organ playing. We took turns, helping with the altar flowers—and at Christmas time there was always the crèche, and the Holy Child in it, and we stayed up for midnight mass. I made my first Communion before I left —I'm glad of that. But I'm sorry not to please grand-father. It's hard, isn't it, when the things you love best don't please some one you care for?"

A thousand conflicting thoughts were racing through David's bewildered brain. Was it possible there were Catholics in the world who were *good*? That there were children who *loved* to go to church, and grieved because they were deprived of doing so? Half of the little girl's words were incomprehensible to him, but her feeling was clear enough. Hamstead, the Mecca of his dreams, repre-sented Egyptian exile to her.

"What do you *do* all the time here?" she went on bravely after a minute. "Besides being no churches—real churches, I mean—there are no shops, and no parks, and no theatres, and no *people*. Nothing but grass and trees!"

He laughed, a little bitterly. "If you'd ben fetched up out back instead of to Paris," he said, not unkindly, "you'd think this was quite a place. It looks awful good to me. When I get a chance I read; but mostly I do chores for people—weed gardens, and drive cows, and milk 'em after-wards. Now that hayin's come, I hope I can get some money ridin' the rake. I'm trying to earn enough money to go to the University of Vermont by and by and learn to be a doctor—I'm going to, too!"

He spoke with a sort of savage superiority. Poor and ragged and ignorant though he knew himself to be, he felt vastly superior to this little French "heathen" with her changing moods, her quick gestures and many questions, and her self-assurance. Suddenly it occurred to him, that in spite of the fact that she was so generally unsatisfactory, she might be a means to an end. He jerked out an embarrassed query.

"Say—your grandfather don't want any extra help, does he?"

"Help—about what?"

"Some one to work. You don't s'pose he'd let me come and live at his house and do odd jobs after school hours—and read his books, do you?"

Jacqueline shook her head. "I'll lend you all the books you want," she said, "but I don't believe he needs any more servants. I'd love to have you come though—come back to supper with me, and we'll ask him." Then noting his look of dismay at the mere suggestion, "Oh, do! I'm so lonely, I shall die here pretty soon! And I've got a big box of chocolates that have just come from Maillard's—and—and there's a skeleton—a real live skeleton—I mean a real dead one—well, anyway, a *bone* skeleton up in the attic. I'll show him to you."

David's face kindled. "Mother'd lick me good," he said thoughtfully, "if I went anywheres on Sunday—barefoot, too. But—a big one, is it?" he wavered, and Jacqueline, with the precocious instinct of her sex, saw it—knew too, that he longed to go, not to comfort her loneliness, but for the sake of the possible "job," and the certain cheer of chocolates and skeleton. It caused her a slight pang; nevertheless, like Eve, she held out her apple bravely.

"Oh, yes—an awfully big one," she murmured, and she began to hum again, that little tilting, merry song, with the words that David could not understand, as she turned and danced away from him, looking back to wave her hand, and smile over her shoulder.

Without another word he followed her.

CHAPTER III

IN WHICH TWO FAMILIES ARE INSULTED

"You've brought a friend home to supper, Désirée? I didn't know you had made friends here—in fact, I fear there are no suitable playmates for you in this place."

The man laid down the book he was reading, and drew the breathless child on his knees, smoothing back her mass of curls, and kissing her flushed little face. His own seemed as finely tempered, as clear-cut, and as cold as a steel rapier, but it softened slightly as she threw her arms around his neck.

"Well, he's not a very old friend. I ran away after dinner——"

"We hunted everywhere for you—you have given us a most anxious afternoon. Promise me you'll never do it again, my dear."

"Well, we'll talk about that later," she said, settling herself comfortably on his lap and kissing his nose. "I found a lovely lane leading to the meadow, behind the big barns, and I walked down it to the river. It's beautiful down there. And I found a boy."

"Jacqueline——" The little girl had no way of guessing the bitter memories and still more bitter dread for the future which her impulsiveness stirred in the man. Where was heredity to lead this gay and wayward little dancer who had become so unspeakably precious to him? His one instinct was to cage her, above all to keep her to himself. She rippled on, either ignoring the anxious severity of his face, or unconscious of it.

"His name's David Noble—and oh, grandfather, he says his daddy used to go fishing with mine. He has awfully bad manners, and dirty finger nails, and he's barefoot, but somehow I like him. He wants to be a doctor some day, and is trying to find some kind of horrid work he calls 'chores' so that he can earn enough money. He asked me if you needed any more help. I was surprised because I thought *he* needed the help, and I do so want to give it to him! He's waiting out in the hall until I say David. I'm going to say it now—David."

If Jacqueline had given the boy a new vision of femininity, no less did this wonderful house give him a new ideal of a dwelling place. The hall in which he stood waiting was wainscoted in mahogany, there were thick soft rugs in rich colours on the polished floors, and draperies at doors and windows even softer and richer; paintings in heavy gold frames hung on the walls, and there were ornaments of burnished copper on either side of a great gilt clock which stood on the mantel-piece; through an open door he could see into a white panelled dining-room, with sideboards laden with silver and crystal; a man-servant, dressed in livery, was laying a fine embroidered cloth, edged with lace, on the large round table in the middle of the room, and putting a bowl of crimson roses in the centre of it. On the stair-landing, against a red velvet curtain, stood the gleaming white statue of a beautiful, undraped woman. Through the dazed bewilderment of David's brain, a new determination took shape.

"And when I get to be a doctor," he promised himself, "I'll have a house just like this—only much handsomer."

When Jacqueline called, he started, and pushing aside the brocaded portière, entered the library. The dream of the future was rudely shattered by the agonizing reality of the present. He took a few steps forward, then stopped abruptly, his shabby cap in his hand, his head hanging; he could feel the redness of his cheeks, the length and bareness of his legs, the raggedness of his clothes, with a consciousness that was painful to a degree of torture. But for the sake of plenty of books, the sight of a real skeleton, and even the possibility of a "steady job" he was prepared to suffer much.

Mr. Huntington's greeting was hardly of the nature to be reassuring. He swept the boy from head to foot with a glance that pierced through him like a March wind, and spoke in a voice as cold and cutting as the thin March ice that gathers so quickly towards evening on the little pools of water bravely melting in the brief sunshine of a March day.

"Miss Huntington," he said, "has no authority to engage my servants for me. When I require them, I select them from reliable sources, I do not pick them up from the highways and byways. Moreover, my present needs are quite filled. Neither has Miss Huntington the age nor the discretion to select her own companions, and the fact that your father and hers—if it is a fact—were acquainted does not interest me. My son was not always fortunate in his choice of friends. I shall endeavour to assure myself that his daughter does not consort with tramps and beggars."

"Grandfather!" cried Jacqueline passionately, but David interrupted her. He pushed her aside, and strode forward, his hot, bashful face raised as if by magic, his voice blazing with anger.

"I ain't a tramp or a beggar," he cried. "I didn't ask to come to your house—I come because she plagued me so I couldn't get out of it. But I'm ten times as respectable as she is—I ain't got a drunkard for a father nor a cheap actress who had to be married out of pity for a mother, neither. I'll never set foot in here again, not if it was to save your life nor hers—they ain't worth it."

He plunged out of the room and through the front door, slamming it after him; but Jacqueline, too quick for her grandfather, was beside him before he reached the walk. She caught hold of his arm.

"Grandfather wasn't fair," she cried. "You needn't ever come there again, until he takes back all the hateful things he said. But you shall have the books just the same—I'll bring them down to the river—and the skeleton too, if I can manage. But tell me—whose father was a drunkard, and whose mother was an actress? Don't people get married because they love each other? David—you're not angry with me, are you?"

He did not answer her, but shaking her off roughly, started down the dusty street on a dead run. She could easily have caught up with him; but her wounded pride, and her bruised and bewildered mind, drove her back to the house. She flung herself into her grandfather's arms in a torrent of rage and tears. Before she would be pacified, he was obliged to tell her, for the first time, something of her parentage, to promise her a certain amount of freedom of movement, and to pour such other balm as he could on her outraged little heart, himself furious with resentment that his own hasty speech had indirectly brought about such a necessity.

As to David's parents, their anger knew no bounds, when the boy, too enraged and insulted to maintain his customary reticence, hurled out the story of his afternoon; and it would be difficult to tell which of the two families went to bed that night with the bitterer feelings against the other.

23

CHAPTER IV

THE FIRST RUNG OF THE LADDER

DAVID kept his word rather better than most people do; for it was nearly five years before he entered Mr. Huntington's house again.

Jacqueline kept her word a great deal better than most people do; she managed not only to take the books but the skeleton down to the river, and after going there on three successive afternoons without finding David, she went to his father's house.

Mrs. Noble opened the door in response to her gentle rap, and looked out at her through the narrow crack with sour disapproval.

"You kin run right along," she said sharply, "whether you're sellin' soap for a premium or solicitin' for a fair, it's all the same to me; I ain't got no time to trifle away with you."

"I don't understand," said the child, much puzzled, "I'm Jacqueline Huntington, and I've come to see David. I've brought him the books I promised him, and when he's read these, I'll bring some more."

"Well, if you're Jackaleen Huntington, I certainly shan't let you in," was the furious answer. "David's a perfectly decent, self-respectin' boy, and it won't do you no good to run after him and try to pervert him, you little furrin' heathen!" and the door slammed in the little girl's face.

Mrs. Noble happened to be in a frame of mind compared with which her usual acidity was sweet indeed. It is a mistake to overestimate the feeling of democracy in small villages, and she had that afternoon been mercilessly snubbed at a meeting of the Ladies' Aid, by Miss Manning, one of Hamstead's aristocrats. Of course the family at the Big House "didn't count"—they were simply "summer people" and Hamstead never "called" unless it wanted a subscription to Foreign Missions or a contribution to the Annual Church Supper, or something of that nature. But the Mannings and the Grays and the Elliotts and the Westons—the families, in short, whose ancestors had founded the village and those about it, and had lived there, in the same houses which their great-grandfathers had built, ever since—were apt to look down on new-comers, especially if they came from " out back " with a superiority such as Boston itself feels over its humbler suburbs. It did not matter that Miss Manning was so homely and so " peppery " that no man had been known to " keep company " with her; that the Grays were as poor as church mice, and their handsome son, Austin, was " wild as a hawk "; that Mrs. Elliott was a tireless gossip, and that the Westons, father and son, drank too much—any more than the same failings would have mattered on the Back Bay—where, as a matter of fact, they exist quite as frequently. These same persons had their good qualities too. Miss Manning was generous to the point of bounty, Austin had a wonderful mind, the Westons had dispositions like sunshine. They formed the society of Hamstead, and the rest of the village recognized it. So, when Mrs. Noble and Miss Manning disagreed as to the number of eggs that should go into an angel cake, the Ladies' Aid promptly and unanimously sided with Miss Manning, though she was but an indifferent cook, and Mrs. Noble an unusually good one. Even through the long shut-in winters in the little cottage at West Hamstead, when most women would have found it well-nigh impossible to set a good table, Hiram's family was remarkably well-fed. This undeserved slight was too much for human nature to stand.

" I never used more'n eight eggs in my life and I never had one fall yet. I've heard the remark passed lots of times that no one had such luck with angel cakes as I have."

" Well, some women do well that way, but I was brought up to use the best of everything, and plenty of it. (Pass me the bastin' thread, will you, Mis' Gray? Does that hem look even to you?) I wouldn't dream of greasin' the pan with anything except butter, either."

" I don't grease my pan at all, and I don't have a mite of trouble with its stickin'. To my way of thinkin', a good cook can manage with a few things a sight better than a poor one can just by bein' extravagant. Don't you think so, Mis' Gray?"

"Land! It's so long since I've felt I could afford one at all, I've forgotten how I used to do. But Miss Manning always sets an elegant table. You'll say so yourself, when you've been here a little longer, Mis' Noble."

"We all know what Miss Manning's tea-parties are like," said Mrs. Elliott with a simper.

"All of us that gets invited to them, of course you mean," added Mrs. Weston. "I've always thought your cakes was remarkable, Jane."

"I don't wonder that woman's husband drinks," snorted Mrs. Noble, in an audible whisper to Mrs. Gray. "She's the worst toady I ever see in my life."

"Oh, no she ain't—she's real nice," the good-natured Mrs. Gray hastened to whisper back. "It's natural she should agree with Miss Manning—they've been real intimate always, same as their mothers was before 'em. Heathen wear more clothes than you'd think, judgin' from some of the accounts in the missionary papers, don't they? My back is most broke runnin' that machine this hot day."

Bitter as it was to have to "swallow Miss Manning's angel cake whole—and I'll bet it was a fallen angel cake at that," as Mrs. Noble said in relating the experience to her husband—this was not all. Not a single woman had noticed—or at all events mentioned—the calla lily and Martha Washington geranium in her parlour window, though she had raised one of the shades in that sacred apartment—at the incalculable risk of fading the carpet—because there was no other place where they would "show to the street" as the earnest workers went past to the vestry. Her skill with flowers was as noteworthy as it was with cookery—that, too, had been overlooked—probably on account of Miss Manning's old-fashioned garden! Immeasurably wounded herself, it was like balm of Gilead to Mrs. Noble to be able to turn Jacqueline, hurt and bewildered, from her door.

But Hiram took another view of it when his wife related the episode with pride that night at the supper table.

"Wal, I admire her for keepin' her promise," he said, pausing in the act of pouring his tea from cup to saucer before drinking it. "I never s'posed she meant a word of it. She must have to do some plannin' to get 'round that grandfather of hers. But Sol Daniels says she's real cute that way—not exactly what you'd call sly—but she manages! He see quite a lot of her when he was finishin' the last of the paintin', and he says every one on the place just worships her, and she twists all that gang of foreign servants round her little finger till they don't know whether they're a-foot or a-horseback. And that kind and thoughtful and generous, Sol says, that she'd take the shoes off her feet and give 'em to you if she thought you needed 'em. Next time you see her go by on horseback, I'd stop her if I wuz you, David, and thank her. Pass me a few more of them cucumbers, Lizzie, seems as if they wuz unusual tasty tonight."

Mrs. Noble's spirits revived at this well-merited praise of the garden products which she had striven so hard to raise. The events of the afternoon were momentarily forgotten in the pleasing remembrance of the morning, during which she had taken her husband's place at the post-office for a couple of hours while he went " out back " to confer with the seeker for simplicity from New York in regard to further purchases of land.

" There was an uncommon large mail come in on the ten o'clock," she remarked as she complied with his request. " I dunno when I've seen so heavy a bag. I dunno but what we shall soon be havin' two, they take so many papers and magazines up to the Big House. Sol Daniels says he got a stitch in his side luggin' it all in one. And the Grays always have more readin' matter comin' to them than their means warrant. Austin is writin' real regular to a girl up in Wallacetown, too. He might better save the money that goes into postage. She writes back on pink paper. Thomas came in for the mail this mornin' and I blushed to hand him such a lookin' envelope. Austin ought to think more of the awful example he's settin' those younger brothers and sisters of his. They're all smelled up, too. Stop your snickerin', David, you know perfectly well it was the pink letters I was talkin' about, and not . . . Miss Mannin' had two mail order catalogues from firms in New York City, but land! with that face on her, it don't make much odds where she buys her clothes, she can't look no different. Jack Weston had a postal from a feller in White Water askin' him to come up and spend Sunday with him and go fishin'. You can talk about the depravity of the heathen, but I couldn't help thinkin' when I see that, we've got our hands full with depravity right here in Hamstead. Fishin' itself would be bad enough, of course, but we all know what goes with it. I hope he'll get sobered off before he comes home. Well, just as I was glancin' at the postal to make sure who 'twas for—of course it would have been an awful thing to put it in the wrong box—Mis' Elliott come in and wanted to know what was on it. I do hate a curious woman, above all things, but of course I had to give her the gist of it, so's not to have trouble. I suppose it'll be all over town in no time now, but I done my best to stop it. I told her I should feel awful if it got around. Then right on top of that she says, 'Ain't it too bad about old Mis' Brown?' and when I says, 'Why, what's the matter with her?' she says, 'Why, that's what I'm tryin' to find out.' She does beat all. She told me she just got back from her cousin's funeral, down in Maine. 'Twas the handsomest she'd ever see. A mahogany coffin, and two floral harps and a pillow with 'Rest in Peace' on it, besides lots of ordinary tributes, of course. He was real well-off, she may get a little something herself, though the widow is awful graspin', seems to think he'll leave practically everything to her, as long as there weren't no children. I don't know when I've enjoyed hearin' about anything so much—— Well, maybe you're right about that French young one. David kin do as he likes for all me."

David had already decided that he had been somewhat too rash in flinging away the possibilities which a friendship with Jacqueline might possess, and the revelation that his father would not disapprove of the acquaintance offered a ready excuse to his pride for trying to get in touch with her again. She rode nearly every day, accompanied sometimes by her grandfather, but more often by a groom, who kept at a respectful distance; and the next afternoon David met her with the latter, as he was driving home Sol Daniels' cows—one of the "chores" which was slowly but surely, in quarters and dimes, bringing in the precious money that was in time to send him to the University of Vermont. She seemed to bear him no malice for his mother's rudeness, for she stopped, jumped off her pony, and held out her hand, saving him the embarrassment of speaking first.

"I've been to the river every Sunday," she said, "but you did not come. So finally I went to your house, but a cross woman in a grey overall slammed the door in my face, when she heard what I wanted. You ought to tell your mother to get rid of that servant."

"I'll come to the river next Sunday," said David. "That warn't a servant—we don't keep no hired girl. It was my mother."

"Oh, I'm sorry! I didn't guess—please forgive me! I wouldn't say anything—against any one's mother—for anything in the world."

David's conscience smote him. "That's all right," he said awkwardly, "I know you didn't mean nothin'. I must get along now, but I'll see you next Sunday, sure."

Jacqueline turned to the waiting groom. "Oh, Thomas," she said casually, "lead Frou-Frou home, will you please? I think I'll walk. You may meet me at the foot of the driveway with her in half an hour."

"Very good, Miss. A little this side of the driveway, perhaps?"

He was perfectly grave, but the corners of his mouth twitched.

"You always understand me perfectly," said Jacqueline soberly. Then, as the man rode off, she turned to David coolly, "Which way do you go? I'll walk along with you a little way—I think I have a better plan than the river now."

David felt as if the leaping of his heart must surely be visible in his face. "What is it?" he said, with elaborate unconcern.

"You know grandfather has a farm, and a foreman to run it. He lives in the lodge."

"The——"

"The little house down by the big gate. Sheldon's his name. He's an awfully pleasant man."

"Well?"

"Well, I heard him talking to grandfather the other day, and he said he needed more workmen—'help,' he called it, just as you do. 'If you'd let me hire men around here, Mr. Huntington,' he said, 'they'd be more contented than the ones you get from the city, and understand their work much better. I could get more out of them.'"

"Well?"

"Grandfather said all right, to do as he thought best. Of course Sheldon has nothing to do with the house-servants, or the men in our own stable. Thomas's father, Grimes, is coachman, and they both live with Mrs. Grimes in the cottage by the coach-house. They don't 'mix' with the farm hands at all. And Sheldon hires all of those himself. Oh, David, why don't you see if he wouldn't hire you?

"He wants a boy," she went on breathlessly, "to sleep in the big barn. It's really a lovely barn, and there's a nice little room in it on purpose for you—for some boy, I mean. You see he wants some one right there nights, with all those valuable work-horses, and cows, and—things," she added hurriedly, and a little vaguely, unconsciously admitting to David that her agricultural education had been much neglected, in spite of her superior wisdom on many other subjects. "I know Sheldon hasn't found one yet, for he said he wanted to be sure to get one who wouldn't all the time be running off to balls in Wallacetown, and you wouldn't do that, would you, David, because you aren't old enough, and besides you want to study? And grandfather goes to sleep every evening right after dinner, and Mademoiselle goes to her room to write to her relations in France as soon as she's put me to bed—and then I can get up again, and slip down to see you, and bring you books—and you can have the skeleton for company."

Perhaps it was this last attractive appeal that carried the day. At any rate, David went to see Sheldon.

Less than a week later he was installed as "general boy" on Mr. Huntington's farm. The village, which, of course, immediately heard of this, did not entirely approve. And Mrs. Elliott, with her usual lack of delay, decided to tell Mrs. Noble so, in case—as she had reason to hope—no one else had forestalled her in this agreeable task. She accordingly sought out her new neighbour after supper, and found her in the garden, picking string-beans for canning, assisted by two of her younger sons, while Susie, her thumb in her mouth, and a sugar cookie in her free hand, hitched up and down on the path with one foot tucked under her.

"Good evenin'," said Mrs. Elliott, breathless with haste, "warm, isn't it? Awful tryin' weather we've had this season."

Mrs. Noble wasted no time in greetings. "I ben so druv I ain't noticed the weather," she responded, snapping off a bean.

"Well, I sh'd think you'd need all your family to home to help ye, busy like you are."

"I dunno's a woman's family's always a help to her," said Mrs. Noble, going on down the trim line of vegetables without stopping. "I kin git more done when I ain't hampered too much by anybody in the family—or out of it, as fur as that goes."

Mrs. Elliott had never heard of *double entendre*; nevertheless, at that moment, though she could not have called it by name, she became vaguely and uncomfortably conscious that there was such a thing.

"But I make 'em work when I kin," went on Mrs. Noble vigorously, after a slight pause, "though 'tain't much, of course. Sam! take that bushel basketful inter the kitchen, and tell Leon to start in stringin'. Don't trip over Susie and *spill* it! If your father's in from the post-office tell him I want he should make sure there's plenty of wood in the fire, and that it's kept so. I can't keep a-runnin' in all the time. And then you hurry right back, and help Harry to start fillin' the basket agin down to the other end of the garden. I guess that second batch I planted is ready, too. . . . Hev you done much cannin' this summer, Mis' Elliott? I've put up over a hundred quarts of vegetables so far, and that's a fair beginnin', with strawberries an' currants, an' raspberries besides, of course! But I can't do as much as I used to do on the farm now that I hev to be in the post-office so much—an' hev neighbours runnin' in all the time."

Still uncomfortable, Mrs. Elliott decided that the only thing to do was to take the bull by the horns.

"I hear," she said sternly, "that your boy has gone up to the Big House to work."

"Which boy?" inquired Mrs. Noble, as if this was the first time she had heard of it.

"Land! David, of course!"

"Get out from under my feet, Susie!" cried Mrs. Noble, sharply and suddenly. "I 'most fell over you. Here—take a carrot an' chew on that awhile, now your cookie's gone."

"It's true, ain't it?" insisted Mrs. Elliott, perspiring slightly.

Mrs. Noble wiped the carrot on her gingham apron, and handed it to her daughter.

"There! . . . Kitty'd like a taste, too, ef she comes around! . . . Why yes, it's true. Has anyone said it ain't?"

"Not that I know of. Leastways—but no one could hardly believe it. I'm sure *I* couldn't. I shouldn't want a son of mine to go there, and every one feels the same way. The minister is real surprised. I shouldn't wonder a mite ef he spoke about it in prayer-meetin'. There's all kinds of queer stories about the Big House, and the folks that lives there. Likely some of 'em ain't true. But I've heard——"

"I've heard it, too," said Mrs. Noble crisply.

"Heard what?"

"The same as you hev, I s'pose. But it don't frighten me none."

"But I ain't told you yet *what* I heard."

"I know you ain't. You don't need to. It don't frighten me none, whether I know what 'tis or not."

"Oh," gasped Mrs. Elliott, looking a little frightened herself, "well, as I sez before, I shouldn't want a son of mine to go there—that's all. I sez to Joe, the minute I heard, 'I must go right down an' tell that boy's mother how sorry I feel for her. I know he's an awful stubborn boy. I know he's hard for her to handle. I kin tell by the look of him. His looks ain't like my Fred's at all——'"

"I've noticed that myself," said Mrs. Noble.

"But, I sez to Joe, 'Maybe she'd think of some way she could stop him, ef she had a chance to talk it over with some other woman.' And Joe sez, just as kind, 'Yes, why don't you go down an' pass the evenin' with Mis' Noble?' He's real unselfish—some men wouldn't feel they could spare their wives a whole evenin', that way. But he urged me to come right along, and not to hurry back. He's settin' on the back kitchen porch readin' last week's *Wallacetown Bugle*. He makes it a point not to read the paper till it's a week old, so's he kin hev the pleasure of hearin' the news first from the neighbours."

"Well," said Mrs. Noble, straightening herself up suddenly, "you kin go home an' tell him a piece of news from me, which, so fur as I know, ain't in the paper yet: And that is that I don't blame him mite for wantin' to hev peace once in a while, but that I don't feel no call to help him git it by stoppin' my work to let you tell me what to let my young ones do, and what not to let 'em do. I've had seven of my own to your one, an' I wuz the eldest of ten myself, so I've had some practice in raisin' 'em. Dave didn't consult me none in makin' his plans, but I don't know as I'd hev hindered him much ef he had. He's fourteen years old, an' when a boy gits to that age, he's kinder apt to take the bit in his teeth, one way or another. If it happens to be a curb bit, it cuts him up some, an' he goes round with a bloody mouth for a while, but them wounds don't last. Not as *I've* noticed."

She tucked Susie under one arm, and lifted her brimming pail with the other.

"On your way home," she said tartly, "you might run in and tell Mis' Weston it's a pity Jack drinks so. An' then go an' ask Mis' Gray if she knows where Austin is tonight —an' who with—an' what time she expects him back. That'd give yer husband time to read his paper real thorough, an' I'm sure them other women would be grateful to hear what you think of their sons, and the success they've had bringin' 'em up,—same as I'm grateful to hear what you think of mine. I'm sorry to leave you. But I cal'late to git all them beans ready for the stove before I go to bed, and some of 'em on tonight, so's I kin git the job finished the first thing in the morning. Good-night, Mis' Elliott!"

Hiram was pushing a stick of wood into the already crowded stove when his wife entered the kitchen. "I see you hev a caller," he said with interest, turning.

Mrs. Noble set down her baby and her pail, and slammed the lid, which her husband had lifted, back into its place.

"Yes, an' I guess we're likely to have some more," she retorted. "I told you what sort of things was bound to happen if you left the farm. But if any of them callers trick you inter sayin' you don't admire David for gittin' up an' startin' to *do* somethin', 'stead of sittin' on the post-office steps all the time tellin' what he thinks some one else ought to do—well, you'll hear from me, Hiram Noble, sure as that's your name! I'd a sight rather see a son of mine wearin' out the soles of his shoes than the seat of his pants!"

Mr. Noble stared at his wife, open-mouthed.

"Why, Lizzie," he stammered, "when you first heard David was agoin' to the Big House—I mean that he had *gone*—you wuz so mad you said you'd lick the hide off'n him, the first time you could lay your hands on him. What's come over you?"

But Mrs. Noble did not even deign to reply. She snorted, and began to string her beans.

.   .   .   .

So, as we have said before, David was installed as general utility boy on Mr. Huntington's farm, with the acknowledged privilege of going to school in term-time, eating at the farm house, sleeping and studying in the comfortable little room at the end of long line of stalls,—and the unacknowledged one of seeing Jacqueline very often indeed. Night after night, after she had been warmly tucked up and was supposed to be soundly sleeping, she stole through the gardens and across the wide lawns, easily concealed by the abundant shrubbery, down the shaded paths that led to the big barn. Sheldon, discovering, as was perhaps inevitable, the state of friendliness between the two children, not only never mentioned it, but guarded it from the detection of others. David did his work with a kind of fierce thoroughness that was a marvel of speed and efficiency, and when it was done, he never stirred off the place, but sat "with his nose in his books" until all hours of the night. Sheldon, after years of bitter and aggravating experience with flighty and stupid "general boys," knew that it would be a long day before he would find such a treasure again, and realized that anything that contributed to his content must be looked upon with a lenient eye. Moreover, he was quick to realize that Jacqueline was always the seeker, that David never presumed upon her favours, and was at times almost impatient at her interruptions. Had things been the other way around, Sheldon's conscience might have troubled him—as it was, he sincerely rejoiced that the lonely child had found some one to amuse and cheer her. Mr. Huntington, who had grown old before his time, took but little personal interest in his estate; he seldom saw David, and failed to recognize, in the unobtrusive and exemplary young farm hand, the ragged boy whom Jacqueline had once so thoughtlessly introduced to the seclusion of his library, into which he retired more and more. David's parents, blissfully ignorant that he came into any contact with the family at the Big House, and more than gratified at the wages he drew from the big purse, were supremely content. And so matters drifted on uneventfully enough until David was in his last year in the Hamstead High School, and nearly nineteen years old, and Jacqueline, who did not go to school at all, but taught David almost everything worth knowing that he knew, was not quite three years younger.

It could hardly be expected that they would drift much longer.

CHAPTER V

THE AWAKENING

IT was a mild, starry evening in mid-May, and David, who had been up most of the night before with a sick cow, had nearly fallen asleep over his books. They were piled high around him, a motley collection. There were his school books, almost falling to pieces from hard use, for several other pupils at the High School had had them before him; there were the daily papers, slightly out of date, for they went from the Big House to the farm house, and from the farm house to the little room in the barn; there were several agricultural periodicals—*Hoards Dairyman, The Holstein-Friesian World, The Rural Outlook*—which he read conscientiously from cover to cover, before he turned to devour the two old medical books, sadly behind the times, which the village doctor had discarded as no longer useful, and given to him; and finally there were two or three shabby novels from the Hamstead Public Library.

The window of the little room was wide open, and David, yawning and stretching his arms above his head, walked over to it, and stood looking out into the calm and silent night, feeling vaguely restless and lonely. Jacqueline was in New York. As she grew older, her grandfather became daily more proud of her, and at last he shook off his inertia and desire for solitude, and began to seek out his old friends again, that he might have the satisfaction of displaying his treasure. He had buried himself in shame because of his son; he was emerging with pride because of his grandchild. The success of the first venture into his old world after an absence of many years was so great that it was soon and often repeated. Jacqueline was personally too lovely and winning, and financially too great a prize for the dimming remembrance of the scandal connected with her parents to carry much weight. Occasionally some matron whose own daughter lacked partners at a party remarked acidly that of course it was not surprising that Désirée Huntington danced so well, or some father whose son failed to make even the most halting progress with his books sought public consolation in the statement that Hal Huntington's girl was naturally a good linguist: but for the most part, if they spoke at all, every one said that of course there was likely to be a black sheep in every family, and the Huntington family was no exception to the rule, but still, it was a fine family just the same, one of the best—and yes, indeed, the child had wonderful charm, and it was easy to see that she was going to be a great beauty. The Big House, which for years had been so quiet, was filled with guests much of the time, and trips to New York, to Washington and Baltimore, and even to Boston, which Mr. Huntington had expected never to visit again, became more and more frequent.

David had seen less and less of her these last two years. It was now six weeks since she had been in Hamstead at all, and there had been no intimation of when she was likely to return; in fact, there had been some talk before she left of the possibility that she might enter a fashionable boarding school for the spring months.

Sheldon, who by this time loved David as if he were his own son, could not help boasting about him from time to time to the less fortunate farmers in his vicinity, whose "hired men" were the vexation of their lives. There was just cause for his satisfaction. The boy worked hard and faithfully, and he saved his wages. The account at the Wallacetown bank, started four years earlier with a grimy dollar-bill, had crept up until it had already passed the thousand-dollar mark. He spent nothing on amusements, little on clothes, yet his appearance was always creditable. He had shot up tall and slim and he carried himself well, neither slouching nor stalking. The determination of his mind seemed reflected in his body—the strong shoulders were flung back, the dark, lean face and head of heavy black hair rose defiantly above them. Almost any man can look well in broadcloth and fine linen; this one contrived to give grace and dignity to a pair of cotton overalls. His record at school, moreover, was excellent. He was to graduate in a few weeks, valedictorian of his class.

"And he's as straight," Sheldon invariably wound up, "as a ramrod; as clean as a whistle."

This was true. However, David deserved less credit on this score than Sheldon and his audience gave him. He had a single-track mind, and the train that ran on it was an express to the city of material success. It made no stops at the way-stations of idleness and folly largely because he had no inclination to do so—they would have used up valuable time. Moreover, the boy worked, physically and mentally, from five o'clock in the morning until late at night. He was too tired when evening came, and still had too much ahead of him before he could go to bed, if he were not only to reach the goal ahead of him, but live up to the standard he had already set, to "run with the crowd." He had gained much by the course he had chosen; but he

37

had also lost something as well. He had made few friends, and if there were no evil in the boy, neither was there much unselfishness, or gentleness, or human sympathy.

None of the girls in his class at school had interested or attracted him in the least; and when he thought of Jacqueline at all, which was seldom, it was with a sense of passing and grudging gratitude for the fact that without her help he would not have been able to travel so far already on his single-track railway. He never missed her when she was gone; sometimes, when she appeared at the barn, he was glad to see her, for she was merry company, and he had no other; at other times, he was merely impatient with the unwelcome interruption of his work. If he had analyzed her at all, he would have admitted that she was pretty, that she was loyal and generous, that she was tender of heart. But he had never done so—never until he stood by his window on that May night, feeling dissatisfied with himself and all the world. Then suddenly, he realized it all. He felt, with the realization, that he would give anything in the world to see her, that he was hungry and thirsty for something he had never wanted before, and that only she could give him —and, as he stared out into the starlight, he saw her coming towards him, and caught his breath, a flame of violent feeling sweeping through him.

She was clad in a soft muslin dressing-gown, that fell to her feet, showing, as she moved, almost every line of her exquisitely slender and graceful figure; the wide flowing sleeves hung away from her arms, leaving them bare far above the elbow; the deep cut V of the waist showed her throat and neck gleaming white and bare; her hair was gathered into a great knot at the nape of her neck, and escaped in delicate curls about her lifted face. She was singing softly, a little French song, as she had been the day he first saw her. He could understand the words readily enough now, but they meant nothing to him. All that mattered was that she was there, that she was coming towards him, that he wanted her more than anything else in the world. . . . Pallas Athene, draped in the garments of wisdom, helmeted, spear in hand, had advanced sternly towards him through the groves of learning during five years

38

of steady toil. He had accepted her challenge, and won her grudging favour; she was no longer a stranger to him, but a friend and mentor; but when he first knew her well, he could not have told, nor did he care. But Aphrodite rose suddenly from the sea-foam, where an instant before there had been only the calm and sunny water of a blue ocean, dazzling in her unashamed loveliness, pearly-white and beautiful as the shell upon which she stood, a smile of invitation on her parted lips. . . .

Jacqueline caught sight of him. She nodded; waved her hand, and walked nearer without hurrying; then with a sudden impulse, ran to the window, and caught his hand in hers.

"Oh, I'm so glad to see you!" she cried. "We came home on the evening train; but we only decided to do it at the last moment, so that our telegram saying we were coming reached Grimes barely in time to meet us at the station—you didn't know, did you? We had dinner, and after I had seen that grandfather was comfortable for the night—he was pretty tired, for he isn't very strong—I got out of my travelling clothes, and had a bath, intending to go right to bed myself, when suddenly it came over me that I couldn't wait another minute to see you. So I slipped into the quickest thing I could and came out. Isn't it a heavenly night? Lift me up, David, so that I won't have to go around through the barn!"

It was a request that she had made dozens of times before. To come in through the window saved considerable time, and greatly lessened the danger of discovery. He leaned over and took her in his arms; then instead of releasing her as soon as her feet touched the floor, he crushed her to him with all his strength. She flung her arms around his neck with the candid and affectionate embrace of a happy child.

"My, but you're strong," she said admiringly, "let go, David, you hurt. I'm sure Cyril Wainright couldn't pick me up like that."

He released her, almost savagely. She did not understand—did not even see how he felt. His sudden passion had been so unreasoning that he had blindly taken for

39

granted an instant response to his own emotion. And there she stood, looking at him with clear, smiling eyes, telling him that he hurt, and speaking to him about another man.

"Who is Cyril Wainright?" he asked thickly.

"A boy I met this spring. Oh, David, I've had such a good time! I haven't been to school after all, just visiting and doing the nicest things all the time! But I'm going next fall, for a year, and after that I'm going to 'come out' in New York, and then grandfather's going to take me to London to be presented. Won't it be wonderful?"

"Is Cyril Wainright going, too?"

Jacqueline burst out laughing. "I don't know—but just at present he seems to manage to go everywhere that I do, so perhaps he will. Anyway, he's coming here to spend next Sunday with his grandfather, who was a great friend of my grandfather when they were in college. His father and mother are both dead, just like mine. You see we have lots of things in common. He's ever so old—twenty-one, and a senior at Harvard. He—David, are you sick, or what's the matter with you?"

"I was up almost all last night—I'm sleepy."

"Too sleepy to be glad to see me?"

"I'm glad to see you," he said fiercely, "only——"

"Well, I must say you don't seem *very* enthusiastic——" she turned towards the window. He stepped in front of it.

"Jacqueline," he said, "don't——"

"Don't *what*? I'm going back to the house, I'm sleepy myself—but I'll come again tomorrow night if I can manage to. You're right in my way—that's better—why, no, I can jump down all right alone! I always do."

He watched her out of sight, then sat down, and tried to force his seething brain to map out a plan of action, too unsophisticated to know that he was by no means the first man to find his desires and his sense of elementary righteousness as far apart as the two poles. Jacqueline had gone away hurt, he knew, by his strange reception, and very far, he saw also, from guessing the cause of it. And proposing to come again the next evening! These lonely intimate visits must stop instantly—that was his very first decision. Sooner or later he would be bound to betray himself, and now that he reasoned the matter out, he saw with tardy gratitude that it would be the worst possible return for all her goodness to ask her to wait indefinitely for a man who was not fit to tie up her shoes, who had, indeed, for several years, been her servant, milked her cows and groomed her horses! Besides, what would he gain by telling her that he loved her? She would laugh, and ask him how old he thought he was, anyway. Inquire if it was not a little sudden, considering that he had only tolerated her, all this time, for the sake of a skeleton. Point out to him that ladies were not in the habit of marrying their stable boys; and come again the next evening as if nothing had happened. And if he persisted, told her that some day he would surely be worthy of her, forced her to see how he felt, tried to touch her—that, he knew, would mean instant and disgraceful dismissal, and the complete overthrow of all his hopes. Daylight found him no nearer a solution of his troubles—he went to his work after a second sleepless night, though for a very different cause than his first one.

It was hard enough to be not quite nineteen, and know that you were poor and ignorant and in love; but how much worse this condition of things could be made by the power of jealousy, David was shortly to discover also.

Jacqueline did not come to see him the next evening after all. Cyril Wainright and his grandfather came several days sooner than they were expected, and arrived that afternoon; but she saw David, very unexpectedly, the next morning. Thomas was away on his vacation, and Grimes was smitten with sudden illness; he telephoned down to the big barn, and asked Sheldon if he could send his chore-boy up to the stable to do the morning work, and take Frou-Frou and Sophie around to the Big House for Miss Jacqueline's morning ride.

She was standing with her back to the path as he came up, laughing and talking with her guest, a slim fair youth, irreproachably dressed in London riding togs, who was smoking a cigarette, and smiling at the girl with an expression half-amused and half-provoked. She was quite evidently teasing him.

"I'll make you take back that speech before we get

home!" he warned her, lazily.

"You'll keep me out for ever then!"

"I'd like nothing better."

"Pshaw! You'd be keen for it until about lunch time. Then you would be ready enough to come home."

"We might take lunch with us; something we could put in our pockets. Haven't you ever heard of feasting on bread and cheese, and kisses?"

"Yes, but I don't care for bread and cheese, and I don't think you can put kisses in your pocket. *Why, David!*"

"Grimes is sick, and Thomas is away, you know."

"I hadn't heard. No, thank you, Mr. Wainright will help me up. That's all, thank you."

"You had better have that boy discharged, Jacqueline," Cyril said, as they started off, quite loudly enough for David to hear, "awfully bad form, you know, coming to the door in overalls like that, and not even touching his hat and calling you 'miss.'"

He did not hear the girl's reply; she was off at full gallop, laughing. Laughing—as if it were an amusing thing to have that long-legged, tow-headed dude talk about keeping her out for ever, and feeding her with kisses, and offering her advice on the subject of her affairs! It was all right for him to lift—not help—her into her saddle, and be damned slow about—she didn't tell *him* to let go, that he hurt! All day long David thought about it, and the longer he thought, the more unfair and intolerable it seemed to him; and when evening came, for the first time in his life, he asked Sheldon for a "team" to go to Wallacetown.

Sheldon hesitated.

"I don't begrudge you a horse and buggy, Dave," he said kindly, "you ain't asked many favours sence you ben here, and you've done a good many. I ain't one of those that thinks Wallacetown's the den of iniquity that some does, either—it's a real smart, up-and-comin' place. Still, 'tain't just the spot I'd choose first to turn a boy of your age loose in, and it's pleased me considerable that you ain't never seemed to care to go there. I kinder hate to see you start in."

"You don't expect to see me shut up with a pile of books for company every night for the rest of my life, do you?"

said the boy, hotly. He seemed to be unable, these last few horrible days, to escape for one instant from his newly wakened, throbbing senses. If they could not be satisfied in the way for which they seemed to cry aloud, perhaps there was some chance of surfeiting or deadening them. And because he was hurt himself, he wanted, desperately, to strike back—to hurt some one himself, by doing something foolish, or wild, or wicked——

"No, I expect to see you make your mark in the world. There ain't many young fellers, David, has got your talents and your grit, and I look to see you do better with them qualities than throw them away in the pool-rooms and saloons in Wallacetown; but you kin have the team."

Sheldon waited up for him in the little room in the barn that had so long proved so safe a sanctuary. David was both surprised and insulted to find him there. It was a rainy night, and he was soaked to the skin; he did not know how to dance, and the "ball" he had attended had gored him to extinction. He was not the first person to return more out of temper than injured by his maiden attempt to "see life."

"Did you think I'd be so drunk I couldn't get to bed alone?" he asked with bitter sarcasm; and after the kindly farmer had departed with awkward apologies, he muttered to himself, "But I will be next time, if no one thinks any better of me than that."

The events of the following day did not tend to improve David's frame of mind, or to raise his spirits. He was set to weeding flower-beds and clipping shrubbery, and his work took him—and kept him—near the deep veranda of the big house, where, the weather having become suddenly unseasonably hot, Jacqueline and her guest had ensconced themselves in big willow chairs, with a frosted pitcher of lemonade and two tall, slim glasses between them, and several volumes of poetry for company. The "general boy," dirty, dishevelled, and perspiring, could not lose sight for one moment of the vision of Cyril Wainright, clad in white trousers, white tennis shoes, white silk shirt, silk socks and blue coat, not a hair of his sleek blond head out of place, a fragrant rosebud—presumably pinned there by

Jacqueline—in his button-hole, a cigarette between his long, slim fingers. What was worse, he could not escape from Jacqueline's voice. Her "education" had reached that point where the English poets, by means of diagrams and synopses, were being "taken up"; and, given this dry and meagre opening, her own temperament, tastes and talents, were causing her to drink far more deeply from these wellsprings of beauty and emotion than her teachers would have either imagined or approved. With her usual impulse of wishing to share with some one else that which she herself enjoyed, she insisted on reading aloud to Cyril; and though he cared very little for the rhapsodies of Shelley or the melting sequences of Keats he enjoyed tremendously the effortless hours passed on the shady piazza with Jacqueline beside him, and, to secure and retain these, he would have listened without objection if she had seen fit to read to him pages from Webster's dictionary—and would have derived about as much inspiration from them. But to David the poetry, overheard from the bushes, meant something very different; and when the girl, after reading "Bright Star, would I were constant as thou art," closed her book and sat looking out over the meadows with an expression of hushed joy on her face, while Cyril murmured politely, "Well, that chap *did* know how to write, didn't he?" David flung down his scissors with a muttered oath, and crept up closer to where the others were sitting.

"Think you could be as constant as all that?" drawled Cyril after a comfortable pause, reaching for a fresh cigarettee.

Jacqueline gave a slight start, coloured quickly, and drew in her breath. "Oh, *yes*——" she breathed, "if—if—I ever loved any one the way Keats loved Fanny, you know! And Fanny didn't love Keats! It seems so strange! She treated him dreadfully! I'm sure I should feel more like Juliet."

"A funeral vault, eh? Faithful unto death and all the rest of it. Well, I think you might brighten up even a tomb considerably. You're the most *alive* kid I ever saw! Light this for me, will you? I can't reach the matches."

"The funeral vault of course—if—if that had to be part of it—but I was thinking of something else." She picked up another book, and, her fingers trembling with excite-

44

ment, began turning the pages rapidly. Then she read,

"'Romeo: Oh, will you leave me thus unsatisfied?'

"'Juliet: What satisfaction canst thou have tonight?'

"'Romeo: The exchange of thy love's faithful vows with mine.'

"'Juliet: I gave thee mine before thou didst request it. And yet I would it were to give again. . . .
My bounty is as boundless as the sea;
My love as deep; the more I give to thee
The more I have—for both are infinite.'"

"Go on," said Cyril encouragingly, "that's a pretty scene, when it's well acted. Ever seen it played? I suppose you haven't—I keep forgetting how young you are. I'll take you to it some time."

"No, you won't," answered Jacqueline slowly. "And I don't want to read any more. You don't feel the same way about it that I do. You don't feel it *at all*!"

"But it's only a silly story about two mooning idiots, after all, you know——"

"It isn't! It isn't! I don't quite understand it, of course, but it's *real*—and it's—a sort of *creed*——"

"Oh, good Lord," interrupted Cyril, flinging down his cigarette and bending over her. "You take things too seriously, baby. I feel enough for *you*, anyway, you cute little thing——"

David picked up his shears, got to his feet, and strode away. That night he asked for a "team" again.

But it was not until Sheldon, undeterred by the boy's ingratitude on the first occasion, had seen him come back three times in the grey of early dawn exhausted and intoxicated and profane, that he decided he must have immediate help if David were to be made to behave himself; and with the unreasoning but unerring instinct of real affection, it was to Jacqueline that he turned for assistance. Cyril had departed. Sheldon felt sure that before long she would go to the barn. He deliberately lay in wait for her in the garden, and he did not have to wait long.

"David ain't home," he said abruptly, as she approached, "if you wuz thinkin' of tryin' to see him. And I guess I shall have to discharge him."

" *David!* Why, I thought he was the apple of your eye! What's the trouble?"

" He goes to Wallacetown every evenin'."

Jacqueline laughed.

" Is that all?"

" That's enough."

" Because he takes the horses too often, you mean?"

" No—but because of the places the horses take him to." The foreman blushed, a deep, honest brick-red. " It's hard to speak to a young lady about such things; but I know you've always been real friendly to Dave. Maybe a word from you——"

There is something in the intelligence back of a young girl's innocence that senses the black things she does not know. Jacqueline came nearer to Sheldon, and he saw that there were tears in her eyes.

" I know," she said, " that is, I'd heard—that men—but not *David!*" She stopped, her lips quivering. It was the old cry, her woman's heritage from the centuries that had gone before her. Other men may sin, but not this one whom I trust! " I'll try—to help. You—you love David, don't you, Sheldon?"

" Love," like " God "—are we not told that the two are synonymous—is a word seldom used in rural New England. Sheldon's blush deepened.

" Yes," he muttered shyly.

" So do I," said Jacqueline quietly.

CHAPTER VI

THE ROAD TO WALLACETOWN

" SAY, I guess you don't remember me—I met you at the ball last Thursday night."

David, who was standing on the kerb-stone opposite the Wallacetown station, watching the arrival of the New York express, turned to see a girl of twenty-one or thereabouts beside him, and holding out her hand. She was short and plump, with a mass of lustreless black hair, much puffed out under a sailor hat, bright red cheeks, and small snapping black eyes, and was dressed in a cloth skirt and a pink silk blouse, not very fresh and trimmed with cheap lace.

"I'm afraid I don't," he said, vaguely polite. "I don't dance much; but I want to learn; and I'm real—I mean, very—glad to meet you again. What was your name?"

"It was, and *is*, Elsie French," the girl responded with a laugh and a coquettish toss of the head. "Seems as if I'd seen you round here several times lately—aren't you gettin' more sociable than you used to be?"

"I never have been much in Wallacetown," David responded.

"There's an awfully jolly set, once you get acquainted," said Elsie. "Course we don't like to pick up with any one that comes along, so there's some that says we're stuck up, but there ain't a word of truth in it. We'd be real pleased to see you any time. I work in Sawyer's store, and I'm going to meet some of the crowd at the drug store for an ice-cream soda, and then go to the show at the Opera House. It's a real show, not home-talent, 'Out in Idaho,' and from the posters I should say 'twas just grand. What do you say to comin' along with us?"

"I'd like to," he said, "let me treat you to the soda, won't you? That's the drug-store you mean, right over there, isn't it?"

While he was speaking, the door of the apothecary's shop was thrown open, and a girl came out and stood on the step, looking up and down the bright street with eager interest. Wallacetown was at that time the only place in the vicinity which boasted electric street lights and concrete pavements, and two or three of the leading citizens had already invested in automobiles, and were driving back and forth doing their Saturday evening shopping. The crowds from the train were pouring across the street, and the restaurant near the drug-store was doing a lively business, while the town band, a short distance off, was playing the airs that had been popular in New York six months before. She was bareheaded, and dressed in a white linen habit, her slender figure clearly silhouetted against the dark door behind her. Elsie stared at her with curiosity.

"I wonder who that girl is," she said. "My, but she's

got a swell figure! She seems to be all alone, don't she? It won't take any one as good-lookin' as she is long to pick up a feller, though; likely she's waitin' for some one now."

David's heart leapt to his throat. "I'm afraid you'll have to excuse me," he said hurriedly, "that's—that's Miss Huntington, from Hamstead. I work at her grandfather's farm, you know—something must be the matter——" and without waiting for an answer, he strode towards the drug-store. "Jacqueline," he said thickly, "what are you doing here?"

"Why, David," she said, turning with cordial surprise, "what are *you* doing here? I supposed of course you were grinding away as usual, only too thankful not to be inter-rupted! Grandfather is ailing again, and out of his pet tonic, so as I wanted to ride anyway, I came up here to get it! It's such a relief not to have Mademoiselle dodging every footstep I take, you can't imagine! If I'd realized how much more satisfactory a lady's maid would be than a governess, I'd have managed to make this change for the better long ago! I supposed I'd get home earlier than this, of course, but Sophie went lame, and I had to walk her the last half of the way!"

She went across the pavement as she spoke, towards the hitching post where Sophie was tied.

"I'd like to stay here a little while," she continued. "I've hardly ever been here, and never in the evening—it's like a little city, isn't it? I love the country now—do you remember how I hated it at first?—but I'll never outgrow my early taste for lights and music and people, I'm afraid! But I suppose it's just as well that I get back before any one finds out I'm gone—and begins to worry." She laughed. "I saddled myself—I wish I'd taken Frou-Frou instead— I haven't liked the look of Sophie's foot for days! Now I'm afraid I'll have to lead her all the way home, and walk myself. Unless you'd let me ride back with you—if you weren't doing anything special?"

David untied the waiting horse. "Get on," he said, vainly trying to steady his voice, "and ride until we can get out of this place. She can't be too lame for that. I'm on foot myself tonight—I've had a team several times

48

lately, and I didn't want to ask again—so I can't drive you home. But I'm coming with you, of course."

He lifted her into the saddle, as he had seen Cyril Wainright do it, handed her the reins, and started out beside her in silence. Twice before they were off the bright street, he stumbled, and he took hold of the bridle and gripped it; the third time that it happened, they had already reached the dusty highway. He glanced up at Jacqueline. She was looking straight down the moonlit road.

"Jacqueline," he said.

She turned and smiled down at him.

"Yes, David," she said gently.

"I want to tell you something."

She put her hand on his shoulder. "Yes, David," she said again.

"I couldn't let you come home alone—promise me you won't ever go out—this way again. But I haven't any right to be with you. I've—I've been drinking, Jacqueline."

The girl slipped from her horse, and thrust a small, cool hand between his hot clenched ones.

"I knew that all the time," she said quietly.

He wrenched his hand away, and turned his head. Of what stuff was this girl made? He knew only too well the torrent of abuse, the lamentation, the sour recrimination, that such a confession would have called forth if he had made it to his mother. An overpowering sense of shame for what he had already done, a sickening fear of what might have happened if he had not met her when he did, seemed to surge about him, and drag him under and drown him. He tried to shake it off, to reason that she was there with him now, that nothing was strong enough to prevail against her presence—it was of no use—he seemed actually to hear the roar of the waves——

"Let's sit down for a minute," Jacqueline was saying. "I love this curve in the road, don't you? There's no better place to see the mountains, and the river, and the valley, all at once—it's almost beautiful enough to be Heaven, in the moonlight, isn't it?"

He sank down beside her, gratefully, on the green bank.

Gradually the roaring ceased. He reached for her hand again.

"I want to tell you something else, " he said. "When I saw you I was just going into the drug-store with a girl I didn't know. I was going to treat her to an ice-cream soda, and take her to a show, and——"

"There!" said Jacqueline, "I knew I was spoiling some kind of a good time! Why didn't you tell me before, and let me come home alone? I wouldn't have minded a bit."

"Oh!" he said, and set his teeth. There is no one in the world more unwilling to bruise the fragrant blossom of a young girl's innocence than the boy who loves her. "You don't understand. I didn't know her. She spoke to me on the street. She——"

"Oh, David," cried the girl, "it breaks my heart to see you so dreadfully unhappy! You *didn't* go with her—everything's all right!"

There was silence for several moments. He clasped the hand that he held to his heart, and held it there—Jacqueline could feel the beating. When he spoke again, his voice was clear and steady.

"I promise you," he said, "that I will never drink too much again—or do anything else that you would be ashamed of."

"I know you won't," she said. She made no attempt to take away her hand, and he gripped it hard. The worst was over—he had sinned, confessed, been forgiven, and started afresh; but he knew, that before he could be happy again, he must rid himself of jealousy as well as shame.

"Would you tell me something, too?" he asked.

"Anything you like."

"Did Cyril Wainright kiss you that day you went out riding with him—or any other time that he was here?"

For a moment the girl sat very still. He felt her hand tremble a little in his. There was no anger in her voice when she answered him, but there was more reserve than he had ever heard before.

"Don't you know without asking me?" she said.

"You and he were joking——"

"Oh, *that*! People say all kinds of things! It's rather

puzzling, but I'm learning. It's only the way they talk—in society. It doesn't mean anything."

"Then he didn't? He or anyone else?"

"Of course not," she said; she drew her hand away. "Come," she said, very quietly, "we must go home."

Something like a sob rose in the boy's throat. She had trusted him far, far beyond the measure of his deserving, and he had rewarded the sweetness of her charity only by doubting her dignity, grieving her to the heart; still, even though he should hurt yet more, he could not let it rest there.

"No," he said, snatching her hand back again, "no—I can't—not until—I'm going to kiss you myself—I'm going to be the first——"

Then suddenly he poured it all out—unworthiness, jealousy, longing, love. Incoherent words, broken sentences, came tumbling through his quivering lips. He hadn't meant to tell her—honestly, he hadn't—not for years and years—until he was rich and great—and then not like this. He wasn't telling her himself, really; it was telling itself. . . .

"And you thought I wasn't glad to see you," he cried at last, "when I didn't—didn't dare—to let you know——" He swept her into his arms. "But I've got to now——"

When at last, trembling in every limb, he raised his head, Jacqueline lifted hers, clinging to him, and the light that he saw shining in her eyes told him that at first touch of his hungry lips she, too, had been granted the vision of Aphrodite, rising pearly-white and beautiful from the calm and sunny sea.

CHAPTER VII

THE BOUNDLESS SEA

On the morning following the evening that Jacqueline and David had spent together on the road to Wallacetown, the boy walked up and down the vegetable garden, between trim rows of infant potato-plants, spraying them with Paris Green. A less congenial—not to say less romantic, occupation for one who had recently and exultantly become an accepted lover would be hard to imagine. He was tired—

51

weary, for the first time in his life, to the point of exhaustion, not only from the hard "spring work" on the farm, which always lay heavily upon his shoulders, and from the almost sleepless nights which, for more than a week, he had been passing, but from the inevitable reaction after the excitement and triumph through which he had passed. His head and back ached, with a dull, stupefying pain, his eyes smarted, his throat felt choked and dry; his overwrought brain seemed stubbornly to refuse to work at all, much less to be spurred into increased activity, as he had vaguely expected it would be, by sensations of ambition fulfilled and desire gratified. He had "got what he wanted" —something equally despaired of, and longed for—and instead of being overcome with joy and rapture he was overcome with discouragement and fatigue. The events of the night before, viewed in the light of a blazing and relentless sun instead of a silvering and sheltering moon, seemed to take on a very different aspect. His sudden and overpowering passion for Jacqueline appeared not only presumptuous and hopeless, but senseless as well. His vision blurred, and two or three scalding tears fell quickly on the grimy hands holding the sprayer. He dropped to the ground, and threw his arm across his face . . .

At the further end of the garden, he could hear Sheldon talking to some one. The foreman seemed to be in high humour—his loud, jovial voice and raucous laugh grated on the boy's nerves—well, in a minute he would stop roaring and guffawing, when he came down the path and found his farm-hand literally—"lying down on his job." And of course it would all be laid to those trips to Wallacetown, when he had asked for the "team"—to *all* the trips to Wallacetown, which had, after all, been harmless and even boring, except that last one. . . . He would probably be fired. It didn't matter—nothing mattered, so long as this deadly weariness following his wild folly—a folly that was as ridiculous as it was wicked—a folly that would ruin his career—had taken possession of him. Then he realized that it was to Jacqueline that Sheldon was talking. . . . And still he did not move, even when the sound of her footsteps, coming in his direction, told him that she was getting nearer, that she was hunting for him. She called him twice, but he did not answer. Probably she wanted to tell him that she, too, realized the madness of what had taken place the night before, the utter impossibility of his remaining at the Big House. Well, he would get ahead of her—he would tell her himself, first, when she found him. But he wouldn't bother to *help* her find him. . . . Then, suddenly, he felt her arms around his shoulders, her cheek laid against his. . . .

"Oh, David," she was whispering, "isn't it wonderful to wake up—the morning after—and find that it isn't just a beautiful dream—that it's all true?"

Mechanically, he turned his head towards her, blinking back his stupid tears, and gulping as he did so.

"Do—do you think so?" he asked numbly.

"Do I *think* so? *Oh, David!* . . . And what do you suppose? You're going to have a day off—a whole day—and we're going back to that heavenly bend in the road where—where we sat last night—and see it all over again."

He pulled himself free, almost roughly, and got to his feet.

"Some one may see you," he said in a hard voice. "You mustn't touch me like that. Besides, you'll get all dirty—I'm covered with every sort of filth. And I can't have the day off—I never do. The work's way behind as it is. Sheldon wouldn't listen to it for a minute."

"He has listened," said Jacqueline calmly. "Quite pleasantly. About five minutes ago. Sheldon always listens when I talk to him."

"You mean you've asked him already?"

"Of course. And packed the lunch. Chicken salad and olives and sandwiches and angel cake. And lemonade in one of those queer new bottles that keeps things hot or cold, just as you want them to. Have you ever seen one?—Well, you'll be interested; they're quite ingenious. And grandfather's very miserable this morning," she ended cheerfully, " a splitting headache. There's not the slightest chance of his feeling any better until the sun goes down, and he won't ask for me before that—and then we'll be home. I'll devote the evening to him—except, of course, for running out, for a minute, to say good night to you."

David hesitated for a minute: then, without replying, he picked up his sprayer and resumed his work.

"Do you think I care," asked Jacqueline softly, "how much dirt there is on the outside of your clothes—as long as you're clean *inside*? And as for being afraid that any one will see me touching you—oh, how I wish I could tell the whole world that—you really do love me! I've been so afraid that you didn't! And I've loved you—ever since I can remember!"

"Jacqueline," began the boy desperately, "you—I— we've got to talk this thing over a little. Last night—we couldn't."

"Of course we couldn't! And of course we must! That's exactly why I've made this lovely plan for us to spend the day together—so that we can! And then you raise objections! Why don't you stop—delaying things, and put those hateful tools in the barn and come along— I left the lunch basket in your room."

But even when, the dusty highway behind them, they had climbed the little hill overlooking the river where they had sat the night before, and had eaten the dainty lunch from the English tea-basket, David still found himself unable to talk, and Jacqueline, apparently, had no wish to do so. She looked more like a little girl than at any time that he had seen her that spring, dressed in a frilled sunbonnet, a straight yellow smock of crisp linen, a short white skirt and heelless white canvas shoes; the loveliness of her figure, which the flowing negligée and the tight-fitting habit had both so effectually, though so differently, revealed, was completely hidden, to David's vaguely-felt relief. And her sunny contentment, her calm acceptance of their changed relations and her joy in them, seemed unpenetrated and impenetrable by the doubts and fears that were assailing him. He watched her, without offering to help, while, singing under her breath, she repacked the remains of their lunch carefully and neatly in the basket, and then sat stolidly beside her, staring away from her, without the power to break the silence which was rapidly becoming intolerable to him, until, for the second time that day, Jacqueline laid her cheek against his. He turned his head and kissed her, not because he especially wished to do so, but because he realized that she must be wondering why he had not done so before.

"You're a little dear," he managed to say, huskily, "I—I think a lot of you. And I want to talk to you, ever so much. But I can't seem to get the words out—or to do anything, but sit here like a bump on a log! I'm dog-tired—I can't imagine why; and I can't think of anything except how tired I am—and how I wish I could go to sleep, and forget—about everything for a while."

"Wouldn't you like to lay your head down on my lap and try to go to sleep?" she asked, gently. "We've lots of time, and I'm sure I could make you comfortable. When you get rested, then we can talk." She held out both her arms—"Please—dear——"

"I'd—I'd hate to muss you up, you're so clean and pretty——"

Jacqueline laughed. "I've told you once before today that I don't mind about *your* clothes," she said. "I'm sorry if you care so much about mine. Won't you come?"

Suddenly David knew that there was nothing on earth he wanted to do so much as what she was urging. He almost tumbled into her arms, and buried his face in the cool soft fabric of her dress. Then he felt her fingers, stroking, ever so gently, the hair back from his temples. . . .

It was late in the afternoon when David, having drifted first from a profound slumber to a delicious semi-conscious-ness, and then into a drowsiness so comfortable and satisfy-ing that he had no wish to stir and break it, opened his eyes. The sun had gone down behind the Vermont hills, and the quiet place where he lay was full of lengthening shadows; but, across the limpid river, the mountains in New Hampshire were turning from blue-green to rose-colour in its reflected light—slopes and mounds and peaks transfigured with its fiery glory. Through the stillness, a church bell was ringing for an early evening service; some-where, very far away, a whip-pool-will was singing. . . .

Without moving his body, he looked up at Jacqueline. She had taken off her smock, after he had fallen asleep, and folded it into a pillow to tuck under his aching shoulders, which, miraculously, no longer ached; but her neck and arms, left bare by her sheer cambric underwaist, were partly veiled by the cloud of bronze-coloured hair which she had let down and thrown about them, to shield his smarting eyes—which, miraculously, no longer smarted from the light. She was still unaware that he had wakened, and was gazing straight ahead of her at the rosy hills; she was very pale, and there were violet circles under her eyes; he realized, for the first time, with a pang of contrition, that she, too, had probably not slept the night before, that she, too, had passed through a new and bewildering experience; her face seemed to have lost something of its fresh childishness; but there was something in its place—an exaltation—a consecration even—passing far beyond the hot ecstasy of the night before, and yet containing and embracing that also. For a long time he lay, immeasurably rested and refreshed, immeasurably comforted and strengthened, watching her silently; and, as he watched, he knew that there was no need of speech between them, no need of doubts of himself or of fears for her; knew, too, that she had taken him out upon that "boundless sea" of bounty of a woman's love, revealing to him the new heaven and the new earth which contained treasures that he had never glimpsed before, and which were now his for the taking.

"Désirée," he said at last softly.

She bent over him, her tired face brightened with tenderness, her arms tightening about him.

"You feel better now," she said happily, "you're all right again——"

David drew a long breath. "Yes," he said slowly, "I'm all right again. I'm going to stay all right—the rest of my life—for you."

CHAPTER VIII

DAVID BURNS HIS BRIDGES

HAMSTEAD went to bed early. Evening chores were not over until nearly eight, morning chores began between five and six. It was therefore necessary to retire soon after the former were finished, in order to refresh oneself for the latter, and insomnia was not one of the complaints which the village doctor was called in to treat very often. By half-past nine, practically all lights were out, and after some event of unusual hilarity, like the annual church supper or a reception to a new minister, when later hours necessarily prevailed, the next night was pretty sure to see the maple-bordered street shrouded in darkness sooner still. But on the balmy June night, following the one on which he had seen his eldest son graduate from the High School, Hiram Noble was still lying awake when the village clock struck twelve, wide-eyed and rigid with excitement, not daring to give way to his longing to toss about for fear of rousing his sleeping spouse on the other side of the feather bed.

The boy had done so darned well. Hiram said it over and over to himself, and his pride increased each time he said it. There wasn't another fellow who could hold a candle to him in looks, in the first place, as he stood up to take his diploma, with that black head of his thrown back, dressed in new ready-made blue serge—bought, of course, for the occasion in Wallacetown—and stiff, snowy linen. And that crimson tie he wore—someway it hadn't looked like a Wallacetown product, but then, where else could David have got it?—wasn't any brighter than his glowing cheeks. Then that valedictory speech—how did a boy nineteen years old—not quite that, come to think of it—have sense enough to know all those things, let alone brains enough to write 'em down on paper? Most valedictories were kind of flowery and wandering, but this was straight stuff. And on top of all this, to have him win the Manning prize, bestowed yearly by Miss Manning, Hamstead's one wealthy and aristocratic spinster!—well, it was almost too much glory——

"The boy's done darned well," muttered Hiram again, and grinned in the darkness.

Mr. Huntington and Jacqueline had attended the exercises, and Hamstead, which affected to scoff at the Big House, preened itself with satisfaction. Sheldon, going to the old gentleman with the farm accounts, as was his custom the middle of every month, had lingered a moment after gathering up the scattered sheets.

"Very satisfactory indeed, Sheldon. You ask me to take more personal interest in the farm, but really there's no need, while I have a man like you."

"I'm glad them's your feelin's, Mr. Huntington. But I'm afraid we shan't make quite so good a showin' after David leaves."

"David?" asked Mr. Huntington vaguely.

"Yes. He came here as a chore-boy, you know, it'll be five years ago, come August—to sleep in the barn, and do what odd jobs he could after school-hours and during vacations. His father's the postmaster. Now he's goin' to graduate from High School in about a week, and he aims to go to college in the fall. I don't know whether he'll stay the summer or not, but I'd like real well to keep him until after hayin', no matter what I had to pay him. He does the work of any other two men I kin get, and keeps his mouth shut about it. There ain't no yap about overtime, or this or that bein' some one else's job—no, sir, not from him."

"It seems a pity," remarked Mr. Huntington, "that so valuable a workman should have mistaken ideas of his calling, and desire to educate himself above his station. College for chore-boys! What are we coming to? Perhaps a word from me——"

Sheldon shook his head, coughing to hide a smile. "I wouldn't try to argue with David if I wuz you," he said. "He's been plannin' this thing out—his 'career,' he calls it —ever since he was a little shaver without a quarter to his name. Now he's got twelve hundred dollars in the Wallace-town Bank. He ain't thinkin' nothin' 'bout his 'station,' except the station where he's goin' to take the train away from here to go and learn to be a doctor. But I tell you what, Mr. Huntington, if you and Miss Jacqueline could feel to go to the exercises when he graduates, I think 'twould be a real proper thing."

Mr. Huntington had always felt the relation of country squire to tenant in England to be extremely picturesque. There seemed to be few opportunities for him to play such a rôle in Hamstead, but though a High School Graduation was hardly the same sort of an occasion as a May-pole festival or a barn-dance, it would serve the purpose. He graciously signified to Sheldon, as he waved his hand with a suggestion of dismissal, that he would attend. And that night he informed Jacqueline of the fact.

"My dear," he said at dinner, "have you ever noticed a boy about the place named David Noble?"

Jacqueline was buttering a cracker. It seemed to be a fairly absorbing process.

"Why, yes," she said at length, "I met him down by the river years ago, when we first came here, and brought him to you myself. Don't you remember? You turned him out in short order, but later Sheldon hired him after all, and now he thinks the sun rises and sets on David's head. He's the paragon of hired men. Why?"

"I recall the incident, now that you speak of it. Perhaps I was a little hasty, but I've always been so afraid . . . Well, it seems the boy has done very creditably at the High School, and is to graduate there shortly. Sheldon thinks, in view of his long and faithful service, it might be well for us to attend the exercises."

"I think so myself," said Jacqueline.

So, as has been said already, they went, Jacqueline in a pink, crisp, frilly dress, the like of which Hamstead had never seen before, with little satin slippers and silk stockings to match. In larger places, like Wallacetown, the "Graduation Ball" was a separate and very grand event, but Hamstead, where dancing was still more or less frowned upon, contented itself at that time with a "promenade," after "speaking was over." And David, coming straight down from the platform, walked across the floor before any of the rest of his class had stopped whispering and giggling behind the curtain, to the place where she sat beside her grandfather.

"Will you lead the march with me, Miss Huntington?" he asked.

All this, of course, Hiram Noble had seen, and the whole of Hamstead beside. Saw, too, that Mr. Huntington—his mind revelling in mental pictures of the squire's daughter dancing with the handsome young tenant—smiled his approval, and that Jacqueline, instead of merely nodding her assent, according to the village custom, swept David a low curtsy, and slipped her arm through his; and after the "promenade" was over, she came, at her own request, and was introduced to the Noble family, from Hiram down to Susie—who was pretty sleepy by this time, and alternately nodding and staring—and stood chatting with them, "just like folks" for some minutes. Then when the music began for the next number, taking David's arm again, she went back to her grandfather's side, and David held up a wonderful shimmering velvet coat, lined with white satin, and wrapped it around her, and went out of the hall to help them both into the waiting carriage—and came back, looking as unconcerned as if graduating exercises, and rich, lovely girls to promenade with were everyday occurrences in life.

And what Hiram and all the rest of the village had seen, Lizzie Noble had inevitably seen also. But not once, on the drive home from the Town Hall, did she open her closely pressed lips, or even glance down at Susie, sleeping serenely in her lap, wrapped in an old shawl. She sat staring straight ahead of her into the fragrant, misty June night, as unseeing as she was silent. And having descended unaided from the carryall, telling the boys to "go help their father put up the horse," she lifted the key from its hiding place under the door-mat—where everybody in Hamstead always hid their keys—entered the dark house, fumbled for the matches on the table in the front entry—those were kept in a small china lamb—lighted a lamp, and, without waking Susie, undressed her and put her to bed. When Hiram came in from the barn his wife was standing in front of the small pine bureau in their bedroom, unfastening the cameo brooch that had been her mother's. Her back was towards him. But, through the dim light he could see in the cracked and blurred little mirror that her hands were trembling.

"Why, Lizzie," he said, "you're shiverin'—this hot night! Hev you took cold?"

"No, I ain't took cold," she replied tartly, sticking the brooch in the red bead pincushion vindictively, and remov-

60

ing her only other ornament, a hair-bracelet that had been her grandmother's.

"Are—are you mad at somethin'?"

"No, I ain't mad—and I ain't one to stand an' spend the night in idle talkin' neither, when I got to be up an' stirrin' at four in the mornin'."

She unbuttoned the black silk dress in which, twenty years before, she had been married, turned it carefully inside out, and hung it in the shallow closet. Then, gaunt and unbeautiful in her coarse cotton undergarments, she faced him.

"But even if I ain't, I know a promisin' boy when I see one," she said with a note of fierce pride in her voice that Hiram had never heard there before, "an' when sech a boy's my own son, I guess I kin take some satisfaction in him, same as any one kin."

"Why, Lizzie!" gasped Hiram.

"An' I know a lady when I see one, even if I ain't one myself," she continued in the same voice, "an' if that pretty-spoken, nice-mannered little Huntin'ton girl ain't one, for all her mother was a lost creature an' her father was a drunkard, I miss my guess, that's all. There's somethin' back of her good-looks that's worth a heap more'n her handsome hair an' pink cheeks. I could tell the minute I saw her step out in the promenade, before she come an' spoke to us. And after I'd heard her talk I was dead sartin' of it."

"Everyone likes the girl, an' that's a fact, Lizzie," agreed Hiram, "but I don't see what that's got to do with David."

"You don't, eh?" snapped his wife. She flung the straight, scanty locks she had been braiding back over her shoulder, and sank on her knees beside the bed. "I thank Thee, Lord," she said distinctly, "for all Thy mercies. For—a son like David, for—that pretty, pretty, little critter that kin give him all the things his mother's ben too druv, an' too ignorant, an' too sharp-tongued to give him—if she only will. O Lord, please make her feel to give them to him! For Jesus' sake. And bless them both. Amen."

As she rose and slipped into bed, Hiram saw that her rough, thin cheeks were wet. He longed, dumbly and

miserably, to comfort her. But this would have been difficult for him to do at any time, and in the light of her
recent emotion—for he had never seen her display emotion
before—it was impossible. He was infinitely relieved when
her regular and not over-quiet breathing assured him that
she was asleep. After a few moments he dismissed the
recent scene without much trouble from his mind, allowing
it to revert to the pleasing spectacle of his firstborn, with
Miss Huntington's velvet cloak on his arm, escorting her
from the hall.

The sequel to this Hiram did not yet know. However,
if he had, no amount of terror inspired by the fear of waking Mrs. Noble, and the consequences if he did, would have
kept him from tossing about. When David, all festivities
over, reached his little room something after midnight, he
was startled to find Jacqueline, still in her crisp, frilly, pink
dress, curled up on his bed, half-asleep. She sprang up
with an expression of joyous welcome, and threw her arms
around his neck.

"Oh, David," she cried, "it was splendid! Your speech
was great! I don't wonder you got the prize—and the tie
I gave you is so becoming! And wasn't it wonderful to
march together? I could hardly wait for you to get home
to talk it over with you."

He put his arms around her and kissed her, more tenderly than passionately, and drew her down beside him.
Since the little straight chair by the desk was the only one
in the room, they were forced to sit on the bed if they were
to be side by side.

"Look here," he said gently, "all this has got to stop."

"All what?"

"Coming here to see me; and letting me make love to
you; and kissing back when I kiss you."

"You mean—you don't love me any more?"

"I love you a great deal too much to let you get into
trouble; I've got an awfully guilty conscience."

"If you were half French, like me, you'd have less conscience and more intuition."

"Well," he said smiling, "I guess that's true—and you
intuitions have sure suited me all right so far! But it look

to me as if they were all the more reason why I'll have to have conscience enough for both of us."

"What have you done so very dreadful?"

"Stolen," said David grimly.

"For heaven's sake! What?"

"You," he answered briefly.

Jacqueline burst out laughing and shook him. "You miserable wretch!" she exclaimed. "I thought from your manner it must be the Chinese porcelains, at the very least."

"I wish you wouldn't joke. It doesn't look much like a joke to me. You know we haven't any right to see each other like this."

"But we've been doing it for almost five years, and you haven't minded."

"We weren't doing it just like this, were we?" he asked, suiting his action to his words. "I should say the situation had changed a good deal since the night we went to Wallacetown. It makes all the difference in the world if you know in your own mind that what you are doing is all right —as it was before—or all wrong——"

"*Wrong!*"

"Not in itself, darling, but under these circumstances— as it is now. Besides, we were lucky never to get caught, except by Sheldon, but if we had been, when you were eleven, and I was fourteen, we'd have been scolded, and told to keep away from each other, and that would have been all there was to it. But if we're caught now—do you think I want to make a scandal—out of you—for the servants?"

"David! We're engaged!"

"We haven't any right to be engaged."

"Because we're too young, you mean?"

"Because you're a lady, and I'm your servant."

She put her hand over his mouth, trembling, "No, no, no," she cried. "You shan't talk like that—I can't bear it."

He took the hand away, kissed it, and held it fast. "It's true," he said, almost roughly, "and you know it. And until it isn't—listen," he broke off abruptly. "I'm going away—immediately. I ought to go anyway, if you want me to go to Harvard, instead of to the University of Vermont. I ought to go to Cambridge, and take the entrance examinations. I probably can't pass them all with the preparation I've had, and if I can't, I ought to stay there all summer, working off conditions, so that I can start college with a clean slate in the fall. But before I leave, I'm going up to the Big House to tell your grandfather how things stand between us. I'm not going to put up thi miserable sham another minute!"

She tried to break away from him, panting with grie and anger.

"I think you must be stark, raving crazy! Do you know what will happen then? I'll be clapped into a convent in disgrace, and you'll be discharged."

"I can't be discharged if I discharge myself first, can I? And you won't be disgraced—I'll say this was all my faul of course."

"But it isn't."

"Well," David smiled again, "don't get so terribly angry darling. It's really about half-and-half, and that's the way it ought to be. But I think myself a convent would be a pretty good place for you—no knowing where those 'intuitions' of yours may lead you, without a little restraint— straight off to Cyril Wainright, for all I know! Of course he's going to try to make them, and I won't be there to prevent!"

"It would serve you right, because you *weren't* there to prevent. You ought to think of staying around to take care of me."

"Lots of fellows," said David, more truthfully than grammatically, "spend their time hanging around a girl to take care of her, when she needs to be protected from them more than she does from any one else. Cyril won't hur you—he's a perfect lady. But the other thing will be ou case exactly, if you won't listen to reason."

"What do you call reason?" sobbed Jacqueline.

"Well—doing this out in the open, or not at all—and o course I know that means not doing it at all, at presen But when we're old enough—I'll come back——"

"I won't be here."

"Probably not. But I'll find you. If a fellow reall

64

wants to see a girl, he'll do it, if she hides in the desert of Sahara, or on top of the Himalaya Mountains. Five years from now you'll be old enough to marry whom you choose, no matter what your grandfather says; and I'll be fit to have you, by then. But neither of those things is so now."

"You'll find me," she flared. "And I'll be married to some one else! And it will serve you right."

For a moment the boy hesitated. How could he tell this sweet, loving, wilful, hurt, innocent thing that he was fighting not only her but himself? That if he had not been . . . the little, quiet, dark room seemed suddenly to close around him . . . he got to his feet, almost hurriedly, pulling her with him.

"No, I shan't," he said, "not if the road to Wallacetown meant as much to you as it did to me. And if it didn't . . . I don't want you now—or then—or ever—— Did it?"

They clung to each other, both too shaken to speak, a minute—two—five—possibly longer. Then he lifted her to the window-sill.

"Good night, darling," he whispered, "and good-bye—unless you'll meet me in your grandfather's library to-morrow night, and we'll tell him together . . ."

All of this, of course, Hiram did not know. Nevertheless, the village clock struck one, and still he lay, perspiring and quivering, and staring into the darkness.

There was a slight noise beneath his window. Bristling, he raised himself on his elbow.

"Dad," whispered David's voice outside.

Hiram crept cautiously out of bed and across the room. The vogue of pyjamas had not reached Hamstead. He confronted his son in his abbreviated night-shirt.

"Don't wake your ma," he breathed. "What the heck's the trouble?"

The boy laughed softly. "Nothing," he said. "Come out to the kitchen and let me in. I'll be quiet—but I want to speak to you."

Hiram pulled on his trousers, and taking his shoes in his hand, tip-toed from his chamber, closing the door behind him an inch at a time. Then he lighted a lamp, and sped to the kitchen door. David stepped inside. He had on the blue serge suit in which he had graduated the night before, the same snowy linen, and strange crimson tie, and he carried a cheap new suit-case, a battered old carpet bag, and an armful of books tied together with a halter.

"Do you think," he asked calmly, "that you can drive me to Wallacetown in time to catch the two-thirty express?"

"Where for?" gasped Hiram.

"For Boston."

"Land of Goshen, David! What's come over you?"

"Mr. Huntington. I've just been into his house for the second time, and got kicked out for the second time. The first time I wanted a job—and I got it after all, without his help! This time I want his grand-daughter—and I'll get her, too, when I'm the greatest doctor in New England—as I'm going to be—and take her to live in a place that will make the Big House look like thirty cents!"

Hiram stared at his son as if he thought he had suddenly gone mad. David, having delivered himself of his modest purpose, seized his father by the shoulder.

"Come on out to the barn and harness," he cried. "We've got to hustle to make that train. I'll tell you all about it—on—on the road to Wallacetown!" he ended, with the excited, exultant laugh of eternal youth starting out to seek its fortune.

PART TWO

CHAPTER I

JACQUELINE'S BIRTHDAY

On an unseasonably chilly afternoon in May, almost five years later, three persons were sitting before the cheerful fire in the drawing-room of a house in London, drinking tea, smoking cigarettes, and talking. They were apparently all excellent friends, and enjoying themselves to the fullest measure.

The man who sat nearest the fire was about twenty-seven years old, very fair, very slender, and noticeably well-dressed. Everything about him was eminently correct, from his faultless tie to his perfectly manicured nails. His voice was that of an American, with a carefully cultivated English accent. The warmth of the fire seemed welcome to him, and indeed it is doubtful whether so super-civilized a being could have been comfortable without one.

The second man was at least ten years older, shorter, stouter, and also faultlessly dressed. He spoke English, indeed, instead of American, but with the decided accent of a foreigner. The fire apparently held few charms for him, but taking his cigarette from his mouth, he leaned over the table, and poured a generous contribution of cognac into the cup his hostess had just handed him.

She was a girl, who, at first glance, seemed to be about twenty-five years old, so self-possessed, so perfectly poised, and so splendidly developed did she appear; but closer inspection revealed that she was considerably younger, revealed also the rather singular combination of extreme sophistication of manner with an unusually clear and direct gaze from a pair of deep hazel eyes, and an almost childlike outline of chin and throat. There was something about her as baffling as it was fascinating, a fleeting impression— almost instantly dispelled, to be sure—of very deep feeling —was it joy or sorrow, or a capacity for both?—suppressed beneath a mask of levity because it did not dare to show itself, of some sort of faith so betrayed that it would be slow to trust again—or was all that mere imagination, and was she merely a beautiful "society girl" of unusual brilliance and charm? She was dressed in a very low-cut tea-gown of white Liberty satin, long and very scant, and her knees were crossed, revealing plainly that she wore little beneath but a generous length of white silk stocking, and white satin slippers with big rhinestone buckles. Great masses of golden brown hair, obviously all her own, were piled high on her head in a simple regal fashion, fastened with a great comb set with diamonds, and a single string of enormous pearls hung almost to her waist.

"Tell us something amusing," said the younger man, flicking an almost imperceptible ash from his knee. "She's not so amusing as usual today, really, is she, Gustav?"

"That I should hardly say," replied the other, bowing as gracefully as his cigarette, his cup of tea, and his avoirdupois would allow. "She is more still—more *en repos*, shall we say? But then she is never dependable, two days the same. In that doubtless lies much of her fascination for us poor victims." He might almost have been discussing a china vase or a handsome animal. "What says your immortal Shakespeare, 'Age cannot wither'—here she has reached another birthday, very old!—'nor custom stale'— has she not been our constant custom this long time?— 'the infinite variety of her charm.'"

"Oh, not Cleopatra, please, Gustav," cried the girl, leaning forward and throwing her cigarette into the fire—"she was always playing to the gallery, and roping in some man with theatrical effects! Think of the rug she rolled herself up in, and the painted galley! She didn't dare to be simple! And that asp story—I haven't any use for a woman who can't stick things out, no matter how bad they are. I'm not especially disturbed at her morals, but I think her tastes were dreadfully middle-class. I'm afraid I'm *not* very good company—but I'm pretty tired; partly because the season's been so awfully crowded, I suppose—what would Queen Victoria have said to the pace her descendants lead us?"

"Mon dieu, Désirée! Blame you the poor king because you ride miles and miles in the Row, go out to luncheon, go to a picture exhibition, to a dinner, to a ball, and then walk home at four in the morning, two miles, with Freddy Lambert!"

"Jealous, Gustav?" she asked lazily, half shutting her eyes. "I never can bear to get into a closed car when I've been dancing all night—and dawn is really a lovely time for a walk! And Freddy is such a comfortable person! It wasn't yesterday that tired me especially—that was like lots of other days, no fuller—and I often take those early morning walks—is this the first one of which you've happened to hear? Sometimes with Freddy, sometimes with other people. The exhausting thing happened after I got home. When I reached my room I found a note from my first love on my dressing-table."

Both men burst out laughing. "You are amusing, after all," said Cyril. "Who is he?"

"His name is David Noble. He used to be a stable-boy on my grandfather's estate in Hamstead, Vermont—you know what a perfectly barren time I had there for several years, while I was growing up, until grandfather finally made up his mind to venture out into the wicked world again. This fellow was very attractive, and I'm afraid I flirted with him—when I was between fifteen and sixteen years old. He had more conscience than common-sense, so one day he went to grandfather, and insisted that we should be engaged—it wasn't proper, in his category, to have a little *affaire de cœur*, unless the road to the altar was in plain sight. Of course he got discharged for his pains, and I got clapped into a convent—I've never felt especially grateful to him for his candour! What he is now, I haven't the least idea—the letter was on Claridge's paper."

"By Jove," exclaimed Cyril with an expression of real interest, "I remember that fellow! He came to Harvard when I was a senior, and was so extraordinary that he was conspicuous among four thousand men. He was very striking-looking, as you say, and strong as an ox—he played a fine game of football, made the freshmen team right away. It was the only thing he did play—no one ever saw him drink or gamble or dance or go to the theatre. It was reported that he turned up in Cambridge in the June before college opened, and drove an ice-cart all summer, while he was working off his condition, living in the cheapest kind of a lodging house,—oh, respectable enough—he committed no pleasing human follies! In the fall he got a job as choreman for several of the professors—looking after their furnaces, you know, and that sort of thing—and lived with one of them, working free for his board and lodging. He haunted free lectures and museums and libraries and even churches when there was unusually good music, and I don't believe he missed a single free demonstration of surgery at any hospital within ten miles of Boston! How he managed to crowd in so many things no one could imagine and, as he didn't try to make any friends, no one found out."

69

"How thrilling!" said Jacqueline, evidently without a single spark of interest.

"Isn't it? I ran across him one day on Tremont Street, looking in a jeweller's window, at a really marvellous display of rings. He was such a queer devil that I wanted to hear what he would say, and I asked him if he was thinking of buying one. He turned and stared at me a minute as if I had committed an impertinence, and then he said, 'No, none of them is handsome enough for my purpose,' and walked off. Towards spring, he slipped on one of the icy walks he took care of, and hurt himself quite badly. He was run down—no other human being could have stood his pace half so long—and got pneumonia when his leg was set—but even that turned into a piece of luck. The doctor that was called in to look after him—Ross, a great friend of Professor Hildreth's and an awfully big bug, don't you know—took a tremendous shine to him, and asked him home for the summer. His wife was dead and he'd just lost his only child—a boy about Noble's age— under very tragic circumstances. It looked to every one like a tremendous chance—but I never heard definitely what happened after that—you know I came abroad as soon as I graduated. I wonder what he did next—did his letter give you any clue?"

"It said very little—ran something like this—'Dear Jacqueline, as tomorrow is your twenty-first birthday, I shall come to see you sometime during the afternoon. I am very busy, so I can't tell at what time I shall be free, but if you are not in when I get there, I will wait. Faithfully yours, David Noble.' That's the first syllable I've heard from him in five years."

"I say, what perfectly colossal effrontery!"

"It suddenly came over me," Jacqueline went on, fingering her pearls, "that he had insisted at the time of that volcanic eruption in my grandfather's library, that when I was twenty-one, legally of age, that is, he would appear again. He has. From what Cyril tells me, I imagine he has been fairly successful already along certain lines; from what I know of him, I imagine he expects to be very successful—along others. And I expect to have the most interesting experience of my life paying him back for his self-confidence."

She laughed, a laugh far too worldly-wise and weary for a girl twenty-one years old.

"If it weren't for giving him his deserts," she said, "I believe I would marry him—just to get out of this rotten life, and away from all the rest of you!"

The portières parted. A footman stood in the doorway. "Dr. Noble, if you please, miss," he said.

The two men sprang to their feet; the girl cast a mocking glance back at them, and advanced with outstretched hands.

Her laugh died as quickly as it had risen. A perfectly dressed man, so tall that he seemed fairly to tower in the great room, his black head flung back, his dark eyes full on the girl's face, came forward silently, bowed to her companions, and stood waiting for her to speak.

It was no more the shamefaced boy whom Jacqueline had kissed on the road to Wallacetown than she was the fresh-faced, heartbroken little girl who had clung to him, weeping because he was forcing her to say good-bye.

CHAPTER II

THE STABLE BOY

JACQUELINE recovered herself quickly, "How do you do?" she said coolly, without holding out her hand again. "This is a very great surprise, and of course a delightful one. I think you know Mr. Wainright? May I introduce my friend Count Saxburg? Gustav, this is Mr. Noble, of Hamstead, Vermont.—Let me offer you some tea."

David bowed slightly a second time. "I think the Count and I met once in Paris last summer," he said; and turning from the Austrian, who stared a moment, and then coloured violently, muttering a few words unintelligibly, but in visible surprise, "Thank you, yes—clear, please—no sugar—no lemon—no cognac."

"And a cigarette?" she went on, as he sat down on the great sofa beside her. "We have all been smoking, but we got so interested in your note—I have been telling Cyril and Gustav about it—and your probable arrival in its wake, that we seem to have stopped. Have you been long in London?"

"About two weeks. There is a clinical congress here, as possibly you did not know. It meets in various capitals from year to year. Last summer it was in Paris, and next year, I believe, to be in New York. Will you try one of mine?" he added, taking a cigarette case of engraved gold from his pocket, and offering it first to Jacqueline and then to the two men. "They're fair, I think."

"But surely you are not a doctor yet?" She was extremely conscious of the grave eyes of the man beside her as she leaned forward for Gustav to light the cigarette between her red lips.

"I was fortunate enough to get my degree at Harvard in three years, and we get our title after two in the medical school; that of course would not admit me to the congress, however, if it had not been for the kindness of Dr. Ross, with whom I am travelling, and who was good enough to do a little wire-pulling for me."

"In—er—just what capacity are you with him? Cyril has been telling us something of your very interesting career during your first year at college, but was obliged to stop short at his own graduation, leaving you in the doctor's hands, more or less disabled, but planning, as he understood it, to be his chauffeur that summer."

"I am grateful," said David, "to Mr. Wainright for abbreviating the story I had to tell you—I feared it might be tediously long! With one year already accounted for, I shall be able to be less tiresome. Yes, I went there first as a chauffeur—do you remember how crazy I was for an 'ottermobile' when I was a boy? I still do all our driving, but his kindness took me out of the rank of chore-boy sooner than I could have hoped without it. My second year in college I was able to have a room in one of the less expensive dormitories, and to do tutoring instead of minding furnaces; and by the third—my last year—I had time to begin to make some friends, and enough money saved up after my second summer with the doctor to feel I

7²

wouldn't be 'sponging' if I did. The fellows—and their families—were all awfully kind—and so much less critical of the verdure of the Vermont hills, which I knew covered me pretty completely, than I expected! Dr. Ross insisted on my going to him for good and all as soon as I graduated. It's a little hard to answer your very natural question 'in what capacity?'—I'm not his chauffeur any more—that is, I think he would hardly allow you to call me that, though I shouldn't mind in the least! He's planning to call on you and Mr. Huntington very shortly himself, if you'll allow him, so perhaps he can give you a more satisfactory explanation than I can. He wanted to adopt me legally—funny, isn't it?—but my own father wouldn't part with his ugly duckling. I'm to be his assistant later on—and that, of course, means succeeding to his entire practice in time—a long time off, I hope! Meanwhile he indulges me most shamefully—aren't you ready for another cigarette, Jacqueline? You've let that go out. Allow me to light it for you this time——? I hope I haven't bored you? Ever know a fellow named Bobby Hutchinson—just between us in college—Mr. Wainright? He'd have told that same story so that you would have been shedding tears of amusement and sympathy and interest—he says I'll never be any kind of a doctor, because I don't know how to talk. He ought to know—he's getting to be a very successful one himself. I think I've heard him and his sister Nancy speak of you. . . ."

Jacqueline glanced at Cyril. He was flushing no less painfully than Gustav had done a few minutes earlier. He rose, however, with dignity.

"I believe both brother and sister are noted for their wit," he said icily. "In our society we should call it vulgarity. Are you planning," he said pointedly, taking Jacqueline's hand and bending over it, "to get a little rest before your party tonight? I fear you are greatly overtired."

"I'm saving the first dance for you," she said gaily, "and I haven't half thanked you for your wonderful flowers—and all the wonderful birthday wishes that went with them—I'll surely answer your note very soon."

"And mine, Désirée?" the Austrian also bent over her hand, but looked at her lips.

"Yes, and yours. *Auf Wiedersehen.*" She turned to David. "I'm having a ball tonight," she said, "in honour of my birthday. It would give me great pleasure——"

"I am sorry," he said, "I have already made other plans. But I will see you again before I leave London. May I not," he added, "take either of you gentlemen somewhere? I have my car at the door."

All three went out together talking. Jacqueline bit her lip, walked to the fire, and kicked a half-burnt log viciously. It fell apart, blazing again. A footman came into the room, and took up the tongs.

"Dr. Noble has sent me for his cigarette case, miss," he said, when the log was in place again. "He thinks he must have dropped it. Will I disturb you if I look for it, miss?"

"Will you ask Dr. Noble," said Jacqueline slowly, "whether he will not come back and search for it himself?" and as David re-entered, and the footman withdrew, she put out her hand again.

"Won't you shake hands with me?" she asked. "And won't you let me tell you—that I wish to welcome you very warmly, and that I am filled with admiration and surprise."

"And I," he said quietly, "am filled with disappointment, and grief—and shame."

CHAPTER III

JACQUELINE'S SIDE

"Can't we sit down?" he asked, as the girl gave an exclamation of amazed anger, "and really talk? You know I never did like shams, and I see by your tastes that your 'intuitions' have been playing you false, just as I feared they would."

"My tastes?" she flared.

"Yes—in friends—and little customs like cognac for afternoon tea, and dresses—like this. We doctors believe a great deal in heredity and environment, you know, and are always quarrelling as to which is the more powerful. I should say that in your case they were pretty well matched."

Jacqueline sprang to her feet, and reached for the old-fashioned pull-bell that hung by the door. David was too quick for her.

"Don't have me put out quite yet," he said more gently. "I'll go directly, anyway, if you really want me to—I shouldn't have said that. You were fairly insulting yourself, you know, when I first came in—and I was so surprised that I am still a little stunned. You see, I've been hoping and waiting and working for five years to be worthy to come to the most loyal friend, the truest lover, the fairest girl God ever made. And when I thought I could, without too much presumption, do so, I find—she doesn't exist any longer. What happened, Désirée? I think I have a right to ask on—on account of the road to Wallacetown. You seem to me, in spite of all this splendour, so tired, and so bitter, and so lonely."

"Don't," she said quickly, "I don't want to talk to you. It's hardly fair—after all these years—to remind me of a silly episode in which I played a very foolish part."

"Is that the way it looks to you? It hasn't been an episode to me—it's been a lodestar to decent living, and high ambition, and success. It's seemed to me, all along, that the part you played would have been that of a guardian angel, if it hadn't been so divinely flesh and blood as well! You were a spirit and a saviour, but a sweetheart, too—don't you believe me, my dear?"

"No," she said slowly, "I don't. If that is the way you felt, why did you leave me to face everything alone? Don't you realize, that in all those years, you never once tried to see *me*? It was always I that sought *you* out! Even the—the road to Wallacetown wasn't an accident! I went out that night because Sheldon had told me that you were in danger, and I wanted to help, if I could! I lied to you about the reason for my being there, just as I'd lied, or acted a lie, to other people, over and over again, in order to be with you. And that last night when I went to your room and you turned me out—oh, you were right to do it,

75

of course! There wasn't a moment, ever, when you weren't
a truer gentleman than any I've known since—but think,
when my grandfather trapped me, of the part I had to
admit I'd played. Boldness—'shamelessness,' he called it
—for the sake of—a servant! And a servant who—I had to
admit it—had never made the slightest advances to me!
At whose head I'd flung myself! Who must therefore hold
me so cheap that—that——"

"That he had probably proved how cheaply he did
hold you?" asked David with a strange quietness.

"Yes—just that. He accused me of having done things
—of having let you do things—which up to that moment
I'd been only vaguely conscious that—that any one did.
Young girls—sheltered young girls, I mean, like me—have
certain intuitions—and—and theories of course—they're
not fools—but everything is so—blessedly hazy in their
minds! I was so stunned—so horribly stunned and terrified
when he made his hideous charges that——"

"That he saw how mistaken he'd been. Yes. He would
do that." David's mind was travelling back to the lovely,
impetuous child sitting beside him on the narrow bed in
his dark little room. "He couldn't very well help it, if he
was in his senses."

"But not until he'd taught me, when I was far too young
and unprepared—truths I couldn't forget again. Awful
truths about human nature—oh, why do they have to be
true? I've never got away from the horror of the fact that
they are!"

"No," said David.

"And then," she went on, "I was put into a convent.
And the Sisters were told not to give me any liberty at all
—a girl sixteen years old, with no outlet for her overflowing vitality! I—'needed to be watched.' If I'd been a boy,
I'd have gone—straight to the devil, of course. But I only
—didn't sleep. For nights and nights I lay awake, because
my mind, which they couldn't confine, was so much more
active than my body! And when I lay awake I cried for
you—very quietly of course, so no one would hear me—a
sort of strangling sobbing—missed you till I ached all over
—longed to see you for the tiniest minute, hungered for

76

your touch! And I never had a letter or even a message—not a single word to tell me that you still cared—if you ever had cared, really! So of course I came to believe that my grandfather was right. That though you hadn't held me quite as cheaply as he had thought at first, still—— I think I suffered as much as I possibly could—as much as any one possibly could—and then I grew very hard. I'm hard still. I suppose I always shall be."

So far she had looked at him steadily. Now she turned away, her lips quivering.

"It had all been as mystical and beautiful and holy to me as—as the Eucharist," she said in a hushed voice. "And to you it had been merely——"

"No, it hadn't," interrupted David fiercely, "it hadn't—*it hadn't*! Oh, you poor little girl!"

The sincerity of the startled grief in his voice was unmistakable. Before she could prevent it, he had seized both her hands, and pressed them against his heart with a sort of rough breathlessness that was at the same time infinitely tender.

"And I never thought of all this before," he said in a voice which showed plainly that the thought, now that it had come, was utterly unendurable. "It—it was a sacrament to me too. It was because I wanted to keep it so that —I did what I did. That little room had been a sanctuary —and it wouldn't have been, any longer, if I had let you stay! I knew I couldn't stand it—the way things were going. And you were so little and sweet, and innocent, that you couldn't understand—and of course I couldn't tell you! But I hoped—I thought—you'd trust me even if you didn't understand. I thought you knew I loved you—that you couldn't help knowing that—though you couldn't guess how much. If you couldn't believe this before—won't you believe it now?"

She drew her hands away, quite gently and without haste, her self-possession, apparently, strangely restored by the fact that he had been shaken out of his.

"Yes," she said, sitting down on the sofa again, "I believe you now. I—I can't very well help doing that. There's something about you that's—very convincing. But if you

77

haven't thought of my side, isn't it largely because you've been thinking of yourself—your side of it—all the time? Isn't that what you always do, unless you're very much moved, just for a moment, as you are now? Isn't it a question of *your* viewpoint—*your* happiness—*your* success always? How much have you ever helped your family—gone home to see your mother, had long talks with your father, tried to see that those three brothers and that little sister of yours didn't have to face the odds that you have? —Oh, you've succeeded, wonderfully! But you couldn't have done it if you'd loved any human being as much as you love your career! And now you've come here, expecting me to fall into your mouth like a ripe cherry, and be a suitable ornament, in time, to your very successful establishment! I'm not too blind to see what would happen if I did, even if you are! I should probably fall in love with you over again, if I'd let myself, and then you'd fail me again, worse than you did before! And that would affect you very little indeed—and it might affect me a good deal. You'd pursue your career—unhampered. But it might be rather difficult for me to find something that I would care to pursue!"

David, entirely calm again, was lighting a cigarette. The vivid colour from the flame of the match flashed across his face for a moment, flared, flickered, and went out, leaving it in the shadow.

"Your opinion of human nature seems to be almost unnecessarily pessimistic," he said coolly. "What you so cheerfully predict might happen, of course, but it seems to me extremely doubtful."

The girl had expected as hot a denial to her statement as the one which he had made five minutes earlier. She made no effort to control her rising anger.

"Don't forget what brought about my present opinion of human nature in the first place," she said, "or forget that since then I've had nothing to raise it—only one thing after another to lower it. Since I left the convent I've had three years 'in society'—on both sides of the Atlantic. Do you realize what that means—to a girl like me? It means that almost every man who meets me tries to marry me, for one thing—that I'm flattered and courted and cajoled and—desired, and that all that is called—'love'! It means also that I'm watched, night and day, by women who are jealous of me—and there are many such; by men whom I haven't favoured—and there are still more of those —who are hoping I'll make some kind of a little slip, that I'll soil my satin skirts just enough so that they can shriek to the Heavens that they're dirty! They haven't been able to yet, but I have to be eternally on my guard that they shan't be—and hating and despising them through it all! But dresses like this one—which you don't need to tell me isn't modest, or even decent—and friends like those you found here—and I know what sort of men they are—and cognac and gambling and flirting and dancing—and—and all the rest of it—everything that makes up a modern belle's existence—are just second nature to me now! I was shocked—oh, far more shocked than you are—at first—but now I never even think of it—in fact, I couldn't live any other way! You're perfectly right—that girl you used to know doesn't exist any longer. She was careless—because she was so innocent that she could be. I am careful, because I am very, very worldly-wise. She gave her favours freely, because she loved so much. I give none, because I love no one at all. You are wasting your time to come here. Just before you came I promised those two men you found with me to let them know tonight which one I am going to marry."

"Everything you've told me," said David, "is true, perfectly true, except that. You are going to marry me."

"I am not," said Jacqueline hotly, "if for no better reason than that you wouldn't want me to if I told you the rest of my conversation with them."

"I am open to conviction," remarked David, smiling.

"I told them—about our engagement. I pretended that I had almost forgotten—but that it was just a silly case of calf-love—a pastime for a bored girl—a . ."

Not the slightest change came over his face, and he made no effort to interrupt her, but she stopped, horror-stricken at something hidden beneath his perfect self-control which she could divine and feel.

"Can't you understand why I did it?"

"No," he said slowly, "I can't. I believe it's the only thing you ever did in all your life that wasn't—splendid. And you've just accused me of not realizing that—our love was a sacrament. If *you* realized it, how could you defile it so?"

"Because I had lost faith in the sacrament. Since I had nothing holy left, there was no profanation. An atheist can't blaspheme."

"I think I see," he answered; "I'll—I'll try. Perhaps it was my fault anyway, not yours, if all these years I seemed to be robbing you of your holy thing. I wasn't though, really. I must convince you of that before we go any further. May I sit down beside you and show you something?"

The quiet question was almost a godsend. It caught Jacqueline back from the torrent of pent-up emotion, which, for the first time in years, had swept her off her feet. She steadied her voice, and spoke quietly and courteously.

"Why, yes," she said gently, "anything you like. And please—let's try to be friends, after all, can't we? I meant, when I found you were coming, to 'pay you back in your own coin'—to insult you and hurt you. I can't do that, no matter how hard I try; you are too invulnerable. I'd only hurt myself. I see that clearly now—what did you know about Gustav and Cyril that upset them so? Lots of people are clever—but *you're* powerful—as the rock of Gibraltar, and just as hard, I'm afraid! I don't think it will be safe for any woman to marry you until you are ready to give up your career to have her—and to do it then to serve, not possess her! But you're very wonderful, David. And now that I've told you my side—if I've made you see it—I'm proud, very proud, to have you here——"

"I see," he said, "that the girl I used to know does exist, after all. I thought she did, if I could only find her. Look!"

He drew from his pocket a little package wrapped in soiled paper and tied with a frayed string.

"You never had a letter from me while you were at the convent," he said, "because I was afraid it would only hurt you, if you did—that your mail would be opened and scrutinized and reported upon. Wasn't that so?"

"Yes . . ."

"But I wrote to you—from the time I left you that night in your grandfather's library and started for Harvard. Regularly, every Sunday night, before I went to bed. We've been talking of sacraments—well, that was my Evensong. Of course the letters in themselves—weren't much. They just told you that I'd got a new job, or what marks I had in my courses, or how much money I'd put in the bank. Once in a while—not often, partly because it was so hard, at first, for me to express my feelings on paper—I'd never tried to do it before, you see—and partly because I didn't suppose it was necessary—I told you that I loved you. Then I used to date and seal and address the letters—and put them away. When there were enough of them to make a little package, I tied them up—like this. I brought one of the packages with me today, because I thought it might interest you—I didn't realize that I'd need it—to prove my case! Will you open it, please?"

Jacqueline's fingers trembled over the knot. David took out his pocket-knife and cut it. Half a dozen cheap envelopes, covered with a sprawling, boyish handwriting fell from the crackling paper. He picked one up, opened it, and handed the scribbled sheets to her.

"This one is dated in December, in my first year in college," he said. "Suppose you read it aloud? . . ."

"Dear Jacqueline"—the letter ran—"It is awfully cold in my room because I have no fire and I am writing with my mittens on, so I suppose this will look worse than usual.

"We have been having some awful 'tests' called 'hour-exams.' I have passed them all, but nothing to brag about. Some of them I just skinned through. Most of the fellows learned more at school, before they came here, than I could in Hamstead. Lots of subjects we didn't take up at all. But I guess I can do better next year.

"Everyone seems to be getting ready to go home for Christmas. I have looked up the fare to Hamstead and its $5.91. So I don't think I shall try to. I wish I could send you a nice Christmas present. Some day I will.

"I think about you a lot, especially how I went to sleep with my head in your lap. You were awfully good to me that day. I'll never forget it.

"Well, I guess I must close now, with love from David.

"P.S.—If I could put kisses on paper I would cover this whole page with them instead of words."

He took the letter from her, folded it, and putting it back in its envelope again, opened another. Jacqueline stretched out her hand.

"No," she said unsteadily, "not—not now. I'd like to have them all—not just this one package—if you'll give them to me. But I'd rather read them when I'm alone."

"Then let me show you something else."

He took her hand, touching her for the first time, and laid it palm-upwards on her lap; and into it he dropped a ring, a ring more beautiful than the girl, surfeited as she was with jewels, had ever seen. The stones were large, but it was the quality rather than the size of the gems that was so remarkable. Jacqueline knew that there was a fortune in the gold circle set with a ruby glowing between two diamonds, knew instantly the symbol as well as the value —the red heart of love burning to the white heat of passion. She rose, and taking it to the fire, whose dying coals gave the only light to the darkening room, turned it over slowly again and again. At length she spoke.

"This ring cost a great deal—not just money, though of course I know how valuable it is—but heat and cold and hunger, slights and deprivations of every sort. It explains why, though you started out with twelve hundred dollars, and made more money all the time, you drove an ice-cart, and slept in miserable lodgings, and took care of furnaces. It represents five years of sacrifice—and I thought you had been thinking only of yourself!"

"Since you put it that way—yes."

"Five years of sacrifice for some one who does not exist —'the most loyal friend, the bravest lover, the fairest girl God ever made!' A lady who kissed her stable boy, and— rightly—gloried in her kisses. And what have you found in her stead? A woman in whom 'heredity and environment are pretty evenly matched'—in other words, the frivolous

82

daughter of a drunken reprobate and a ballet dancer!"

"From the bottom of my heart," he cried, "I ask you to forgive me those words!"

"And from the bottom of mine," she said, going to him quickly, and kneeling down beside him, "I know that they are true! And now, please, go away!"

She slipped the ring back into his hand, and as she did so, he felt the tears falling on it.

"Jacqueline," he commanded, "look at me—get off your knees! Go *away*! Why, I've just *come*!" Then as she burst into convulsive sobs and tried to break away from him, he lifted her in his arms, and held down the hands that strove to hide her face.

"Do you hate me," he asked, "because I didn't understand? Because I thought only of myself—remember I was suffering too! Because I didn't guess how much you'd have to face when I told your grandfather, and left you with him? In short, because I was an ignorant, egotistical boy, trying hard to be square?"

"No—no—you know I don't!"

"Then why do you tell me to go away?"

"Because I know how much you must despise me—if I can measure it by the way I despise myself!"

She tried once more to wrench herself free, but this time she might as well have struggled against the strength of the sea.

"And if I told you that I didn't despise you—that I love you with all my heart and soul, and that I know, in spite of everything you do and say, that you love me, the same way, and always have?"

"It wouldn't make any difference. Grandfather——"

"I saw him *first*, this time. He feels rather differently than he did before."

"There are a thousand other reasons then. We're as far apart as the two poles in our habits and tastes and ideals. I'd surprise—and shock and grieve you. You were jealous before—you'd be jealous—with much more reason—now. I couldn't satisfy you, no matter how hard I tried. And you would come first to me—but I would come second to your career. . . ."

David laughed, a low, happy, triumphant laugh. "Who's jealous now?" he whispered. "You're fighting, just because you've made up your mind not to yield. But you will. I asked you once if any one but me had kissed you, and hurt you dreadfully, because you thought I shouldn't need to ask. I don't this time. I know, that in spite of yourself, you've been waiting for me."

She felt the wonderful ring slip on her finger, and the hand that bore it raised to his lips. Then his arms closed around her once more. She knew that she was powerless against his strength, his will, his love, and a feeling of glory in her weakness swept over her. He was kissing her hair, her forehead, her throat. In another instant she thought it would be her mouth. But there he stopped.

"I have taken the rest," he said, "won't you give me that—*Désirée*?"

CHAPTER IV

THE ENGAGEMENT

FOR five years every battle that David had fought, with himself and his surroundings, had resulted in victory— triumph spelled in capital letters. It was therefore not strange that, with the usual healthy egotism of youth, he had come to regard defeat as an impossibility. It was equally natural that, having had little time for amusement, and little inborn taste for dissipation, he should have scant understanding, and less charity, for the frivolity of others. Persiflage puzzled and horseplay disgusted him—without being consciously a prig, he saw no reason why every one else should not be as serious of purpose and as austere of life as he was himself.

His natural dignity of bearing and character, his self-confidence, or rather, egotism—the natural result of his success against heavy odds—made him appear much more thoroughly a man of the world than he really was. The only world he knew was a very small one, and as severe in judging other spheres which revolved differently from itself as it was satisfied with its own revolutions; and even in the world which he did know, he had taken time to make so few friends, and these were so relatively unimportant in his scheme of life, that his knowledge of human nature of any kind was extremely superficial. Jacqueline, who as a child had been so refreshingly naïve, and who still seemed, at times, to have retained much of her naïveté, was, in truth, mondaine to her very heart, though that heart constantly overflowed with sympathy and understanding and affection; while David, who seemed—and believed himself to be—entirely master of this and any other possible situation, was ignorant of the very A-B-C of the society into which he had so confidently flung himself—a fact which would, unfortunately, have disturbed him very little if he had been wise enough to be aware of it.

His engagement to Jacqueline, announced instantly, on the night of her twenty-first birthday—for he had refused to consider "the sham" of keeping it a secret—seemed merely another step—an important one to be sure, but by no means warranting a change in schedule, or undue satisfaction on having reached an important capital on time—on his single-track railway. Did he not deserve her? Had he not worked and waited long and faithfully for her? Was he not in every way her equal, in many her superior?

But if the betrothal scene which was only a few hours past had not brought elation to David, it had brought an exquisite torture to Jacqueline. She had fallen under the spell of his presence, almost as soon as her fortress had been besieged, her surrender had been both complete and unconditional. For the vulgar insinuations, the criticism, the sneers at her choice, which she knew were bound to come, she cared not at all, knowing the sterling metal of which the man she had chosen was made; that he had chosen her, that he still wanted her, in spite of everything, was a matter for thankful prayer; but that there was a moat between them, which would be difficult, if not impossible, to bridge over, unless the conqueror possessed greater engineering skill than she believed—she realized with a pang of something very like terror before she was fully awake the next morning; nevertheless, she rose at once, lest she should not be dressed in time for the visit which she expected would take place at the earliest possible moment. Her room was filled with flowers, her bed-side table piled high with notes of congratulation, messages and gifts arrived steadily all day; but it was four in the afternoon when David finally appeared. She expected explanations, apologies for his tardiness, the caresses and regrets of a lover no less disappointed than she herself at the delay. Instead, he seemed to have no idea that he had been remiss: gave her a glowing account of a hospital he had visited that forenoon; a sketch of the maturing plan for his trip to the Continent, now less than two weeks off, and which he apparently saw no reason for giving up; a humorous description of his experiences in a fashionable shop; then after a scant hour with her, rose to leave!

"You say you wish me to join you to a fancy dress ball this evening—such things aren't much in my line."

"I rather hoped you'd dine and dress here, and that we'd go together."

"I can't arrange that—Dr. Ross and I have already made engagements for the evening—but I'll join you about midnight, if you really insist."

"I don't insist—you must do as you prefer. But it is only fair to tell you that if you don't, considering that the engagement is already announced, it will probably provoke considerable comment."

"From persons whose opinion isn't worth having! Well, I'll come! But don't accept any further similar invitations if you can help it."

"I am going to Lady Thornington's place near Oxford on the fourteenth for the week-end. She has just sent me a message saying that she had written you asking you to come too. You made a most favourable impression on her last night, and that is a family and a house which I know you will enjoy."

"I liked her, too—I'll gladly go there. Good-bye, my dear, I'll see you later."

Five o'clock found her alone again. With a desperate resolve to shake off her depression, she ordered her horse, and was putting on her habit, when she was told that Mr. Wainright was waiting to see her in the library; if she were disengaged, he wondered if she would receive him.

"Tell him I'm just starting for a ride, Hodges; but if he'll have a cup of tea with me first, you may serve it there at once."

"So that's how you settled it?" was his greeting as she entered the room.

"Won't you sit down? Yes—I'm sorry, Cyril—I mean I'm sorry things didn't come differently for you. I realize that I had led you to think that perhaps they would. You don't feel very badly?"

"I? Oh, no—it is of course the most trivial of disappointments. I especially wish to embrace the first opportunity of extending my congratulations to your fiancé."

"Cyril—if this is one of your sarcastic days, would you mind going home?"

"I should, very much. I did not expect the pleasure of tea alone with you, and I shall certainly not forgo it—I think I see it coming now."

"David has only just left," said Jacqueline, handing him his cup.

"It isn't necessary to sound so apologetic—he's not dining with you then?"

"He had some previous engagement—a medical dinner, I believe."

"Of course the Continental trip is given up?"

"No, indeed, it's too great an opportunity."

"Then you're not to be married immediately?"

"No—that is——" the girl stopped suddenly, her face flooding with colour, realizing that the question had not even been brought up. "Not at present," she ended, rather lamely.

"And Mr. Huntington?"

"Oh, grandfather's disappointed, of course; but he's more reconciled than I had dared to hope."

"He had some other choice, perhaps?"

"Cyril, you have no right—you know very well what he wished."

"Can't you prevail upon Dr. Noble at least to establish himself in London? I really fear that a separation from you might bring about serious results with Mr. Huntington, and he would hardly care to move again, now that he is so congenially placed. Besides, I hate to think of you going to waste in the provincialism of Boston, Mass. Of course you know that every one is saying that you are absolutely demented to throw yourself away like this?"

"If they knew the man I am going to marry as well as I do, they would not say so."

"As well? Forgive me—but isn't it five years since you have seen Dr. Noble?"

Jacqueline rose. "I'm afraid you'll have to excuse me," she said rather coolly. "I don't like to keep Sophie Second waiting too long. Will you go and see grandfather for a few minutes?"

"I'm riding myself—I'd much rather come with you, if you don't mind——" Then, as she hesitated, "Surely, we haven't got to give up all our good times—isn't old lang syne to count for something—in this very brand-new engagement?"

David, on reaching Claridge's, was told that Dr. Ross had just gone out, leaving no message. He waited as long as possible for him, then, disturbed and puzzled, he went to the dinner without him; no word had been received from him there, either; finally, when David returned to the hotel to find their suite a second time deserted, he became genuinely alarmed, and when the door at last opened to admit the doctor, wreathed in smiles and apparently unaware that he ought to be the cause of either anxiety or censure, the boy flung down the wrap he was holding and greeted him with the angry anxiety that came from long waiting.

"I was just putting on my coat to go out and hunt for you! Where on earth have you been?"

"Where I should think you would have been—with your fiancée!"

"Good Lord! I knew you meant to call on her some time soon; but did you forget all about the Savoy? They delayed the dinner nearly an hour for you, and we telephoned to every club in London, I believe."

Dr. Ross regarded his protégé blankly for a minute, then

burst out laughing. "What a joke!" he exclaimed. "I did forget it completely."

"You don't seem to take it very seriously," said David stiffly. "You broke an engagement, you know."

"My dear boy, do calm down a little. Supposing I did? If I were a little younger, I should certainly try to break yours—I think that girl's the most glorious creature I ever saw in my life."

David unbent sufficient to smile. "You like her then?" he said, with evident satisfaction.

"*Like her!* Why didn't you describe her to me a little, so I wouldn't be so completely dazzled! She was just coming up the steps after a ride, with a tall, fair fellow, when I got there, and there's nothing like exercise like that to show off gorgeous colour, and nothing like a black habit to do justice to a perfect figure. The whole thing nearly knocked me over! She gave me a glance, and then she held out her hand, and said, 'I think this must be Dr. Ross.' It was one of the most charming and graceful things I ever saw done."

"A little unconventional, wasn't it? You might have been any one else in the world."

"Yes, but you see I wasn't. I fancy that girl's a good guesser. She turned to this blond squire with the air of a queen dismissing a subject, and remarked without much enthusiasm, 'I'll see you again tonight, I suppose—I'll try to save you a dance, but I won't promise——' and then she devoted herself exclusively to me."

Dr. Ross took a whiff at his cigar, and glanced at David, who was still pacing the floor of the tiny drawing-room.

"She took off her hat when she got inside," he went on, "and her hair—loosened by the wind, I suppose, tumbled down and fell all around her shoulders—I bet it's down to her knees! So then she went and fetched her grandfather to see me, while she was 'gone to get tidy.' He wasn't enthusiastic, but he was decent, and he asked me to stay to dinner. I wouldn't have missed it for a dozen Savoys. She was in pale yellow when she came down the next time—soft and sheer—— You can go to medical dinners every day, but you meet a girl like that once in a life-time.—

David, how soon are you going to be married?"

"Why—I hadn't thought. In about three years I suppose."

"Three years—what's to prevent your making it three weeks?"

"We'll be in Stockholm by that time, won't we?"

"You're not serious, are you?"

"Certainly—why not?"

Dr. Ross rose, and with some embarrassment, laid his hand on the boy's shoulder. "Look here," he said, in a voice so gentle that he tried to make it sound a little gruff, "you're not making that—ridiculous plan—on account of —lack of funds, are you? Of course you don't want to be the dependent husband of a rich wife—and I wouldn't for an instant hear of that haughty old scoundrel being given a chance to do more than provide Jacqueline with pocket money. But I've meant—ever since you first came to me, David—that the money my poor son inherited from his mother, which she asked he should have intact as his wedding gift—should be yours, when you married, my dear boy. It isn't a fortune for these days, but it's rather a substantial sum, just the same. And ever since that girl came laughing up the steps I've been thinking—if you'd only bring her to live in my old house—how that laugh would sound to me, ringing through its emptiness, what it would mean to me, in time, to have a little child there again—I had some lonely years, David, before you came to me——"

David gripped his hand. "And I had some lonely ones, too, before you took me," he said gratefully, "but I can't do what you suggest. Even if it weren't accepting more than I am willing to—I don't feel a man can do first-class work if he tries to combine school and matrimony. I've always felt a good deal of scorn for the fellows who married before they'd completed their course, and for the girls who let them. A few years more won't hurt either of us—and now I suppose I must go and dress for that damned ball——"

It was nearly midnight when he entered the ballroom, having spent the greater part of an hour between the front door and that particular apartment, so enormous was the crowd at the colossal and splendid house where the party was being held. The beautiful apartment was filled with dancers, and the sparkling light from hundreds of crystal chandeliers, the blaze of jewels, the magnificent costumes which seemed to shift before him with the brilliance and swiftness of a kaleidoscope, gave him an immediate and involuntary sense of exhilaration and intoxication. He felt as if he were witnessing the sudden blooming of a huge, exotic orchid. Then a feeling of disgust came over him for the extravagance, the ostentation and the lack of dignity before him, and he stood, eagerly looking through the dancing crowd, to see if he could distinguish Désirée, and bear her away from this abnormal atmosphere to some more quiet spot where they could have a few minutes alone.

Two other men were standing by the door talking together, and, in spite of a skilful and complete disguise, David recognized the one nearest him as the Austrian Count, by his rotund figure and marked accent. The conversation, which he naturally could not help overhearing, at first proved uninteresting enough to him—a detailed account of the respective merits of several fragile, though shining, "stars" of the music-halls. After singing the praises of various beauties, with whom he stood on various degrees of intimacy, he changed the subject.

"Those are all very good for London," he said lightly, "but we haf them much, much better in Vienna—there, there is really some choice. And ven Miss Huntington is also in Vienna, vat vill you amuse yourselves with here?"

"But Miss Huntington isn't going to Vienna, you fool! She's going back to America with this young doctor who's suddenly turned up out of thin air. All London is talking of nothing else. What did you say this fellow was in the beginning—a blacksmith?"

"Mein Gott! You do not suppose she really intends to marry him? Désirée is *grande coquette*—he is a blind, nothing more,—a tool to increase the infatuation of others by yet more uncertainty. But he will not long be a rival— a man who was with her but one hour yesterday—as I have it from Wainright direct—does know the meaning of a *grande passion*. After his little call she went to ride with our cherub Cyril, and this evening did she come here with

Freddy in his electric brougham."

"Good for her—she has the right idea! As long as she's so impartial, no one can get jealous, and I notice her swains—if she goes about alone with 'em—are all that harmless variety like Freddy and Cyril. Doesn't go much with you, does she, old sport?"

The Count grimaced. "I console myself with the thought that no beautiful woman becomes *amoureuse* of the men she trusts too much," he said cynically. "She promised to unmask early, and I have in vain been trying to discover her. Rest assured, it will be a sight worth going far to find."

Seething with rage, and knowing that if he stayed where he was another moment, he should certainly do some violent injury to the Austrian, David pushed past the two men, through the crowd, and made his way towards the conservatory. It was dimly lighted, the air was heavy with the scent of flowers, and in the middle stood a great pool of water, its calm surface unbroken by a fountain, reflecting the beauty of the luxuriant growth all around it. He sat down on a marble bench near it, leaning his head on his hands, and gazing into its quiet depths, and again a feeling of being entranced and bewitched overcame him. Decidedly, no such houses, and no such parties, existed in Boston. And Jacqueline must be rescued from this atmosphere—would it perhaps not, after all, be better to follow Dr. Ross's advice? But he regretted the necessity—two or three years later would be so much better, from every standpoint. He was actually impatient with her for making him feel, by her choice of living like this, that he ought to take her away——

A low laugh came from the further corner of the great room—to his angry imagination it seemed to fairly ruffle the placid water by which he had found an instant's seclusion and peace. He sprang to his feet and went rapidly in the direction from which it had come. A circle of masked men stood about a seated girl, masked and wrapped in a great cloak.

"Oh, well," she was saying, "it's only a few minutes now, anyway, and if you wish a private view, so to speak, before we go into supper—*me voilà, messieurs!*"

She rose as she spoke, and David, forcing his way forward, stood before her. Apparently Gustav's suggestion of the evening before had not fallen on deaf ears, for she was dressed as Cleopatra. A wide band of dull gold bound her hair, completely covering her forehead; a wider band of the same metal encircled her waist, and there were pendant earrings, studded with gems. in her ears, and a golden fan hung from a jewelled chain from her girdle. Her flesh-coloured gauze skirt was diaphanous; her slim white ankles were bare; her silver sandals glittered. She had clasped her bare arms behind her head, and stood looking at them all through lazy half-shut eyes. As she caught sight of another masked figure, she took a slow step forward and held out her hand.

"Welcome!" she said slowly. "Cleopatra is holding court tonight for all her friends alike. These gentlemen are about to cast lots as to which shall take her out to supper. Will you draw?"

He nodded without answering. The man nearest him was tearing up a slip of paper into narrow strips. He straightened them in his hand.

"The longest wins," he said, and turned to each man in succession. The longest slip fell to David.

Still without speaking he bowed, and offering her his arm, walked towards the ballrom with her. At the entrance to the conservatory he paused.

"If you will excuse me for a minute," he said very quietly, taking off his mask as he spoke, "I will go back and get the cloak that you dropped. Then I may feel that you are sufficiently clothed not to mind taking you home."

"*David!* I felt it might be you! Do you mean to say you—don't like my dress? I've been so admired—having such a good time——"

"Do you refuse to come home with me?"

"Of course not—I'd like nothing better—but don't look at me like that!"

"I'm trying not to look at you at all."

He held back the curtains, and she went down the stairs in front of him, slowly, her white shoulders gleaming.

They were in her carriage before he spoke to her again.

"Are men simply so many shuttlecocks to you?" he asked then, almost roughly. "A call from me, a ride with Cyril, 'Freddy,' whoever he may be, as an escort to the ball! Then undecided where to cast your favours next, I find you in the most immodest dress I ever saw on any woman in my life, letting a crowd of mountebanks draw lots for you."

"Oh, my dear, I'm sorry! I never thought of any of it in that light at all—I told you we would be bound to look at things differently. But I waited indoors all day for you, and you wouldn't take me tonight yourself. Tomorrow I'll spend every instant with you—if you'll come to me—and wear a collar up to my ears, and drink cocoa."

"It isn't funny—I heard that vile Austrian talking about you——"

"Gustav? Remember he's dreadfully disappointed—he felt so sure——"

"Then you must have given him more encouragement than I should have believed possible. Is there no limit to your indiscretion?"

"You have no right to speak to me like that. Would you wish me to judge you so harshly—or so hastily?"

"You'll never need to," he said; but something in his voice warned him that he had gone too far. He leaned over and put his arm around her. She made no effort to withdraw, but did not return his caress. The joy had gone out of the evening for her, and when they reached the house she pleaded fatigue, and asked him to leave her. He obeyed, feeling injured—was she to do whatever she pleased, and resent his criticisms? He, too, went home, feeling that the day had been a failure; and neither of them thought, though it was to wring David's heart many times afterward, of the dusty moonlit road between Wallacetown and Hamstead; the slender, clear-eyed girl, riding a lame horse; the stable-boy stumbling beside her; the broken confession, "I've been drinking, Jacqueline," and the quiet answer, "I knew that all the time, David"; the gentle judge who did not condemn, but kissed away the guilt.

CHAPTER V

DAVID's plan for greeting Jacqueline with dignified coolness when he next met her was unpleasantly upset by a
note which was handed him late the following afternoon
telling him that she had been in bed with a severe headache all day, and that, though slightly better, she would be
unable to see him that evening, in case he were thinking
of calling upon her. If she were sufficiently improved to
undertake the trip the next day she and her grandfather
were planning to motor down to Oxford to spend ten days
there quietly at the Inn, before she went to Lady Thornington's, as she realized that she was entirely unequal to
keeping her engagements in town. If David and Dr. Ross
would like to go with them or join them there later, they
would be delighted. If not, she would see him Saturday
week at tea-time at " Boxwood."

"Excellent idea," said Dr. Ross when David handed him
the note, which was quite guiltless of anything of a private
or personal nature. "I'm a little worried about that girl.
She strikes me as an unusually healthy, normal creature,
who's lived on her nerves lately more than is good for her,
and has used up her natural reserves by perpetually overtaxing them. I shouldn't be at all surprised to hear of a
reaction in the form of a serious nervous breakdown before
long. But of course I'm a surgeon, not a nerve-specialist,
so I may be mistaken. If I were you, I should coddle her
up a good deal, and see what it would do for her—it would
be worth a trial, anyway, wouldn't it? Of course we'll
motor down with them?"

The next few days were extremely happy ones. David
had never been to Oxford before, but Jacqueline knew it
well. She surprised him constantly by the scope, as well as
the lack of pedantry, of both her intelligence and her information. They wandered about the beautiful, grey old
city, with her as guide, through courts and churches and
colleges, sitting wrapped in the soft English sunshine in

the ancient green garden of St. John, and under the trees on the Broad Walk of Christ Church; they punted down the river, and had tea at Iffley. She seemed neither sulky nor resentful, but she was so quiet—almost apathetic—that David was frightened. Much has been said—and truthfully—about the inconsistency of woman, but no one has yet done justice to the inconsistency of man. Confronted with the terror of seeing Désirée slip through his fingers, literally as well as figuratively, he forgot entirely that any such thing as a fancy-dress ball had ever taken place. He enveloped her with anxiety and tenderness, and just as a hurt child is reassured by his mother's caresses, and smiles through his tears, Jacqueline gradually laughed and talked again. She loved Oxford, loved showing it to David, loved the river and the old mill at Iffley, loved being quiet alone with him and the two elderly men; she looked sixteen again in her wide-brimmed hats and white dresses. When they reached the top of Magdalen Tower one morning, after they had been in Oxford about a week, they sat down to rest for a few minutes, looking down on the city and the verdant country around it Jacqueline put her cheek against his shoulder, touching him of her own accord for the first time since they had parted years before.

"I wish we could stay on here," she whispered shyly, "like this."

He threw his arm around her, and bent to kiss her. He had been so afraid of startling her back into her defensive shell of passivity, that he had hardly dared embrace her; even now, he ventured only to brush her forehead; she lifted her head, and her soft lips met his. Involuntarily he drew her closer.

"Like this?" he asked, "or—just you and I?" Then, as she did not answer, he said, "Désirée—I don't think we can be married for a long time—are you willing to wait for me?"

"To the end of my life——"

"But in spite of knowing that, I may not be able to hold out much longer—you're very sweet, my darling! If I should ask you——"

Jacqueline smiled. "There are always churches on

every corner—especially in Oxford," she said. And raised her face again.

Perfect as such moments seemed to David, he felt, before their holiday was over, that it was only when he and Jacqueline maintained a strictly impersonal basis as the groundwork for their conversations that such perfection was attained. Jacqueline, indeed, found no fault with anything, and seemed only too content to rest and drift. She was both too tactful and too weary to raise minor points of difference between them, unless David forced an issue. But David, far more analytical, was confronted at every turn with small irritations and trifling details to which most men are blind during their courtship and betrothal, and see in large print after their marriage. The more he saw of Jacqueline's habits, tastes and occupations, the less he liked them. She met his thrift with extravagance, his energy with indolence, his seriousness with levity. He rose at six, to find that she never appeared until ten—unless she were going to early church—a reason which was the last to appeal to him. She took a lady's maid as completely a matter of course as she did a travelling bag. She had never in her life, she confessed, drawn her own bath or picked up her own clothes, and no amount of argument could convince her that there was any earthly reason why she should. She loved to lie for hours among the cushions of a sofa or boat, her hands clasped above her head, her eyes half-shut. When she could be persuaded to walk, she sauntered when David wished to stride. He lectured her perpetually on her shortcomings but made no headway. She replied with an amused and good-natured raillery, and continued to do as she pleased.

On one of their rambles into the country they came to a charming and secluded cottage, almost concealed behind a high-hedged garden. There are, of course, thousands of such cottages in rural England; but it was the first one which David, whose travelling had largely been confined to cities, had ever closely noticed. He waxed enthusiastic over it. If they could find or build one like that, somewhere within motoring distance of the Harvard Medical School, perhaps——

D

"Way off in a lonely place without any neighbours?"

"Why yes. That's my idea of a real home. It's so safe from intrusion. One can live so simply and sincerely."

"You mean I could live there so simply and sincerely while you spent most of your time doing interesting things in the city."

David stiffened. It was the first time she had argued with him.

"You could be busy about the house and garden in the daytime."

"I don't know *how* to be busy about a house and garden."

"You can *learn*, can't you? And of course I'd get home for a late dinner. I could have a laboratory there and do research work evenings and Sundays. If I could live in a place like that I could get married without interfering with——"

"That *career*? Well, it all sounds to me very much like the story on the epitaph on the old tombstone, 'Here lies Mary Anne, resting on Abraham's bosom.'"

"Well?" said David impatiently. He never remembered frivolous stories and did not see the point.

"You know some one came along and wrote underneath it, 'Very nice for Mary Anne, but rather hard on Abraham.' I simply won't be Abraham."

She said it all lightly and happily, but David refused to smile. He continued to look back at the sheltered cottage.

"I want to do things *with you* after we're married," persisted Jacqueline.

"What kind of things?"

"Why, the kind of things we're doing this week—travelling, and going for walks and boating, and—and to parties, too, of course; and I want to keep lots and lots of time free just for *loving*."

David disengaged his hand. "I like to work," he said briefly, "and I am going to. I'd never get anywhere if I lived that way."

"Get anywhere?"

"In my profession. I'd stagnate. I intend to be one of the big men in America ten years from now."

"Whatever else goes by the side?"

"Of course. That's the only possible way to succeed."

Jacqueline pressed her lips together. Then she bent over the grassy edge of the road and began picking violets without answering.

"We might try it," went on David at length.

"Try what?"

"Why, getting married."

The girl burst out laughing. "Mercy, David, how immoral you are! I never should have suspected you of such a suggestion! It all goes to prove that you can't tell by the looks of a frog how far he'll jump, doesn't it? I thought that was what you wanted all the time. I——"

"*Jacqueline!*" cried David, almost roughly, "how can you be so irreverent and indelicate?"

"Why, you started it! You said——"

"You know perfectly well I meant that we might *try a little house* like that and see how we liked it!"

"But suppose you liked it and I didn't?"

"Well, naturally the husband's convenience has to be considered first, doesn't it?"

"Yes, but he ought not to consider his wife as one form of it. I simply refuse to be a convenience to anybody. I want to be——"

"What?"

"*Grande amoureuse.*"

Again David stiffened. "Do you know what that phrase really means?"

The gaiety died out of the girl's face. She sat down on the bank and looked away from him.

"I didn't mean to hurt your feelings," he said after a pause during which she neither answered him nor looked at him.

"I wonder what you'd say if you *did* mean to hurt them?" she asked, raising a flushed and troubled face. "I'm afraid it would be something that we'd—that we'd never get over. And I'm so dreadfully afraid that some time—before very long, perhaps—you are going to say it! And I couldn't bear it—I couldn't! I care so much—so much more than——"

She was trembling from head to foot. David was frightened. He had always held the comfortable theory that women's emotions are never, in love affairs, as violent as men's—or as deep.

"My dear girl——"

"You knew what I meant—just as well as I knew what *you* meant about the little house. Why should it be wrong to be a 'great lover'—unless you *want* to see wrong in it? Don't you ever forget about my—my mother? And even if you can't, why do you feel that she was so—dreadfully bad? She loved my father dearly, even if—— And she gave pleasure to hundreds of people—— If it were wrong for her to do that, why wasn't it wrong for them to go and see her—but you don't feel that! And she was generous and kind-hearted and brave—and so was my father, too! I am not ashamed of my parents, or—or my love for you! If you are——"

"Jacqueline!" interrupted David hotly.

"Well, you seem to be. I'd—I'd rather go home alone, if you don't mind. I wish you would leave me."

There seemed to be nothing else for him to do. He reasoned—or tried in vain to reason—with her for a few minutes, and then strode off down the road alone.

He did not see her again until dinner time. The two older men were inevitably conscious of strained relations, and both, without knowing the cause of the trouble, sided mentally with Jacqueline. Mr. Huntington was glacially polite, and David, who was now quite equal to meeting him on his own ground when it came to icy courtesy, froze perceptibly. Instead of shivering in this chilly atmosphere, Dr. Ross became more and more genial, the girl more and more flippant. If her fiancé were not enjoying himself, she herself was apparently unaware of it, or at least saw no reason why he should not be. And later in the evening, when she had gone to bed, the elder doctor tried again to remonstrate with his protégé:

"David—don't you ever play?"

"What do you mean, play?"

"On general principles. More especially, with Jacqueline."

"We're not children."

"No, but she's dreadfully tired and overwrought—almost ill. She needs to relax. You hurt her all the time, and the only way she knows how to cover it up is by assuming a gaiety she is very far from feeling. Nothing could be worse for her. If she could only be natural—as she must have been as a girl—it would be her salvation. I meant to suggest something like this to you before we came down when I told you to coddle her."

"I believe she has you bewitched," said David coldly, "like every other man she knows—except me. I see her the way she really is."

"No, my boy, you don't—that's just the trouble."

"There isn't any trouble," said David, still more coldly, "and there won't be, if I have my way."

"But you aren't always going to have your way."

"Yes, I am," said David, setting his teeth. "I always have so far, haven't I? She'll see things differently before we start for the Continent."

"You may, too," said Dr. Ross under his breath, as, without further remonstrance, he left the room.

CHAPTER VI

LADY THORNINGTON'S HOUSE PARTY

BUT in spite of the drifting clouds over what both of them knew should have been a shining sky, David and Jacqueline were both extremely sorry to leave Oxford. They ignored the quarrel by the road-side, as if by mutual consent, and though they met with a little strangeness the next morning, this gradually wore off as the day advanced, and before it was over the man at least had almost forgotten it, much the easiest course for a lover somewhat ashamed of himself to pursue. Their last evening was exceptionally happy. They punted down the river, drew up their boat on the grassy slope, and sat for a long time hand in hand, talking very little. The sound of a distant clock, striking eleven, brought them to the reluctant realization that they had been there far longer than they realized, and that they must start back to the city. As they went down the bank, Jacqueline made a suggestion, almost shyly.

"Why don't we take your car and go off for the day to-morrow? Pauline and the luggage will go in another to 'Boxwood' anyway, and grandfather can take Dr. Ross back to London in ours. We didn't agree to reach 'Box-wood' until tea-time, and it wouldn't matter, even if we were late for that."

"Where do you want to go?"

"Anywhere—with you."

"I might never take you to 'Boxwood' at all, once we got started off," he said, with a humorous catch in his voice that was very rare.

"I shouldn't care much."

The abandon of her voice made his instantly serious. "Don't," he said gravely, "you mustn't say such things, even to me. But I like your plan—a long country ride, and lunch at some little inn, and a cathedral or two along the way, I suppose? It sounds good to me, too, dear."

So they had their day in the country together, and it proved to be the happiest one they had passed since their reunion. They went to Worcester for their lunch, then back to "Boxwood" through Coventry, Stratford and War-wick. It was all new territory to David, full of unguessed beauties and undiscovered delights; and again he was sur-prised, as he had been in Oxford, at Jacqueline's glowing and intimate knowledge of English history and poetry and at the power and charm with which she revealed them to him. Worcester porcelain—the river Avon—The Great Duke—Lady Godiva—what had he known of all these before? And what man had ever had so lovely a teacher? There was nothing in this heavenly little journey to anta-gonize or displease him—nothing to separate them and so much to draw them closer together. Not since the day when he had awakened from his long sleep on the Vermont hills, and lain, drinking in the glory of the rosy mountains and the still greater glory in Jacqueline's face, had David's heart been so filled to overflowing with tenderness and thanksgiving. And Jacqueline, sensing this, opened hers to him as an expanding flower turns towards the sun. Late in the afternoon, when they had almost reached their destination, David stopped the car by the roadside near a tiny grove with a brook running through it.

"I'd like to go in there and sit down a few minutes. There's a fence, of course, and a sign 'No Trespassing' in the usual hospitable English way," he said, laughing into her eyes, " but we can climb the fence in any case, and pay the fine if we get caught. I feel as if it would be worth it to get my hands off this wheel for a few minutes."

"Where were you thinking of putting them when you took them off the wheel?" Jacqueline asked demurely.

"I'll show you——"

But the embrace in which he silently folded her when they were hidden from the highway by the sheltering trees showed her far more than this alone——

They reached "Boxwood" barely in time to dress for dinner. A few minutes later, Jacqueline's maid tapped at David's door and handed him a note and a tiny package.

"Dearest," the letter ran, " I'm rather rushed, as Lady Thornington has been in my room raving about you ever since I got here. You're to take her out to dinner tonight. I find Freddy and Cyril and Gustav are all here—now please don't get excited! There are three charming girls as well, and they probably won't notice me at all. But I thought it wiser to break it to you at once. I'm to be quite at the opposite end of the table from you, worse luck, but I promise to be good, even if you're not there to keep your eagle eye upon me. Do wear these little things I'm sending you.—Désirée."

"These little things " proved to be a set of beautiful pearl studs, and David, smiling happily to himself, unfastened his plain gold ones, and put the new ones in their stead.

"She *is* a dear," he said to himself, " just as generous as ever, and just as shy at being caught at it—nothing would have induced her to hand them to me herself. It's been wonderful having those days in Oxford with her and I'm glad we've come here, too! I like Lady Thornington and her husband—they're so wholesome and jolly—and this is certainly the finest old house I ever saw in my life."

Lady Thornington met him with a smile as he entered

the drawing-room. "Jacqueline isn't down yet," she said. "I delayed her, I'm afraid. You're going to take me in to dinner, if you don't mind too much. I'm selfish enough to want you to, and besides, Freddy wrote me a note asking for her more than a month ago—before we even knew of your existence!" she finished, laughing. "Are you going to take Désirée away from us immediately? I do hope not!"

"I need not tell you that I should like to take her at once. But circumstances don't seem to be exactly propitious—I haven't finished my education yet, you see. I haven't decided yet what is best to do."

"But what does Jacqueline think?" Lady Thornington's voice expressed her surprise that the decision should rest entirely with him.

"Oh, she'll do as I wish, of course."

"I hadn't realized that she was so tractable—we haven't considered docility her strongest point! But she's wonderful—of course, you know that you have made a great many enemies?"

"I hope that I have made one friend."

"You have, indeed—oh, there she is now!"

Jacqueline smiled and nodded, but went past them without stopping, straight to a girl who was sitting alone by the great fire.

"That's like her," said Lady Thornington warmly. "Rose Grey, my husband's niece, is only seventeen, and painfully shy. This is her first week-end, she doesn't know any of the men, and regards them much as she would howling hyenas, anyway. Jacqueline knows it, and will do everything she can to smooth the poor child's path. She thinks a match between Rose and Freddy would be quite perfect, and though I never should have thought of it myself, I can see that it *would* be the best thing on earth for them both—they're such splendid, wholesome children! Of course, Freddy's thinking of no one but Jacqueline just now, but that's just a healthy phase—it'll pass all right—and—Rose adores Jacqueline herself—just look at the grateful expression in her eyes!"

Rose was, indeed, gazing at the older girl with mute adoration. She was a pretty little thing, with mild blue eyes, straight brown hair, and peach-blossom cheeks, short and rather plump, and dressed in the simplest of white muslins, obviously home-made. Jacqueline, her slender elegance sharply contrasted against Rose's dowdiness, stood with her arm about her, talking as if oblivious of the other's dumb embarrassment.

"It's a rather charming picture, isn't it?" said Lady Thornington. "Look at her pulling Rose's hair looser over her temples—and she's hanging some kind of a chain around her neck—the child's been so keen for a little ornament—I ought to have thought of giving her one myself— she's poor as a church mouse—and hasn't a particle of intuitive taste! Now Jacqueline's bringing her over to you, because she knows you'll be nice to her—but it's too late, for dinner seems to be served."

The table was a long one, and David could catch glimpses of Jacqueline only from time to time. At first she seemed very quiet, eating little, and drinking nothing at all, he noticed, as he drained his own glass of excellent champagne. It was unlike her to be so still—was she, he wondered, overtaxing her strength to come at all? Possibly Dr. Ross was right, and her recent headache of more import than he had realized. Or was it merely the delicate violet dress she wore that made her look so pale? As the dinner wore on, however, her face regained its animation, and he could hear the peals of laughter which followed some of her sallies. He tried to catch her eye as she left the dining-room, but she was looking straight ahead, talking to Lady Thornington, and when he reached the drawing-room, after an hour over wine and cigars that seemed to him interminably dull, she was already playing bridge, and he was called to take his place at another table. He was extremely fond of the game, however, and quickly became absorbed in it; so when the evening was half over, he was surprised to have her come and stand beside his chair as he was playing with considerable skill a particularly difficult no-trump hand. She waited silently until he was through, and applauded his triumph with the others; she had not, it appeared, come to stay, but the question she asked nonplussed him.

"Have you any extra money about you, David? I've played abominably all the evening, and lost all I brought downstairs. It's such a journey to my room, I thought you might lend me a little."

"Are we playing for money?" he asked, looking across at his partner in astonishment.

"What did you think it was for—love?" mocked the girl. "And thanks to your playing, we ought to get enough to-night for me to buy a new frock with my half. Let's see—five tricks—four aces divided—*and* the rubber—that gives us three hundred and fifty altogether."

David handed Jacqueline his purse without speaking, and took up his cards again. She waited a minute, evidently expecting him to say something, then flushing at the quizzical expression of Cyril, who was at the same table, she moved away. When his own game was finished, David, after silently pocketing twenty-five pounds as his share in the evening's booty, went in search of her, fully determined to deliver his opinion on the subject of gambling in private houses, and to ask her if she ever bought her dresses with the earnings of her bridge partners. But Lady Thornington met him with a laugh.

"Your bird has flown to her nest," she said. "She was pretty tired, I'm afraid—I think she seems rather fagged. She left a good-night for you with me."

And with such rather cold comfort, he was obliged to go to bed, far from contented.

"She seems to have rather original ideas about the way engaged persons usually say good-night," he remarked to himself grimly. "And she's been gambling all the evening—I never should have dreamed that Lady Thornington was the sort that would countenance such a thing in her house. I must get hold of Jacqueline and thrash several things out with her the first thing in the morning."

Again, his plans were upset, and this time their reversal caused him no contrition, but acute displeasure. Miss Huntington, he was informed when he got down to breakfast and inquired for her, had gone to mass with Count Saxburg.

He waited for her in the garden. She came at last alone.

her face shining with a sort of inner peace, her white dress golden in the sunshine. She sat down beside him on the bench where he had settled himself, and slipped her hand through his, then sat looking in silence for some moments over the peaceful English landscape.

"Isn't it wonderful?" she said at length softly. "Sunday morning in May—and church—and country—and you—I'm so happy,"

"I'm glad you're happy. *I* should be more happy if you had spent last evening differently, or gone to church with some other companion. Promise me not to degrade yourself by playing for money again, unless you do it unwittingly, as I did last night."

She raised a pair of troubled eyes to his, and hesitated before she spoke.

"I'll avoid it whenever I can, since you feel that way about it," she said. "I can't give a definite promise."

"Why not?"

"It might be necessary for me to break it, and I have never broken a promise in my life."

"I cannot see how such a necessity could arise."

"None of the friends with whom I am constantly thrown feel as you do—indeed, I do not myself. I might spoil an evening's pleasure for a number of people, by refusing to fill out at a table and make the right number. When I marry you, and go to Boston, I shall of course conform to your wishes, and the customs of the society in which I shall be thrown as your wife. But as long as I stay in my grandfather's house, the situation is entirely different."

"Do you consider that it also requires you to accept the conspicuous attentions of other men?"

She flushed painfully, and bit her lip. "To a certain extent it does. You are going to leave me very shortly, for an indefinite time. I can hardly arrange my life as if I were widowed instead of betrothed. But I certainly shall break no conventions—as I understand them, and I am too fond of you to care at all 'for the attentions of other men' and have always been. It is a little puzzling to me to understand why you have found this so hard to believe. The walk this morning was not pre-arranged. Gustav happens to be the only other Catholic here, and it was natural that he should join me when we were both going to church. I am sorry that you feel it is necessary for me to explain—or excuse—what I do."

"Good Lord, Jacqueline, you always contrive to twist everything I say until you put me in the wrong—if you wouldn't do these things it wouldn't be necessary to apologize or explain, would it? I suppose that you can contend that Wainright is an old family friend and Freddy Lambert just a pleasant, harmless boy, but nothing you can say will reconcile me to Saxburg—I must ask you very definitely to have nothing further to do with him—and if you choose to disregard my wishes, I'm afraid I shan't be very patient with either apologies or explanations. Besides, you know what a cross it has always been to me that you are a Catholic. Isn't there some way of getting around that before we're married? It would be tremendously awkward in Boston. Further South, some of the good old families are Romanists, but in New England——"

She stared at him in bewilderment for a moment, then spoke with a hurt obstinacy which astonished as much as it displeased him.

"There are a few things no one should venture to speak against, David," she said, "and you don't seem to have learned that yet. One is a woman's mother—another her friends—another her religion. I thought you understood clearly that in all mixed marriages, the Catholic retains his or her own faith, and the—the children, if there are any, are baptized and brought up in the Church. Matrimony isn't sufficiently important in your eyes to interfere with a career. I'm willing to follow your wishes absolutely in that regard—we'll be married today, or ten years from now, exactly as you prefer; but neither is it vital enough in mine—though I believe I honour it more than you do, for remember I regard it as a sacrament, and you do not—for me to dream of permitting it to supplant my religion, and I'd enter a nunnery before I'd marry you on any other terms than those I have just mentioned!"

She left him abruptly. Again, he had taken all the joy out of her day; and again David, secretly knowing that he was in the wrong, was all the more angry and resentful on that account. At lunch time Lady Thornington told him that Jacqueline had gone to her room, and did not feel able to leave it. She expressed, moreover, the same fear in regard to the girl's health that Dr. Ross had done, but this time David hardened his heart. "I believe she's using those 'headaches' as a means to make me give in," he said over and over again to himself. "She's wound every man she knows around her little finger for so long that she thinks she can go right on doing it with me. I'll show her she's mistaken." When a singularly empty afternoon had dragged itself almost out, however, he relented to the extent of writing her a stiff little note, saying he was sorry she was under the weather again—the unwholesome excitement and late hours of the night before had of course been the worst possible thing for her, except possibly going to church fasting—and asking if he could see her for a few minutes. He understood she had a private sitting-room. The maid who took this affectionate missive brought back the verbal reply that Miss Huntington was better, but was still unable to receive him.

He glanced at the clock. It was not quite seven—plenty of time for a good visit with her before dressing for an eight o'clock dinner—a quiet, intimate visit before an open fire. If he could only win back again that spirit of glad surrender, of complete yielding which she had shown on the afternoon of her birthday! What time could be more propitious, To be sure, she had asked him not to come, but that was just injured pride. She was better. He had every right. Without hesitation he mounted the stair, and walked rapidly down the long corridor.

Outside the door of Jacqueline's sitting-room, he stopped short, growing cold all over. From within he could hear the hurried accent of a man talking rapidly in German, then Jacqueline's reply, hesitating—almost pleading—in the same language. He was a fair scholar, but they were speaking too softly and too rapidly for him to catch the words. Without knocking, he opened the door and walked in. Standing in front of the fire was Gustav von Saxburg, and Désirée was in his arms.

The Austrian, swearing under his breath, loosened the girl, who fell back with a little cry, her face as white as paper; as she gripped the chair in front of her to keep from falling, the great jewels of her ring seemed to flash in David's face with a consuming fire.

"Is it then American custom to enter a lady's room without knocking?" stammered von Saxburg. "Désirée is my braut—my fiancée—not yours—I have her promise!"

"Gustav—for your honour's sake—if you have any——"

"Do not interrupt—this is one matter between men, is it not, Mr. Noble?"

"Give me your ring," said David between his teeth, looking straight past the Austrian at Jacqueline.

"No—not yet—no——"

"Give it to me! If you don't I shall take it!"

She slipped it off, and handed it to him without another word. Little things obtrude themselves in moments of great emotion. He noticed how loose it was, how white her hands were—and had he thought he was cold? Well, this thing burnt him like a living flame—he threw it into the burning coals. Still his hands seemed to be scorched——

"Perhaps you'll let me have a few words with Miss Huntington alone," he added, courteously. "I cannot congratulate you upon having won her promise, for I fear that carries very little weight—but I've not the slightest wish to dispute it with you." Then, as the Austrian did not move, he continued slowly, "Please do not let us disagree over this trifling matter—I desire to speak to her privately for a moment, and I pass for a very strong man, and am at least ten years younger than you." He held open the door with studied politeness, and Gustav von Saxburg walked out. Turning again to Jacqueline, he found her head thrown back, and her eyes, like blazing coals of fire in her white face from which every trace of gentleness had gone, fixed steadily on his.

"The other night," he said, "I heard this man comparing you with the *première danseuse* of a music-hall. I see that he had reason for his classification. You do not, of course, object to sharing his affections with such worthy rivals. A count is a count, and a stable-boy is a stable-boy."

"When he does not become something much worse."

"I understand many things now that were not clear to me before—among others, why it was 'impossible' for you to receive me this afternoon. I only regret that you did not make my own position clear to me a little sooner."

"The regret is quite mutual."

"I shall go back to London tonight on urgent business, and will send a statement to the newspapers saying that the marriage arranged between Jacqueline Désirée Huntington and David Noble is indefinitely postponed."

A maid entered the room with a tea-tray. David turned to her with his hand on the door-knob.

"Your mistress has fainted," he said coldly, as she gave a terrified cry, and looked from him to the girl lying on the couch. "But you need not be in the least alarmed. It is not serious."

PART THREE

CHAPTER I

IN WHICH AN UGLY STORY INTERRUPTS DAVID NOBLE'S CAREER

THE opening of the Edgar L. Ross Memorial Hospital was an event in the medical world—one might add, without exaggeration, perhaps, in the social world and the philanthropic world—not only of Boston and New England, but of the entire country. Splendidly situated in the Fenway, with grounds and approaches—those details so often sadly neglected in American architecture, to the unspeakable detriment of many a fine edifice—as carefully planned and executed as the great white marble building itself, it rose strong and dignified and enduring, with the promise of healing and efficiency written large upon it from slate roof to cement basement, from end of Right Wing, planned entirely for the convenience of the stork, to end of Left, given over to general surgery, in every rounded corner and thresholdless entrance, from the great sun parlour in the rear to the private suites above it, where anxious relatives and friends of patients could find quarters vying in luxury with those of Boston's newest and costliest hotel. Money, time, skill, knowledge, *heart*—all these had gone into its making. And ready to welcome the sufferers brought to its doors were maids and matrons and nurses, housekeepers and cooks, orderlies and pages and porters; there were, moreover, doctors, of course. And in the *Boston Transcript* and the *New York Times* and the *Chicago Daily News*, and even in less exclusive journals; in the circulars mailed broadcast from Maine to California, as well as in the engraved cards of invitation sent to a more fortunate few for the dedication, who would might read that the Surgeon-in-Chief was Dr. David Noble, formerly of Hamstead, Vermont, assistant—and many thought, adopted son—of Dr. Herbert Ross, who had given the hospital in memory of his only son.

The appointment of any man to so important a post would naturally have aroused some criticism as well as some approval; and the choice of David Noble aroused a good deal. He was still very young—the youngest man, "every one" said, that "any one" could remember had been given such a position. There were many, also, who found this a favourable opportunity to remark that *of course* he would never have obtained it if Dr. Ross had not been so biased in his favour; the boy—he was hardly more than that—was really an obsession with him; and when a man spends money like water on a hospital like this one, *of course*, his whims have got to be considered. The fact that Dr. Ross was himself on the staff, and might be expected to take the more critical cases where his maturer judgment would be essential, was in a way reassuring, however. It was also felt on the Back Bay—and more or less openly expressed—that "one of our own doctors" would have been more suitable for an institution of this standing. Who had ever heard of Hamstead, Vermont, or of a family named Noble? If one of "the younger men" were to have the position what was the matter with—Bobby Hutchinson, for instance.

Bobby Hutchinson himself, whom this opinion promptly reached, of course, sat on it so hard that there was not much left of it. He was a plain, slouchy young giant, with prematurely grey hair, and a crooked smile, and an imperturbable habit of cheerfulness. He was not impressed: indeed, he was not even flattered.

"Who in Hell started that fool idea," he drawled. "The undertaking establishments and the mourning apparel shops would benefit more by that arrangement than the Edgar L. I'd run up more business for 'em in a week than they could handle in a month. I'm not a surgeon, or a specialist, or a what you call 'em—diagno—I never can get the whole of that word. I'm a general practitioner—obsolete as hoop skirts and stove-pipe hats. I wouldn't swap that distinction to go and be diag—— etc., to the Queen of Sheba. It suits me exactly. Who's kicking up all this fool row about Dave and me, anyway? He's strong as steel—can operate thirty-six hours out of every twenty-four if necessary, while I have to keep laying off for smokes and drinks and things. Besides, he's got more skill in his little finger than I have in all four feet—more than any doctor I know of has, for that matter, unless it's that old Frenchman, Norchais, over in Paris, and we've only heard about him. What do they *want* for a surgeon-in-chief, anyway? As far as I can make out from all this twaddle the main requirement is that he should have been born on Beacon Street, and about seventy years ago! If he measures up to the expectations in that regard, it apparently doesn't matter whether he knows a stethoscope from an incubator baby!"

No less a person than Dr. Ross himself had gone to confer with Bobby—people had a way of conferring with Bobby. He laughed, which was also usual when anyone talked long with that individual.

"I notice all your patients seem to get well," he grinned, "so I'm afraid the trades you mention haven't profited by you much yet. And—your patients love you, Bobby."

Bobby pulled away at his pipe. He was sitting on the small of his back in an enormous morris-chair, clad in a pair of trousers which his choreman would certainly have refused as a gift, and a norfolk jacket which all his friends averred he had owned when he entered college and worn steadily ever since.

113

"Don't they love David?" he drawled at length, looking at Dr. Ross lazily through half-shut eyes.

"No." There was a short silence which Bobby gave no sign of intending to break. "As you are very well aware," added the older man.

"Oh, yes," said Bobby, "I know. But sick people—women especially, are such awful fools. They'd rather be ignorantly murdered by some one who really feels sorry for them and speaks to 'em kindly, than saved by a living miracle of dexterity and daring who regards 'em in the same light as he does his car—thrilling machinery, that's all. But just the same, in spite of their stupid taste, what you want at the head of your hospital is the mechanician, and not the murderer."

"He does slip up on his after-care——"

"Simply because he isn't interested. Now I cut folks up if I don't see any way out of it, but what I really enjoy is watchin' 'em get well. It is just the other way 'round with Dave. The *human* side doesn't touch him at all. He's pretty selfish, you know, come right down to hard tacks. That's why he's got along so well. 'He travels the fastest who travels alone,' as my friend Kipling says. Bromidic, but true. He's fond of you and me, but I don't know as he would be, if we got in his way; as it is, we've helped him. He didn't care much—for his mother, for instance, did he?"

"No, I'm afraid not. She was a shrewish, ignorant, unlovely woman, who made his life miserable as a boy. He is hardly to blame for that."

"Well, maybe not. But I don't believe he's especially keen on women anyway. You've seen my sister, Nancy, haven't you, and her friend Helena Castle that's with us so much?"

Dr. Ross smiled. "I'm glad to say I have. They're certainly a sight for sore eyes, and I'm not surprised at the reports that masculine Boston from sixteen to sixty has capitulated to either or both. I suppose you infer that David has never shown the slightest interest in either of them?"

"Exactly. There—isn't any one else by chance, is there?"

"No," answered Dr. Ross rather sharply.

"I didn't mean to be prying. Abnormally ascetic, that's what I should call him. His sort always carves in cold blood. Even your hopeless roué, who tries to ruin almost every woman he meets, is often kinder to 'em than the sort that's never been interested in 'em at all—that is, *they* *think* he's kinder. Not that I'm suggesting a Don Juan for the Edgar L.—as I said before, Dave's just the man for the job—don't know any one who can touch him. Let 'em talk—they're always talking about something. But just the same . . ."

"Well, Bobby——"

"Dave's never made a single mistake yet, as far as I know," said Bobby slowly, "and if he only could—make a huge one—medically or otherwise or both together—and have to go through a perfect hell of grief and contrition and despair and shame—well, then you'd see him come out —if he could come out at all—the greatest physician of his generation. Just now, he's only a clever mechanician, as I said before. And when you get right down to hard tacks, that's why there's some opposition to him. All these other considerations wouldn't count a continental, though the people who're making the row don't really sense it."

He rose to escort his guest to the door. "I feel I've been darn fresh, talking to you like this," he said. "Are you feeling first rate, yourself, sir? It's been quite a chore putting this thing through, and making the success of it that you've done. Couldn't you get a little rest now that it's all over but the shouting?"

"I'm going to—as soon as we're really in running order. I've been trying to persuade David to go to Hamstead to see his family—he's really neglected them shamefully—and when he does——"

"I hope you won't wait till then. The Edgar L. is all the family he'll be interested in for months."

"I'm afraid you're right. Well, we'll see."

But when Dr. Ross finally started on his much-needed rest, a few months later, it was for a much longer one than Bobby had sought to make him take. He had indeed given his whole strength to the erection of the hospital;

and not very long after it was finished, he died, suddenly and peacefully, leaving David stunned by the first real grief he had known in his life, and—incidentally—the sole and unquestioned possessor of his benefactor's enormous practice and substantial fortune. And Bobby, who saw a good deal of him in those days, finally spoke his mind, freely and frankly and without drawling, which was, indeed, a rare thing for him.

"If you don't go off and loosen up," he said, "the Edgar L.'ll have to have a new surgeon-in-chief, and there'll be a sign, 'For sale or to let' in the bay-window of your house. You'll be taking your ease in a pretty little padded cell out at Waverly, or under a neat tombstone marked 'Sacred to the memory of' in the Hamstead graveyard. Now's the time to go and see your family, on your two feet or in your new Napier—excuse me, Mercedes—didn't know you'd have even a car with a lady's name—instead of in a long mahogany box with a pretty wreath on top. After you've drunk deep of the rural delights of Vermont—I understand there is nothing else to drink deep of up there—why don't you run over to Paris, and play around with Norchais for a couple of months? Combine business and pleasure—take the French lady with you——"

"*What* French lady?"

"Why, Mercedes, of course! What are you so touchy about?"

David, after losing some valuable time in reluctant facing of facts, acted on Bobby's advice. He was, as he was very well aware, almost at the end of his long tether, before the death of Dr. Ross had added grief to fatigue, and set his much abused nerves quivering. The suggestion of Paris was extremely good. And his conscience had been reminding him for some time that he ought to go to Hamstead. He entrusted the Edgar L. to the tender mercies of his very able assistant, and turned his footsteps, or rather, the headlights of Mercedes, in the direction of Vermont.

But a week in Hamstead proved more than his patience could stand. The little village, which had once seemed such a metropolis to him, proved stagnant to the last degree. His father had waited with impatient pride to show him the many local improvements which had taken place since he was last at home. The streets and most of the houses were electrically lighted, there was a town water system, bathrooms and telephones abounded where ten years before they had been almost unknown; the public library was no longer a tiny shanty which had once been a blacksmith's shop, but a neat little brick building donated by Miss Manning in memory of her father. The church had been "done over" and there was a new Masonic Hall where dances, no longer taboo, were frequently held. David beheld these marks of progress with an indifferent condescension which left his father puzzled and hurt. He was not even interested in news of a more personal character—that Jack Weston, for instance, was "going from bad to worse," and was "not himself" a large part of the time, and that Austin Gray, on the contrary, had not only "pulled himself together" but was rapidly becoming the "rising man" of the community, and had married a very lovely and lovable girl, who was as rich as she was beautiful, and had endeared herself to all the village; or that Hiram himself, whose sincere and unquestioning, if somewhat austere, faith David had always considered as "countrified" as his habit of drinking tea from his saucer or appearing in public without a collar, had now become a Deacon in the First Congregational Church—a mark of respect seldom shown to a man coming from "out back," and a crowning glory in his simple mind, compared to which his long term as postmaster was as nothing.

To greater and more important changes, the spiritual and mental development which sprang from these more material changes, David was entirely blind. Narrow-mindedness and prejudice were on the wane. The minister, instead of being the chilly and forbidding person of his boyhood, was a "good sort" who mingled freely with his flock, in their pleasures as well as their griefs, and in their week-day as well as their Sunday life; there was a Men's Club which held weekly meetings in the vestry, where the discussion of Village Improvements and town politics was no longer excluded; the average farmer's wife, instead of toiling from sunrise to dark, her only diversions going to church and the discussion of the births, deaths and marriages—and other more or less private affairs—of her immediate circle of acquaintance, went, thanks to "modern improvements," to Wallacetown in her own Ford to do her shopping and attend the "movies," and to the gatherings of The Grange on alternate Saturday nights; she played cards and danced whenever she felt like it, unwearied by her own home tasks and uncensured by her neighbours. But all this David neither saw nor wished to see. He had, in his estimation, "outgrown" Hamstead, and he did not care who knew it—in fact, he rather hoped every one realized it as well as he did. A chance errand to Wallacetown filled him with disgust at the place. It was before the days of state roads, and the highways, deep with dust or mud, as the case might be, were "impossible" for motoring to his mind. Never having made any friendships, he had none to renew, and his family was prosperous, and really did not need him. Sam, already successfully started on a legal career, had gone West. The younger boys had completed courses at the State Agricultural College, and had bought the old Daniels farm, which they were running together. Harry, the elder of the two, had married, and was the proud father of a boy three months old. David vaccinated the child, and told his mother not to eat pickles, a piece of advice which she calmly disregarded; and as both she and the baby were bouncing specimens of humanity, he did not feel that any arguments he might advance in favour of her changing her way of living would have much force. Mrs. Noble was dead, and Mr. Noble, still occupied and contented with his position as postmaster, had gone to live with his sons, taking Susie with him. She was growing up a wild little thing, untrained and undisciplined, and, alone among them, stood in no awe of David. Though she seemed to him entirely uninformed on all important points, she was quick and shrewd, and had already nearly completed her course at the Hamstead High School. David was horrified at her boldness and ignorance, and exasperated by her sharp tongue; she reminded him painfully of their mother. And yet he was forced to admit that there were great possibilities in the girl, and she was the only person who interested him in the least in the complacent household. She was handsome, in a sharp, ungentle way; generous and impulsive and capable; her untrained mind was keen. Reluctantly he faced the fact that he "ought to do something for her." Finally, feeling that he had made a great sacrifice, he offered to take her abroad with him, and place her in school in Paris, where he could see her well established while he was studying with Norchais. The following summer he would see that she travelled under proper chaperonage; and at the end of that time she could decide whether she would prefer to continue her education in Europe, or return to America and prepare for college at some good school near Boston. He was appalled by her ingratitude when she flatly refused to consider his proposition for one moment.

"I like it here with Pa and Hattie and the boys," she added decidedly. "I'd rather mind the baby than go to Paris. Besides, I'm nearly sixteen, and there'll be a lot going on here this winter. I guess I'll have a better time where I'm acquainted, than over in that heathen foreign country where I couldn't understand a word any one said to me, for if you think *you'd* be any company to me, you flatter yourself! I think you was born with a poker down your back, and an icicle in each eye, and alum in your mouth—and for all I know, you'd etherize me the first good chance you got, and quarter me, just for the fun of sein' whether you could sew it together again so it wouldn't show!"

In the end it was Hiram who won a reluctant consent from her. Unbiased by the fact that the two sons who had remained at home were the prop and mainstay of his declining years, while the two who had gone out into the world looked down on him and, indeed, almost ignored him, his proud affection overflowed for Susie when her "chance" came, just as it had done first for David and later for Sam. If none of his boys occupied quite the same place in his heart that his eldest had, his only daughter was dearer to him still. And Susie, sharply divining, in spite of her youth, the unselfish desire for her own good that lay behind his awkward arguments that "she had better go along with Dave, like a nice girl," capitulated after one final outburst.

"Well, I'll go—but it's not because I care a whoop about having 'a chance,' it's because you're so dead set on it, though I don't see why you should be. Do you want me to be mean and selfish and stuck-up the way Dave is? Do you want me to despise my family and home the way he does? Hear him talk about Hamstead, you'd think it was a regular hole in the ground. I think it's awful to feel that way about the place you was raised in, especially if it's a *lovely* place, like Hamstead is. He hasn't been near Mr. Sheldon since he got here, and Sheldon just counted the days to seeing him after he knew Dave was coming. I just hope he gets his come-uppance, that's all, some day, and that I can have a share in it!"

"Susie! Don't you lay out to bite the hand that's goin' to feed you!"

"Hoo! It isn't Dave's hand! It's Dr. Ross's money! Much Dave will miss what he spends on me! If he would, you can bet your life he wouldn't spend it!"

"You'd oughter be grateful to Dave, 'stead of slanderin' of him."

"I ain't a-slanderin' of him. I'm tellin' the truth. I'll be grateful to *him* when I see him bein' grateful to some one himself! To you and—and—Ma!"

"David an' your Ma never got on."

"Huh! Well, that was some Ma's fault, maybe, but it was more his. He was too stupid to see that the reason Ma was cross was because she was so tired, workin' her fingers to the bone for us all! Gettin' up at four in the mornin' and hustlin' around till ten or eleven at night don't make a woman feel real *perky*, I guess! Washin', and ironin', and cookin' and' cleanin' an' scrubbin' for seven people year in an' year out an' gardenin' and preservin' too, in the hot summer time, an' helpin' in the post-office so's you could go trout-fishin' in the spring an' deer-huntin' in the fall! An' I've heard Sam and Harry tell, though I can't remember it myself, of course, that when we wuz babies, she useter put us to sleep on a haycock, an' help you pitch on hay out in the fields, an' pitch it off in the barn to save a hired man's wages when they wuz highest, in hayin' time! An' after the Men's Club got started, you wuz free to go to that any evenin' you wanted, while she worked an' worked an' worked! I guess 'twas Ma gave us our real 'chance' if you come to think of it right! We wuz always better fed'n any family in town, without much to feed us *on*, neither! And the house wuz just poison neat, alway, an' I had tattin' on my underclothes when all the other girls wore plain, an'——"

"Why, Susie, I never knew you thought of all them things!"

"Well, I *did* think of 'em, an' I think of 'em still! I wuz ten years old when she died, and I guess I've noticed the difference sence! I ain't sayin' that Hattie ain't pleasant an' good to me—she is—but you can't make the best sister-in-law in the world come up to a sure 'nough mother, even if she is cross!—I didn't care if she was cross. She had *grit*! An' that's more'n lots of awful pleasant wimmen hev got!

"I ain't forgotten, neither," the girl went on after a minute, during which Hiram, conscious of a tightening in the throat, found himself unable to answer her, "that when she wuz real sick, along at the last, she hankered an' pined fer Dave to come home, and she got me to write— she never said a word to the rest of you—that she warn't feelin' first rate, an' that if it wouldn't interfere with his 'career' she'd like to hev him come home an' pass Sunday. And he wrote back that he hoped she'd feel better soon, but that it warn't convenient for him to leave Boston just then. 'Convenient!' An' her a-dyin'!"

"Susie! he didn't know that!"

"Wall, I hope he didn't! But you ain't sure of it, are you?"

"He couldn't 'a realized——"

"Huh! I'd like to *make* him realize some things! When his letter come, she lay so still for a spell, I thought mebby she'd gone already. And at last she sez, 'I kinder wanted to hev a talk with Dave. But then, it don't matter.' Nothin' 'mattered' to her except doin' every livin' thing she could for us! An' after that she never talked much to any one!"

121

Susie snuffled, and wiping her eyes and her nose with the back of her hand, rose, and picked up her hat, which was lying on the floor near her.

"Where you goin'?" asked her father, glad of a chance to change the subject.

"I'm goin' to see the minister. An' Miss Sims; an' Mrs. Elliott. I presume they'll hev considerable to say when they hear I'm goin' to Europe with Dave, an' I guess I might as well let 'em hear it from me first, an' hear it *straight,* before they start passin' remarks around."

"Susie, you do beat all," said Hiram helplessly.

"Well, I'd like to beat *Dave* for gittin' me inter this pickle," she replied, slamming the door behind her.

David, feeling complacent at the turn things had taken next faced the unconsidered difficulty that Susie had no more proper equipment in the way of clothing than she had in the way of manners, and that though she must be made to pass without the latter until she could acquire them, she certainly must be supplied with the former. Hattie, with kindly haste, was running the sewing-machine early and late to supply the deficiencies in her little sister-in-law's wardrobe, and David looked aghast at the garments which he vaguely knew to be "all wrong," which one by one as they were finished, she spread out on the bed in the "spare chamber" for his inspection.

"I've made her four of each," said Hattie with pride, waving her hand in the direction of certain articles of intimate apparel, made of heavy, substantial cotton, trimmed with durable Hamburg edging, which David instinctively knew would give a clumsy and shapeless appearance to whatever was put on outside them. "With what she has already mended up good, she can keep real clean with that many, and change more'n once a week if she should want to. I think that figured challis dress'll be real pretty for best, don't you? I'm goin' to knit her a pair of mittens to wear with that crocheted toque on the steamer, and she's got six shirt-waists, countin' the blue taffeta, to go with her new wool skirt. I think she'll appear real nice. Susie'd be pretty if she didn't look so much as if she was cut out with a pair of scissors. If she hefts up a little, and

122

gets more notion of being pleasant, it would help out considerable."

In desperation, David wrote to Bobby. And Bobby, by return mail, sent back the following answer from his mother's summer place at Manchester-by-the-Sea.

"Dear Dave: How did you happen to have such a brilliant idea? It's the best thing I've heard in a long time. Mother says to bring the kid here for as long as you want. I'm taking a few days off myself, and Nancy is home, and Helena is visiting her, and I bet between them they can lick her into shape in no time. I'll have a good time with her myself. You don't think she would do for me, later on, do you?

Yours,
Bob."

David was much relieved by this epistle, and favourably impressed by the jest at the end of it. Why not, he thought, looking at her as she stood out in the yard taking her leave of a bashful boy who had been one of her classmates, the wind whipping her faded cotton skirts about her lithe, boyish figure, her heavy braids of black hair lying over her breast, her red cheeks glowing like peonies. The girl might well grow up a beauty as well as a wit. Why shouldn't she make a brilliant marriage? Though he had supposed, vaguely—not having given the matter much thought—that Bobby was "interested" in Helena Castle.

It was early afternoon when the Mercedes with its two passengers came to a stop under the Hutchinsons' porte-cochère; and Susie, mute with defiance and shyness and dread, found herself enveloped in a welcome such as she had not dreamed of. These people weren't "stuck-up" like David at all! Why, they were just as simple as—as anything——

"I lived in the country myself when I was a little girl," Helena said that first afternoon, as they sat on the broad veranda which faced the sea, drinking lemonade, "and I remember how terrified I was when I came home from boarding-school with Nancy for the first time to visit. They don't do things a bit our way, do they, Susie? But really—

123

after you get to know them of course—they're very nice."

"I always liked girls from the country better than any other kind, myself," drawled Bobby, at which they all laughed, and though Susie didn't know what they were laughing at it made her feel very comfortable. "I have a nice plan—I think Helena and Susie and I will go off for a picnic tonight instead of staying here for dinner." And off they accordingly went. Then Helena kept the little girl in her own room that night, and brought her down to breakfast the next morning with her beautiful, straight black hair arranged as it should have been, and dressed in a white frock which she had filched from her own wardrobe, and hastily "fixed"—for Helena was wonderfully clever with her needle. That day, and for several days afterward, Susie went to Boston with Helena, and big boxes filled with all sorts of wonderful things—dresses and hats and coats and shoes and linen—began to arrive at the Hutchinsons' house for her. Moreover, Bobby had a way of meeting them and taking them to lunch at big hotels, and to matinées afterwards. In a week, David hardly knew his sister; she had blossomed with unbelievable celerity into almost unbelievable attractiveness; she was happy, she was unembarrassed, she was "catching on" to everything. He motored all day long and every day along the North Shore, rejoiced in the excellent roads, and vowing he would never go near Vermont again.

The night before Susie and David were to sail was damp and chilly, and soon after dinner the five young people betook themselves to Bobby's den, a great half-timbered room with a huge fireplace, built apart from the main wing of the house. It was cold enough for a fire, and they piled it high with driftwood and settled themselves comfortably about it—Susie stretched at full-length on the sofa, with her head in Helena's lap; Nancy in a big chair beside her brother; and David, a little apart from the others, absorbed in the enticements of an automobile catalogue. He was paying but scant attention to the others, when Susie broke the comfortable stillness into which they had lapsed with one of her sudden outbursts.

"Do you know what I wish?" she said abruptly, throw-

ing her arms around Helena. "I wish I was a big man—
as big as Dr. Hutchinson—and do you know what I'd do?
I'd marry you!"

"What an original idea," drawled Bobby. "I am sure
no one else ever thought of such a thing!"

"Well, then," went on Susie, as Helena only laughed a
little and did not answer, "I wish besides that I could stay
here with you and not go to Europe with David at all—
just look at him, sitting over there alone! He looks so
pleased at something, he must be dissecting a bug!"

"But I'm not going to stay here myself, you know," protested Helena. "I teach at a girls' college, where I hope
you'll come some day yourself."

"Will you be there then?"

"I don't know, Susie."

Helena disengaged herself gently, rose from the sofa, and
walked over to the fire. David, glancing up for the first
time from his catalogue, saw Bobby looking at her intently,
and then get up, and say something to her, which he could
not hear, for it was almost whispered. But the girl's face,
which seldom lost its expression of wistfulness, brightened
almost unbelievably. Her eyes were full of tears, but she
was smiling.

"That's like you," she said in a low voice, "bless you,
Bobby." Then after a moment, "Come, Susie, it's time for
you to go to bed; and as I'm rather tired, I think I'll go too."

"So will I," said Nancy, yawning. "Good-night, Dr.
Noble."

She kissed her brother, and left the room quickly, as she
did everything. Susie, who was doing her best to imitate
these wonderful creatures in all respects, walked over to
David and put down her face, though she would never
have dreamed of doing such a thing at home. He kissed
her absent-mindedly, his eyes on the fair-haired girl in the
black dress standing beside his friend. She had held out
both hands to him, and he was holding them, looking
down at her with an expression of wonderful tenderness
and yearning; then they, too, kissed each other and Helena
left the room, her arm over Susie's shoulder.

David laid down his catalogue and came towards the fire.

"I did not know that Miss Castle was engaged to you," he said slowly. "We must have been terribly in the way!"

Bobby knocked the ashes from his pipe, whistled through it, and settled himself in his chair again before he replied.

"She is not," he said at last. "In fact, she is so far from it as to be engaged to another man. I'm surprised you haven't heard the story—I thought of course you knew! Helena's mother made her promise when she was a little girl that she would never marry a man whose family did not approve of the match—her own life had been ruined because she did that very thing. Helena always had more beaus than you could shake a stick at—why, she was grown-up at Susie's age—Susie's a great kid, but she's *just* a kid, that's all—I never saw anything so refreshingly immature! Well, to go back to Helena—when she was eighteen Roger Lorrance came here to visit at the same time that she did. They fell in love at first sight. Roger's family refused to receive her, because of some silly old scandal a generation old, and not long after that, Mrs. Castle died, after extracting Helena's promise a second time. She was left almost penniless. The engagement still stands, for they are hoping that in time circumstances will alter sufficiently to permit them to marry, and still keep to the very letter and spirit of the promise. I believe myself they won't have much longer to wait. Roger's been in California for years, trying to earn a living wage—the last thing in the world he was trained for—and Helena's been as brave as a little Trojan, and teaching herself ever since she got through college. I think public opinion will be too strong for the Lorrances to contend against indefinitely. All Helena's friends—and they're legion—have done what they could for her—but of course it's pitifully little in a case like this!"

"And what," said David, "does her fiancé think of your intimacy?"

Bobby Hutchinson looked at him with surprised unconcern, for a moment, and then answered, drawling more than ever.

"That's not a very pretty question, the way you ask it," he said at length. "Thank the Lord Roger's not that kind of a fool—and I'm not that kind of a blackguard. He's my best friend, and she—well, bless her, she loves him with all her heart and soul."

"And kisses you good-night?"

"Occasionally she honours me to that extent; a few years ago I couldn't have—stood it—but now——

"Your attitude of mind makes me think of a story I heard at a dinner in Vienna last summer," he went on after a minute. "It was a private dinner, and after the women had left the room the conversation turned to love-affairs. Delicate little way Europeans have of talking about such things, haven't they?"

"Very," said David, picking up the catalogue again.

"Well, they discussed the usual conquests of the usual kind, and then one of the men said he could tell a much better story than any of them—that he had once succeeded in winning a wager that he could break up a perfectly regular engagement of marriage between a girl whom he and several other men had been trying hard to get, and who had suddenly announced her engagement to an old sweet-heart of her girlhood whom she hadn't seen for years, and who turned up without warning on the already crowded scene. They had naturally all been much annoyed.

"Everybody—except myself and one Englishman who was there—laughed, and asked for the story. He was only too eager to tell it. It seems that the girl in question, an American beauty living in London, and the fiancé—an American, too, I am sorry to say, for he seems to have been a pretty poor sort—were all at a house-party with a number of others at a big place near Oxford when the wager was made. He'd about given up hope of accomplishing any-thing, for the girl was perfectly crazy about her beau, as we'd say here—one of those cases of a woman who never cares for but one man, apparently, and loves him to dis-traction, no matter how badly he treats her, and turns down a dozen better men, because she's either blind to his defects, or doesn't care whether he has 'em or not. This American certainly had plenty. He was a *parvenu* who'd been successful along his own particular line—the Austrian didn't state what that was—and took it for granted that he could be along every line. His opinions and tastes were to be the final word on everything and he was puritanical and jealous and dictatorial and a general ass. Every one else could see plainly enough that the girl was throwing herself away, but he seemed to feel that the favours were all on his side. Well, at last the Austrian's chance came. The girl got sick. She'd been near a nervous breakdown for some time, and her considerate fiancé had caused it really to arrive. She had a queer heredity, of which she was almost morbidly conscious, and her life as a great beauty and a great heiress in English 'smart society' was just the sort to develop the characteristics she feared she might have inherited, and was trying hard to fight against—and yet longing to give in to. Interesting thing, heredity. Now in this case——"

"What did the Austrian do?" The interruption came sharply. "I'm more interested in the story itself than in your theories about it."

"All right. Usually you like a little friendly argument. Well, he happened to be passing her door when he heard her giving her maid a message—apparently in answer to a note—saying she couldn't see her beau, and at the same time telling the maid to go and get her tea. He jumped at the conclusion that the American would, as usual, disregard her wishes, and decided to arrive on the scene first. He knew perfectly well how that would be interpreted—the American hated him, and thought the girl liked him—he would think she had sent him word not to come because she had another visitor. It doesn't seem credible does it? I know, if—if Roger found a *dozen* men with Helena, he'd never give it a thought—he'd *know*—I supposed any man—any decent-minded man—would, until I heard this story. Though from your question tonight, it seems that——"

"Go on with your story, will you?"

"Why, I *am*, as fast as I can—glad to have such an appreciative audience. The Austrian knocked, and the girl said, 'Come in'—thought of course it was her hostess. She had a private sitting-room, and was lying on a couch in front of the fire. She jumped up and told him, of course

128

to clear out. But he grabbed her, and poured out his undying love—his dirty lust, I ought to say—he timed it pretty well. She tried at first to interrupt him and break away, then kept quite still, thinking that would end it sooner—and just then the American walked in without knocking. He didn't even ask for an explanation. Of course he ordered his rival out of the room but the resourceful fellow listened at the key hole. Then he—the fiancé—spoke to her as if she'd been a—well, a common street-walker, and left her in a dead faint on the floor. Then he departed for London, and the fact that the engagement was broken was announced in the next morning's papers. The Austrian of course won his wager—it was for a thousand pounds, which came in handy, he said, to pay up debts he'd contracted over a *première danseuse* at the Gaiety. He didn't get the girl, though, after all, which he seemed to think was rather strange. She vanished completely soon after—he didn't know what *had* become of her. That was several years ago—I wonder, sometimes, which of those two men was the worst. Of course she vanished—of course she's never looked at—at *a male thing* again without utter fear and loathing. I've wondered, hundreds of times since, knowing she was sick to begin with, if she lost her reason—or only died—or what—and I've hoped—that sometimes she could make the man she loved suffer—the way he made her suffer. I've wondered a hundred times, too, of course, who she *was*—good Lord, David, what ails you?"

For David had risen, and was staggering towards him, his eyes blazing in his grey face.

"Nothing," he was saying between lips so twisted with torture that he could hardly form the words. "I was the man, that's all—oh, my God, what shall I do?"

CHAPTER II

SEARCHING

"Good-bye, Susie, dear; I'll see you again Sunday."

"That's ever and ever so far off."

"Only three days—and I'll bring you something pretty when I come."

"I'd rather stay with you than have anything pretty. It'll be awful without you, David."

"I expect to be rather lonely myself; but it's the best thing for you, honey."

"Oh, David," wailed the child, her arms around his neck, "you're ever and ever so much nicer than you used to be! I do love you a whole lot, and I'm sorry I ever said I didn't. I'll try to learn a whole lot, and grow up to be exactly like Miss Castle; and I do hope you'll find—Her."

David left the prim little French drawing-room, and went out into the bright street, his eyes full of unwelcome tears. It was hard to part from Susie; but it was harder still to face the lonesomeness and bitterness of defeat that lay before him. For nearly three months he had hunted for Jacqueline, and he was no nearer finding her now than on the morning when he and Susie sailed for Europe, and he told her what he had done and what he hoped to do, because, in his misery, he longed to tell some one, who, upon hearing him, would, perhaps, flay him less mercilessly than Bobby Hutchinson had done—the man whose own tragedy he had never guessed, and who was spending the best years of his life in the service of a woman from whom he neither expected nor sought any reward. Would he, he wondered, ever forget the utter scorn and scathing contempt with which Bobby had stung him, after he had traced the story of the lady and the stable-boy from the day when he met her by the river to the one on which he left her lying on the couch of her room in Lady Thornington's house?

"To think," flung out Bobby with biting sarcasm, "that for more than ten years I've considered you the cleverest man I ever met—you miserable fool! You thought she 'might deceive you because she had deceived her grandfather'—the two cases are synonymous, aren't they? A poor, lonely, loving little girl outwitting a stupid old snob in order to be with her only playmate—and later on, her sweetheart, and a grown woman vulgarly tricking the man she promised to marry! The very fact that you could compare them for a minute shows the calibre of your

130

mind! You 'loved her so much that it made you half-crazy with jealousy'? How dare you flatter yourself that you ever loved her—really loved her—for one single second? Because, after watching her with indifference for years, you suddenly itched to get your hands on her when you saw her in a white dressing-gown in the moonlight? That isn't love, you blithering idiot—that's elemental desire, that we all have to face sometimes, no matter how many pretty names you call it, or how much you gloss over the bald fact. Because you went to Wallacetown and made a fool of yourself when she didn't tumble straight into your arms? That wasn't love, it was stupid weakness, and would have been something a darned sight worse, if she hadn't been strong and good enough for both of you—as she would have been this time, too, if you had given her a chance. Because you sent her away from you to cry her eyes out, simply because you knew you didn't have any self-control? Oh, it may have been *right* if you can define right and wrong as easily as black and white squares on a checker board—but it was clumsy and cruel just the same. Because you went without luxury for a few years to buy her a ring? You did that to prove to yourself—and to her —what a wonder you were—to gratify your own pride in achievement. Because it peeved you to see her smoke cigarettes and drink cocktails and play cards for money and wear dresses which weren't like those you'd been used to seeing in Cambridge, Mass.? You've got lots of talent distinguishing between the essential and the unessential, haven't you? Because you've kept *so straight*? Well, how often have you wanted—desperately wanted—to be anything else? If there is anything I loathe it's the Pharisee who goes about thanking God he's not like other men when he hasn't the slightest *wish* to be like other men! I bet she's suffered 'keeping straight' a thousand times more than you have, but neither she nor any other woman gets any credit for it, nor even a girl constituted as she must be. *Désirée Huntington!* Why, I remember meeting her more than once, when she came to Boston as a girl! I suppose that tow-headed simp, Cyril Wainright, who was after her even then, though she couldn't have been much older than

Susie, was one of the lordly suitors who made that devilish wager! She rode horseback a lot, and danced like a—well, like something we'd never seen here before. She had a figure that you couldn't miss in a hundred—no normal man could keep his eyes off it—and a great mop of wavy, bronze-coloured hair and hazel eyes that looked straight at you from a face that was beautiful, and sincere, and lovely——"

"Fod God's sake, stop!"

"I won't stop! And in addition to that face and that figure, she had three or four millions in her own name, and a temperament—of course—all gold and fire! Do you suppose *she* hasn't been tempted? Why, she's the kind of woman that knocks men silly, they want her so—and they will take every known means to get her, too. I would have myself, if it hadn't been for—if I hadn't, that's all. And you had a chance—no, a certainty—of marrying her! Help you to find her? I won't help you to a damned thing—and neither will any one else who guesses half this precious story. I almost wish I need never see you again as long as I live!"

But two days later, when David, having left Susie at the Hutchinsons' and hastily returned to Hamstead to see if Sheldon could give him any information, returned with a white face that seemed to have suddenly grown ten years older, Bobby met him with a sympathy and understanding that were like balm to his wounded spirit.

"Could he tell you anything?"

"I don't know whether he could or not; anyway, he wouldn't. I didn't go near him when I was home before and he lays that—and some other things—up against me. He bought the farm that goes with the estate himself several years ago, and pays the taxes on the Big House for the use of its orchards and gardens; he says he hasn't heard from Jacqueline since this arrangement was completed, though he's written her a number of times—in fact, some of his letters have come back to him unclaimed. I told him I wanted to find her because I thought the world of her when we were kids. 'She thought the world of you, you mean,' he said. I believe what you say is true. No one will be willing——"

"Now, look here, Dave——"

Bobby took hold of him, and swung him into the house, where cooling drinks and wafer-thin sandwiches awaited them on a silver tray. "Of course Sheldon doesn't know where she is—what do you think he is—a clairvoyant? And of course I want to help you. I *was* pretty mad the other night, and I guess I said more than I meant to. But I know you loved her all right. You did your level best to be square as well as straight, and to make yourself worthy of her before you claimed her—all of which is more than nine fellows out of ten in your place, and with no knowledge or experience to steer you right, could have done. And you're a genius—there's absolutely no doubt of that, and it can't have helped going to your head a little. You did slip up very badly in England, but—haven't you suffered any for it? I mean, even before you heard me talk the other night?"

"*Suffered!* What do you think I am? Of course I suffered. But I never doubted that I was right, not for a minute. She wrote me once almost immediately, but I tore the letter in two, and sent it back to her unopened. I——"

"Well, you certainly were a general ass and then some, about that time, as I said before (drink some of this stuff, why don't you, it's good), but of course you'll find her in time. Only don't go about it as if you were trying to track her down——"

"What do you think I am going to do? Use bloodhounds?"

"Well, I thought you might use detectives, and I bet she'd regard them much in the same light. Let her feel, when she next sees you, that you've been seeking, not claiming—just trying for the chance to lay an offering of repentance and—and love at her feet. Don't—don't assume anything. I shouldn't wonder—she cared a lot for you, and I sized her up as the kind that—well, I don't know. Remember, she's been dreadfully hurt—that's why she's hiding. Be gentle first, and last—and all the time—it's a mistake to believe that all women need to be bullied into marriage . . ."

"*Marriage!* Surely you don't for a minute imagine——"

"I'm not imagining anything—personal—I'm only telling you, on general principles. So far you've been honest enough—that's all right, as far as it goes. Keep on being honest. And you've meant to be just—that's plain enough in the light of the fact that you're so darned cut up now that you find you haven't been. But don't be so damned stupid—and crude—and hasty. Wait—and wait—and wait some more——"

A flash of red went by the window; there was a ringing laugh outside.

"Susie," said Bobby with a grin. "She's really a great kid—I'm glad she's going with you. I intend to wait for her to grow up, if she ever does——"

"But I thought——"

"Well, stop thinking. You're so stewed you're in no shape to think. You never had a sensible thought yet about a girl as far as I can make out , . . Do you suppose I'm going to spend all my life hanging my heart on a weeping willow tree? Not much! I'm going to get Susie to take it down and play tunes on it for me . . . The Edgar L. wants you to call up at once, by the way—I almost forgot to tell you. I believe they hope you can be persuaded to postpone your sailing for a week, and come back for that long—it seems some rather ticklish cases have come in——"

"Well, why didn't you tell them for me to go to Hell—and save me the trouble? You know perfectly well I'm off at four a.m.—I've sent in my resignation, anyway—they'll get it on the morning mail."

"You crazy loon, what next? Why——?"

"I can't be hampered with the hospital now that I've got a real job, can I? It may be years before I can get back—Thornton ought to have my place, anyway—I've known that all along. Those old tabbies were right—I'm not fitted for it. I'm going——" Suddenly an old phrase of his floated back to his mind—"I'm going," he said, smiling for the first time in days, "to the top of the Himalaya Mountains, and the middle of the Sahara Desert!"

Susie, leaning over the rail at the stern of the great liner, watching the foam, was intensely interested.

"She was the loveliest lady that ever lived," said David, finishing his story, "and she loved me—Heaven knows why. I've told you what I did—now I've got to find her again."

"Do you think she'll marry you?" asked Susie. "I wouldn't. But then, I don't want to marry any one—ever."

"*Marry* me? I think if she'll let me stay in her presence long enough to ask her forgiveness on my knees she'll condescend too much."

"Well," said Susie sensibly, "I think you did act pretty mean; but I guess she was some to blame herself. I don't feel as if she was a saint and you was a leper, same as Bobby seems to, from what you said. She was a high-flyer, and you was a pill, but I guess folks are apt to be like that when they're courtin'. I know before Harry was sure of Hattie, he was moonin' around like a sick calf most of the time, and he'd leave the chores for Leon to do all alone, and go and lean over the graveyard fence, and hang around just hopin' she'd pass by, and one night when she went buggy-ridin' with Bert Stevens, 'stead of him, he acted like he'd sat down on the stove by mistake, he flew around so. He was an awful trial to live with, I know that —he was stupid and hasty, same as Bobby calls you, only he didn't show it in the same way. You'd have thought to see him then that he'd wait on her by inches, all his life, if she'd only have him, but now when they haven't been married but a year, he lets her get her own water for washin' and drag that great heavy baby around—and if he takes her anywhere he acts as if it was a great favour to her, and put him out terrible. That's why I'm not aimin' to have any love-affairs myself—I've seen how they work out too many times before this.

"Why shouldn't you find Jacqueline?" she went on, as David turned his head away with a slight cough, and without answering. "Probably she'll be the first person we see when we get to London, all married to some elegant English earl, with three or four little earls and earlesses of her own." Then noticing that this picture did not seem to appeal vitally to her brother, "You talk as if the earth had swallowed her, and you had got to dig."

"No, Susie," he explained patiently, "but it's years since

I lost track of her, and of course none of her friends will tell me where she is."

"She may be living right along in the same house."

But she was not, though they went immediately to London in the slight hope that this might be the case. The house was occupied by some brand-new people from Milwaukee, who were anxious to shine in society, and who were willing to admit any one who called.

"Yes, we bought the house from Lauder and Lauder," said Mrs. Beering volubly. "Of course you know Mr. Huntington died four years ago. Yes, I saw his granddaughter once—she came to get a few little things after we moved in. We bought the house furnished, and paid for it that way, but of course we wasn't going to split hairs over a trifle like that, when all she wanted was some nocount little keepsakes. I've kept expectin' to hear that she was married to some Duke or something, she was so downright handsome, as one may say. Was you ever acquainted with her? Well, she seemed like a real sweet girl to me that day she was here. No, I don't believe she's in London, for we keep agoin' all the time to all the swell places, and I've never set eyes on her since then. I read the society papers, too, of course, and I don't see her name mentioned. No trouble at all, Dr. Noble. Delighted to see you any time you'll drop in, I'm sure, and I'd be real pleased to have you come to dinner some night next week—I haven't a free evening before then."

David next directed his footsteps to the office of Lauder and Lauder, Real Estate Brokers; they also received him cordially, but the warmth of their greeting cooled when he stated his errand—he had looked good for a country manor, to say the least. However, they told him that Miss Huntington had placed the property in their hands to be sold, and they had not seen or heard of her since the time of that transaction, when she was stopping with her friend, Lady Thornington; they thought it probable that she managed all her property herself, but if she did have legal advisers, they were not known to Lauder and Lauder. Couldn't they interest Dr. Noble in a beautiful abbey that had just come on the market?

But David was half outside the door already. Lady Thornington! She had been kindly disposed to him—surely, if he went to her and made a clean breast of things, she could not help being convinced of his sincerity! He looked up the address of her town house, and hurriedly betook himself to it; but the footman who ushered him into the drawing-room came back after a moment with the chilling announcement that Lady Thornington could not receive him, either then, or at any other time.

If it had not been for Susie, who trudged patiently beside him as he went from place to place, he sometimes felt that his courage would have failed him completely; but she insisted on taking a hopeful and practical view of the situation, and cheered him in spite of himself.

"Wasn't she half French? Why don't you try France?"

"Why don't I hunt for a needle in a hay-stack? I don't know what her mother's maiden name was, even, or where she came from."

"Well, this whole thing is hunting for a needle in a hay-stack—but if the needle's *there,* you're bound to find it sooner or later. She went to school at a convent in Paris, didn't she? Maybe the nuns may know where she is—probably they keep track of their old scholars, especially if they're rich and good-lookin'—send 'em Christmas and Easter cards, and ask them in to Donation Days. And you said she always had her clothes made there—her dressmaker must know where she had things sent to, and a good many other things about her, besides—I'm sure Miss Simms, at home, don't miss much."

David had to admit that all this was good advice; and Susie followed it up with some that was still better.

"You'd think of some of these things yourself if you'd do something else for a change; your head's so dead beat because you try to work it all the time that it don't work at all. Why don't we have a cute little flat in Paris and a car? Why don't you take a course with the French doctor—Norchais, was that his name?—like you planned to in the beginning, and get some kind of a teacher for me so that I won't be so green when I start in school that I'll *sprout.* You don't take any notice of what I do—I'd still be pickin' my teeth and chewing gum if it wasn't for Bobby. You've met some folks in Paris, times when you've been there before, haven't you? Why don't you look 'em up, instead of tryin' to play a lone hand? You want a list of dressmakers, and a list of convents and a list of schools, and you want to take things easier for a spell, or you'll have us both all tuckered out."

"Susie, you'll be a treasure to some man some day."

"Well, that ain't my plan—I'd a sight rather have some man a treasure to *me*. But I'm tryin' to knock a little common sense into you just now."

To Paris they accordingly went, where they established themselves comfortably and pleasantly, and began to study, David with Norchais and Susie with a wizened little old tutor; to ride about in the new Mercedes that David bought, and to present themselves to his former acquaintances. And in due time, the establishment of Paquin and Worth and Doucet, and other very great personages in the dressmaking world were interviewed—but interviewed in vain. Ah, yes, was the almost invariable answer, they well remembered the young lady of whom monsieur spoke; they had formerly made her gowns; but it was now more than four years since the orders had entirely ceased.

"That is the more strange," he was told at the last of the famous houses which he visited, "as the one time we received a letter from Mademoiselle Huntington saying that she was fiancée, and that though she was not to be married immediately, we were to begin at once to collect the most beautiful fabrics that we could find. We found a white and silver brocade, from Venice, monsieur, that was a marvel, for the bridal robe, and other things—but almost immediately came another letter, saying that, after all, she would require nothing. And since then we have not heard from her. Does not monsieur desire to order for mademoiselle something very charming, very discreet?"

"Oh, David, do!"

"I thought you had no feminine foibles?"

"I don't know what you mean; but I like clothes—oh, yes, that one!"

He bought her the frock in question, and ordered another;

as they went down the carpeted steps together, she squeezed his hand.

"It's a shame that you should be buying dresses for me instead of for her," she whispered. "Say, wouldn't she have looked sweet in that white brocade?" Then, noticing how bleak and drawn his face looked, "Let's start right in at the convents now."

After a long search, they found the one which Jacqueline had attended; the Mother Superior received them; and there was something in the cool and gentle aloofness of her manner that made David believe instantly that she knew the whole story. His heart gave a great bound of hope.

"Jacqueline Désirée is not here now," she said quietly, "but it is true that she lived with us as a child, yes, and that she was called then 'the convent's sunbeam'; and always, for a long time, she returned to us at least once a year—for retreat during Lent, or for her birthday, or for some feast of which she was especially fond; and when her grandfather died, she made us a long visit—she was very weak at the time, for she had had a long illness."

"And you know where she is!" David cried. The Mother Superior touched a bell. A sister entered.

"Pray take mademoiselle into the garden," the even voice went on, "it is necessary for me to speak to monsieur privately." And, when they were alone, "Will monsieur not be seated?"

He sat down, and waited for her to speak again. "Monsieur is not of our Church?"

"No."

"Nevertheless, there are times when men of all faith, or of none at all, know that confession is good for the soul."

David met her look squarely. "I see," he said slowly, "you—you don't trust me. You think, if you tell me where she is, I'll hurt her again. But I won't. I don't ask to see her for more than five minutes. I only want to tell her——"

"Suppose you tell me what is in your heart to tell her, my son."

To the best of his ability, he did so; but he was labouring with deep emotion which he was trying to conceal; and he was speaking in a foreign language of which he had only uncertain command.

"Did you never think," she asked at length, "that the religious life might prove a refuge to Désirée?"

"You mean—that she might become a nun?"

"In truth I have heard her say so more than once. Do you not know enough of human nature, my son, to realize that *la grande amoureuse* and *la réligieuse* are own sisters, and sometimes actually the same person? History furnishes you with many an example. Désirée was deeply attached to her faith——"

David bowed his head. "I know it," he said huskily, "but I—I never thought of *this*. Why, that means——" All that it actually did mean came over him with rushing force.

"It does not mean that you would not be allowed to see her for five minutes, if that is actually all that you desire—but it is true that she is not here. She does not write to me often—suddenly, some day, she comes. When next she comes——"

"I beg of you," was all David could say.

And then October came, and Susie had to go to school, leaving him to wait alone for the five minutes in which he was to see Jacqueline.

He motored a great deal; the country about Paris was still very beautiful, the roads perfect, and he found a thrill and excitement in driving the Mercedes, which the true lover of machinery, no less than the true lover of horses, often experiences. It kept him from thinking.

One Saturday afternoon he chanced to pass through a small village more than thirty miles from Paris just as the bells were ringing for vespers; he sometimes went to services now, aimlessly and faithlessly, but deriving a certain amount of comfort from them all the same, and he was moved to do so on this particular afternoon. The little church was bare and cold, with a few tawdry decorations; the curé was old and rheumatic, and the congregation consisted of a handful of peasants, in rough woollen garments and wooden shoes, and two or three women shabbily dressed in black belonging to the small *bourgeoisie*. David dropped a gold-piece in the alms box as he passed out.

"Somehow I like that place," he said to himself as he got into his motor again. "It was clean and well-aired, and there were fresh flowers on the altar—it seemed different, someway, from most of them." He remembered, suddenly, that he had a dinner engagement, and switched, immediately, into high gear, in spite of the cobblestones of the little square. There was a crossing in a turn to the left before he reached the highroad for Paris; and, as he approached it, he saw one of the black-gowned women who had just left the church start to pass over to the other side of the street. She had plenty of time to reach the other side. He was still some little distance away. But when she was about half-way over, she glanced casually in the direction of the motor, then stopped short, uttering a little cry. David flung himself on the brake, but it was too late—the machine slid over her, and jerked itself to a standstill three yards further on.

David sprang back and bent over her. It was almost dark, but he could see a bright flow of blood gushing through the veil which hung from the small hat she wore, and which completely covered her face. As he pushed it away, the filmy black thing seemed to wind itself about his arm, impeding him. He shook himself free of it, shuddering, and looked into the woman's still face.

It was Désirée.

CHAPTER III

FINDING

ALL his life David was to remember—and marvel in remembering—that his first sensation was a wonderful rush of thanksgiving and joy—the knowledge of perseverance and love rewarded, of fear and despair overcome. *He had found Désirée.* Then, the next instant, came another bounding certainty—*she was not a nun*; and he saw, in one dazzling, throbbing moment, that the most colossal lie he had ever told—even though, when he told it, he had believed it to be the truth—was that it made no difference to him whether she was or not, that he only expected to see her for five minutes, just long enough to beg her forgiveness. As a man's whole life is said to be pictured before him when he is drowning, every word that the Mother Superior had spoken came back to him, so vividly that he seemed actually to hear her voice, and he realized for the first time that she had not really said—she had asked him a question, had given him no hope, had allowed him to believe—but she had only been testing him, trying to see whether this time—oh, *this time* he would prove to her— he gathered Désirée to him with a little cry of triumph. And then the horrible, murderous knowledge of how he had found her burst upon him.

The door of the nearest cottage stood half open. He pushed his way through it, his burden in his arms. A white-capped peasant woman sat knitting before the peaceful hearth-stone of a raftered kitchen. There were copper kettles glowing in the fire light, the fragrance of *pot-au-feu* filled the room. She started up with sudden alarm.

"Monsieur desires——" she began; then seeing what he carried, she cried aloud. Her knitting fell, the steel needle clicking against the stone floor. "There has been an accident!" And coming nearer, she cried again, "Holy Virgin! It is my Désirée!"

"It is *my* Désirée," said David, stupidly, in English; he stared at the little elderly peasant, bewildered, forgetting again. Then he remembered and spoke in French—"She's been run over by a motor car—where shall I take her?"

"Where but to her own room? Follow me, monsieur, and may the Saints preserve us!"

As he mounted the tiny, dark, narrow stairway, it seemed as if he understood only in waves, like a man recovering from an anæsthetic—he had found her, she was not a nun, nothing should ever take him away from her again—she was hurt, dying perhaps, he himself had done this unspeakable thing. If he did not think quickly, act quickly——

"Oh, my God, help me!" It was the first conscious prayer he had ever made. And, as he laid her on her narrow bed, and felt her dead weight slipping from his arms, suddenly, as if by a miracle, his mind cleared. He wrenched off a pillow-slip, and began tearing it into narrow strips, speaking rapidly.

"I'm a doctor. I know what to do. Help me all you can. It's going to be all right. And later, I'll explain. Now every minute we waste may mean this lady's life. Bring me some cold water—have you any ice in the house? Well, would any of your neighbours have any? Find some one to send for your village doctor, *quick*! Tell him to bring morphia, ether or chloroform, too, if he has it, but surely morphia—do you get the word? And—all the instruments he has—*hurry*——"

He made a make-shift tourniquet, wound the linen strips about the girl's head as he spoke, and bent to listen to her heart. The little peasant, he saw instantly, after her first natural outburst of terror, was not going to be hysterical, and the water she fetched him was cold and clean.

"Marthe, *ma bonne*, runs for *monsieur le médecin*," she said firmly, "and if ice there is in Fleursy, that also will be here, in a quarter of an hour. *Et alors*——"

"Fill all your kettles, and place them on the fire—we must have hot water as well as cold. Is there a telephone in the village, and do you know how to use it?"

"*Mais oui, monsieur*——"

Holding his left hand against Jacqueline's temple, he scribbled with his right on a scrap of paper.

"Can you read that?"

She lighted the tallow candle on the little bedside table, and scanned it, slowly, painfully. But in the end her face lighted.

"To Monsieur Norchais, 17 rue T—, Paris. If out, leave the message. 'Come instantly to village of Fleursy, house opposite church, bring instruments for major operation, ether, and a nurse. Life or death. David Noble.' Shall I wait for the doctor and ice before I telephone?"

"Wait for nothing."

"*Parfaitement, monsieur*——" but she had not reached the stairs before she called back, softly, "Marthe enters with the ice, monsieur."

The little maid, tears rolling from her round black eyes over her rough red cheeks, handed him the bowl silently.

143

"You'll have to break that up—use a poker—anything—
and bring it back—then go and watch the hot water——"
His own swiftness found a rival in these untaught women
who flew to serve him; almost instantly the broken ice was
thrust into his hands. He saw soon, that the red stain was
spreading less rapidly, that it was not spreading at all, that
it was drying a little—he reached for a towel from the little
washstand, tore that up too, felt the tourniquet once more,
wound the new bandage firmly over the first one. He asked
for scissors, began to cut her clothing, searching for further
injuries. The right arm was broken—shattered—so were
four of the right ribs—there was, of course, internal damage,
too, though how much he could not instantly determine.
If she regained consciousness before he could procure
morphia, her suffering would be terrible. But when he
raised his head after making his examination, a small,
shabby man stood beside him, extending a hypodermic
needle. David seized it without a word, and drove it into
the uninjured arm.

"I have no ether, monsieur, and only a little chloroform——"

"Enough to keep her insensible until we set that arm?"

"*Que monsieur regarde——*"

David looked, set his teeth, and threw off his coat.

"Of course there isn't—to play safe, but I think we had
better risk it—it's a nasty break, and I think we'd better get
it fixed—there'll be harder things to do later, without
being bothered with that—you have more morphia?"

But when it was all over, and the little room silent and
tidy again, and Jacqueline had been clad in a soft fresh
night-dress, and her bronze-coloured hair gathered in two
great plaits, she still lay, white and serene, with no sign of
returning life. David pulled up a chair beside the bed, and
sat down, his fingers on her wrist. And after he had
watched the younger man, who had apparently quite forgotten him, for a long time, the shabby village doctor
spoke with hesitating admiration.

"I will return when you need me, but there is nothing I
can do here now—I but obtrude my clumsy presence on
your genius, monsieur. With your permission, I will go

downstairs, and try to comfort Mère Thérèse—the poor woman has made no sound, but her heart must be breaking for her granddaughter."

"Her granddaughter!"

"But yes, monsieur, our beautiful Désirée is the granddaughter of the good Thérèse. Her mother, *hélas!* was a lovely, wild little creature, who ran away from home when she was very young, and danced upon the stage in Paris. I have heard that she was ravishing, with the frail charm of a fragile flower. She married a young man who became infatuated with her there, but both died when Désirée was but an infant, and she was brought up far from here by her grandfather—her father's father, a haughty American of great wealth, who never recognized the existence of her mother's family. We had almost forgotten the sad story in Fleursy, and we were glad to forget it, for it had brought shame as well as sorrow for Thérèse——"

"Then Désirée came here herself!" David spoke the words with a kind of excited joy, as one who has suddenly seen a shaft of light in utter darkness. "Wasn't it so, monsieur, four or five years ago, after a dangerous illness and the loss of her grandfather, seeking her mother's family, asking you all to welcome her——"

"Is monsieur then a magician as well as a genius? It was even so. She thought of taking the veil—indeed, she wished to do so, for it was plain she had been through a great sorrow, which had left her crushed and bleeding, though she was so fair and young and rich. In those first days she kept much to herself, thinking, praying—but there was so much to be done here, such misery and want! She was quick to see it, to forget her own grief. No angel from Heaven could have done for us more than she has done. If monsieur could but look from the window, he would see the crowd that has gathered, waiting for tidings! May I say that she is safe, that she will be restored to them through your skill and the goodness of God?"

"Tell them what you think best. And go, by all means —to the grandmother. When I need you——"

"Parfaitement, monsieur."

David bent over the bed again, listening for the girl's

heart-beats; there was no change. He glanced at his watch —eight o'clock! Three hours since—Norchais must have been out, and in that case there was no telling when he would arrive. There was nothing to do but wait. He looked about the room, dimly lighted by two great tallow candles. It was plain, even to the point of bareness. There were in it a narrow bed, a chest of drawers, a washstand, two straight-backed chairs, a small bed-side table. The walls were whitewashed, the floor unpainted, and without rugs. Over the bed hung a crucifix of ebony and ivory. Had Jacqueline actually been a nun, her cell could hardly have been more austere.

Through the open window—the only one in the room— he could hear the eager voices of the people outside, below it, the curses of men, the crying of little children.

"Where is the devil that has murdered her? Let us burn the car! What does monsieur the doctor say? Come to the church to light candles to the Virgin for her recovery! Will the Holy Father have her canonized if she dies? Monsieur the curé is praying for her. I will spend my five sous to buy her flowers——"

Half-past eight—would Norchais never come? David tore fresh bandages, though they were not needed, and laid them in neat piles by the bed-side table; picked up the pile of clothes, which, overlooked, were lying on the floor in a heap in the corner where he had flung them, and folded them carefully over a chair—a plain black dress, with bands of sheer white linen at the neck and sleeves, the simplest of undergarments. As he laid them down, something fell from among the folds to the ground. It was a tiny gold cross on a fine gold chain.

Nothing to do but wait. He could hear the crowd still surging outside, and from downstairs the sobbing of Mère Thérèse and the bonne, their fine self-control broken at last. He called softly and the little woman came and stood beside him. And stumblingly, as he had told the Mother Superior, he told her his story. But this woman understood him better.

"My granddaughter has indeed spoken of you," she said, simply, when he had finished, "but she has told me no evil of you—only that as a child, she loved you dearly, that later you were betrothed. Of the Austrian Count she had also told me—something. But these matters concern you and her, and not me, and it was plainly the will of God that the chance should be given you to speak of them together, else you would not have found her; and since you have done so, we must not question the way in which it has come about."

She laid her quivering hand on his shoulder. "Monsieur——"

"You'll tell the doctor and the curé as much of this as they ought to know—they're wondering of course, and probably resentful. And—you mustn't call me 'monsieur' —I come of very plain people, *petits fermiers*——"

She understood the feeling that prompted everything he said. The hand on his shoulder quivered still more.

"David," she said softly, "*mon fils*——"

He snatched it in his own, and kissed it, his hot tears falling unashamed upon it. And then she left him again.

Nothing to do but wait—for the doctor who did not come, and the signs of life which did not show themselves. To wait, while he thought of the Jacqueline that used to be, the fresh-faced child who came to him, singing, through the moonlit garden and kissed him on the road to Wallacetown; of the radiant beauty surrounded by luxury and frivolity, with her loveliness and her elegance, and her marvellous charm; of the Jacqueline that might have been— the wife in the glory of her passionate surrender, the mother with her final crown of womanhood; and then of the Jacqueline he had found—the recluse of a poor village, the gentle, ascetic divinity—but ever and always—the giver. And in those hours the remnants of selfishness and selfrighteousness, of vain-glory and uncharitableness that still lay on David's soul fell from it, as a dark mantle, freed from a woman's white shoulders, falls to the ground, leaving the fair soft flesh bare beneath it. What, he asked himself, in the slow torture that was beginning to burn away the bitter misery of the last three months—what had *he ever given*? He had *taken*—snatched—squeezed dry. He had crashed ahead, blindly, on his single-track railway, triumphantly sweeping aside all obstacles, had reached the great city which was his terminal, and lo! the city was barren and empty, and not worth the reaching. What were the successes of years, the thousand miracles of skill he had performed, worth to him now if he could not save this one girl's life and set her in a throne in his empty city, so that it might no longer be empty, and fall down and worship her? He fell on his knees now, and buried his face in the coverlet of the bed.

Suddenly, without warning, David felt a slight movement beneath the sheet. He sprang to his feet.

Jacqueline was looking around her with wide, quiet eyes, as a child, waking, looks for its mother; as they turned on the man beside her, they lighted, slowly, as if they had found what they sought. A little fluttering sigh came through her white lips, and then she smiled—the smile of the singing girl coming through the garden.

"Hello, David," she said.

CHAPTER IV

KEEPING

"What happened?" she asked, a little confusedly, after a moment, as he did not answer. "I was crossing the street, coming from church—and then I saw you, driving a car—it startled me, and I stopped—did I get run over?" Then, as David nodded, still dumbly, "I'm not in great pain—am I much hurt?"

"You have had a good deal of morphia—I want to save you all the suffering I can; but I must not give you any more at present, for I am sure you are internally injured, and I'll need your help to locate the extent and position of the trouble. Your right arm was broken; but I have set that—the village doctor had a little chloroform."

He had always sneered at the doctors who "coddled their patients by lying to them." Had it been sometimes as hard for them to tell the truth as it was for him to speak those few sentences?—he knew that he would never sneer again——

"Your head was cut, too. Does it ache much?"

"No—not badly. Don't give me anything more—if you need my help—everything seems a—a little hazy still."

"Yes, but that's all right; you're more comfortable that way."

"You'll take care of me? You won't go away———"

"Never, until you send me," he said, "but I've telephoned Norchais, of Paris—or, rather, your grandmother did for me—he must have gone out on a case, or he'd have been here hours ago! I had of course—nothing with me, and your own doctor has not much, either; Norchais will be able to do much more for you than I can. And I'm going to cable to Boston for a nurse—of course Norchais will bring one, but I want one of our own women from the Edgar L.—the best in all the world—for you. She can get here in a week."

"Do you think there may—have to be an operation?"

"Yes, if what I fear has happened."

"At once?"

"Yes, tonight———"

"You'll—you'll do it?"

He turned away from the entreaty in her eyes. "I think Norchais is more skilful," he said gently, "but it shall be just as you say, of course."

She seemed, for a few minutes, to have sunk back into the merciful stupor into which the morphia had naturally sent her; but presently she stirred again, and held out her left hand.

"I wrote to you," she said, "but the letter came back, still sealed, and torn across—I never—could try again———"

"Yes, I know."

"David, I wasn't—I didn't———"

"I know—I've known for three months—I've been hunting for you ever since———"

"Without a single clue to guide you, giving up everything that you were doing . . . then you must have forgiven me!"

The torture was growing unbearable—surely, the robe that Nessus had worn held no such white heat as this! It seemed to David as if there must be some way in which he could tear it off, as if he must fling himself at Désirée's feet, and cry out with repentance and love and passion, in the hope that, as on the road to Wallacetown, he would be shriven and healed. But this time, he knew, the sin was too great; even if, in her infinite mercy, she could forgive him, he could not ask it; and passion had long since passed from the life of this gentle saint. He took the hand that she extended very reverently and quietly.

"Jacqueline," he said, "I did you the greatest wrong that a man could possibly do a woman. I never can atone for it. Some day, when you are well again, we'll speak of it—but you're very ill now—it isn't good for you to talk, or even to try to think. I am a doctor, and you are my patient; we must try to forget, for now, that we were ever anything else."

"Is there any chance that I may not get well?"

David dropped her hand and walked over to the window. The crowd outside was smaller now, because many had gone to the church to pray; but there were still many there. There was no sign of Norchais. The wind was blowing, and there was not a cloud in the sky.

"Don't feel so about it. I don't. I only asked because, if there is, I want to talk about my money—there's such a lot of it, and the people here are wretchedly poor. You have no idea what their existence used to be. I've been able to help them a little, and they mustn't lose anything, if I have to leave them. You could send some one for the attorney, couldn't you?"

"I think he's outside now. I can hear a woman addressing a hungry-looking little man as 'monsieur l'avocat'——"

"Please ask him to come up."

When he had done this, and the little man, snuffling with grief, stood beside her, David was amazed at the brevity and clarity of Jacqueline's directions. There was no mawkish sentimentality, there were no vague desires or half-formed, impracticable plans. So much was to go to the Church, so much to the school, besides two yearly prizes to be given to the graduating pupils of highest rank, that they might be able to continue their studies further; a sum to be used for general charities at the discretion of the curé; a fund from which five hundred francs should be given to every girl of the village upon her marriage——

"Every girl of good character?" said monsieur l'avocat, writing.

"Every girl," reiterated Jacqueline, "and a hundred francs for every baby born; fifty thousand for grand'mère and all the rest of it——"

She turned towards David; he read her intention instantly.

"I am rich now myself, Jacqueline," he said quietly, "almost as rich as you are. I don't need it any more."

"But you'd know what to do with it better than I can direct—now. Is there a hospital in Hamstead?"

"No."

"Couldn't you have one built—and other things like that?"

"Yes, if you are quite sure it is what you wish done."

"All the rest of my property then," she went on, "real and personal, I leave to David Noble, to be used at his discretion. That's all, I think. Please ask two persons not specified in the will to come in and witness it."

When the little room was quiet again, she lay for a few minutes with closed eyes, and David knew that she was not only exhausted, but suffering again, as the effects of the morphia wore away; but she shook her head at his offer to give her more.

"I think I can show you now where the worst pain is—right here."

He made his examination quickly, asking several brief questions. Did it hurt when he pressed it? Was it dull or sharp? Was it worse here—or here? It was very soon over.

"Is your general health good? You are very thin."

"I'm perfectly healthy. I had a bad nervous breakdown when—several years ago. Since then I haven't had a moment's sickness worth mentioning."

"What does 'worth mentioning' mean?"

"I don't sleep."

The words were simple enough. He guessed at what lay behind them.

"That's all, dear lady. Now you must let me put you to sleep, so that you can save your strength."

"All right. Good luck, David!"

She seemed to be almost unconscious, when she reached for his hand again.

"Do you remember," she said drowsily, "that you said once you'd find me if I was on the top of the Himalaya Mountains, or in the middle of the Sahara Desert?"

"Yes, Jacqueline."

She laughed, softly. "Apparently, you meant it! And do you remember that I said once——"

"Well, dear?"

"That it wouldn't be safe for any woman to marry you until you were ready to give up your career to have her, and do it then to serve her, and not to possess her——"

Did he remember! Could he ever forget the magnificent, firelit room, the beautiful girl dressed in white satin sitting on the crimson sofa, the sweet, wilful, self-consenting rebellion that came before the exquisite surrender——

"David—it would be safe now, wouldn't it?"

"I don't understand," he said stupidly.

"If I am dying—perhaps—I have a right to any of the sacraments which I desire——"

"You wish to confess, to receive communion?"

"That first, of course, and then——"

He had no way of telling just how far she was aware of what she was saying and doing. He put his face close to hers to catch the whispered words.

"I told you, too, once, that marriage was a sacrament, didn't I?"

"Oh, my dear!" he said brokenly. Then he pulled himself together. "Darling, you don't know what you are saying. You can't—mean——"

"But I *do*. I do know, I do mean. David, won't you marry me—that is, if you still——"

"Oh, my dear!" he said again, and stopped for a moment, powerless to go on. "When I found I'd failed you *once*," he managed at last to say, "I insisted that I still had a right to—even though I'd left you where your grandfather could insult you and torture you. And just what you predicted happened—I failed you a second time—and that time it was *I* who insulted and tortured you. Don't think

I'm such a fool—such a wicked and presuming——"

She stretched out her hand. "It seems—to be getting dark—I can't see you, David," she said like a pleading child, "please hold on to me——" And when he had taken her hand, she whispered, "But I never said you'd fail me a third time. And you *wouldn't*—would you?"

"O my God, *no!*" he cried, feeling that his very soul was crumbling within him.

But before he could gather her into his arms, he saw that she was again unconscious.

.   .   .   .

It was after midnight when Norchais reached Fleursy, accompanied by a grey-clad nun, who looked, with her pallid face and her great crucifix, like the very messenger of Death—Norchais, already weary from a tedious vigil which had ended disastrously, and angered at his pupil's unreasonable presumption in calling him to an unknown woman in a poverty-stricken village—Norchais, who listened with scant attention as David, hurriedly sorting instruments, told him the main facts of the accident.

"Deaths as the result of motoring increase in number every day," he said, smothering a yawn. "I didn't know what instruments to bring—'major operation' isn't especially definite, you know—but if your diagnosis is correct there's not one chance in a thousand that you can save the girl, anyway—and you can't see to operate by the light of two tallow candles!"

David was rolling up his sleeves. He turned on the other doctor with a ferocity that was as primitive as that of a cave-man, fighting for his mate.

"This is the thousandth chance," he said, savagely. "I'm going to do it, and do it well—and I would if I hadn't anything but a pair of shears and a piece of twine to do it with, too. Go down and get the acetylene lights off your car, and then scrub up and get ready to help me, and be damned quick about it. Now I'm all ready. Take the ether cone, *ma sœur*."

"There must be something——" the great doctor was murmuring with startled excitement, as he returned with

the flaring lights in his hands—he held them high over the
bed, and broke into an exclamation of amazement. "*Ma
foi*, David Noble!" he cried. "That's no village girl—it's
Jacqueline Huntington, the great American heiress. I saw
her once years ago, and I have never forgotten——"

But David did not answer him. He had begun to work.

CHAPTER V

THE BATTLE

THE leaves in the forest of Fleursy turned from golden to
bronze, and fell, quivering, to the dull earth; October, with
its crisp coolness and mellow sunshine, passed; November
dragged its dark length through, and December came with
its frozen roads, and its futile flurries of snow. And still
Jacqueline lay, very white and quiet, on the narrow bed
under the crucifix of ebony and ivory, while David fought
for her life with the grey shadow of death that hovered
over her, and which over and over again seemed about to
bear her away in its tenuous, powerful arms.

It took ten days for the nurse whom he trusted to reach
Fleursy from Boston, and during that time he did not have
his clothes off, did not go further from Jacqueline's room
than the kitchen, and seldom as far as that. The constitu-
tion which, as Bobby had humorously put it, enabled him
to "operate thirty-six hours out of the twenty-four, if
necessary," stood him in good stead now. He ate his meals
in gulps, he slept, when he slept at all, for an hour at a
time on a couch just outside her door. Like most doctors,
he had seldom watched a patient coming out of anæsthesia
longer than was necessary to assure himself that "everything was normal"—an expression which causes physicians
untold satisfaction, nurses untold responsibility, and sick
persons untold suffering. There was no question of the
"normal" this time. Jacqueline, as sometimes, though
fortunately rarely, happens, was almost completely para-
lyzed by the ether. She could not get rid of it in the
"normal" way, she could not swallow or speak or move.
David had seen this difficulty arise but once before, in the

case of an Italian woman at the North End, in Boston, with whose lividness he had felt nothing but impatience. Why couldn't she drink tepid water, and succumb to nausea, and tell all her life's secrets, and shiver and cry, and then drift off into her " ether sleep "? He recalled the hysterical, noisy, rebellious grief of the Italian woman's husband, the ironical calmness with which he had met it . . . And now here was Jacqueline, lying motionless, the perspiration dropping in great beads from her white forehead, her hair, her night-gown, her sheets, as wet with it as if she had been plunged into a bath, her great eyes fixed on him, asking him, dumbly, why he did not help her . . . Like most doctors, also, he had seldom watched beside a patient through the night; that was a task relegated to a night nurse, while he went peacefully home to bed. He wondered, now, how he had ever done it. Morphia did not make Jacqueline sleepy. She grew drowsy, suffered less acutely for a short time, and then lay staring wide awake again; this, too, was an " abnormality " seldom encountered, " a nuisance " when it had been. He felt he would willingly have been cut in tiny pieces if he could first see her drift off into a painless, dreamless slumber. One night— one hideous, panting, agonized, writhing life-time, that seemed alive with horror—might reveal more to him about suffering—the way it must be endured, the way it must, if possible, be conquered—than months of complacent practice had done. Ten of them, coming one after the other, without respite, made him marvel that he had ever thought he knew anything about bodily pain and mental anguish. One, slightly less dreadful than those that had gone before it, buoyed him into exultant hope. The following one was worse, far worse, than any that had gone before it. He thought of deserts—of mirage—and knew now why travellers killed themselves.

Bobby, David had often told him, " pampered his patients "; they were all " medically babied."

"The clean cut of a surgeon's knife is just like any other clean cut," he had said, impatiently many times. "Why should it be regarded as something so different? It's exactly the same. If you slashed your arm with a sabre—

provided it was sterile—you wouldn't expect to be under par indefinitely, would you? I have my patients out mowing their lawns before yours are sitting up in an easy chair drinking cool drinks."

"I know you do," drawled Bobby comfortably. "Also, six months later, when mine are beginning to mow lawns and have got my modest bill all paid, yours are seeking refuge in expensive sanatoriums. Nerves all shot to pieces, no one can imagine why, 'the operation was so wonderfully successful!' You don't stop to think that they've also got to recover from whatever made that nice clean cut necessary—a trouble hidden, or patiently borne for years, sometimes; from pain, which you underestimate, and which is a bigger factor than you seem to know—it isn't over when it's over, to be rather Irish, but entirely truthful; from shock; from ether; oh, I know some people tell you they 'like to take ether.' One woman who told me that——"

"Well?" Bobby's stories were usually worth listening to.

"She came to me for a major operation which had been made necessary by the stupidity of a former doctor; came all alone, two hundred miles,—she lived in the country—because she 'really preferred to.' She was 'used to being sick'—that was true all right—'didn't mind it a bit; a hospital was a colossal joke.' She was the most magnificent liar I ever saw. There was a husband somewhere in the dim distance; he couldn't stand the smell of ether, so she 'hated to bother him.' Well, I'm glad to say it bothered him a little when she died. Oh, yes, the operation was successful—I'm not such an awful bungler as you like to pretend—but she'd bluffed too much, and stood too much, before it, and there was no one to stand by and help her stand and bluff after it was over. I did what I could, but what she needed was some one to love her, love her good and plenty—oh, hell!"

That was what—between incoherent, formless prayers— David kept saying to himself now: he had, of course, made a "perfectly clean cut," there was "nothing to recover from." He dwelt on the words with scathing sarcasm of his own former theories. There were five years to reckon

156

with, five years which had not been spent "normally," followed by a fearful shock and great suffering. Jacqueline, he suspected, had observed the facts of her Church more conscientiously than she had done its feasts, even if the abrupt change from luxurious living to coarse peasant fare had not inevitably wrought havoc. She was thin to the point of emaciation. Moreover, her taste for beauty and pleasure, her emotions, her senses, had not died the natural death that comes from peaceful middle age; they had been torn up by the roots with her own hands, trampled on with her own feet. She had lain awake for nights, weeping until exhaustion overcame her, throbbing for something she was denied—suffering until the power to throb had left her altogether. "*Nuits blanches*"—"white nights"—David had heard the phrase, had thought it rather expressive—now he knew for the first time what it really meant.

Sœur Célestine he instinctively distrusted. Nuns, he thought, probably essayed to cure their patients by rosaries rather than routine. He watched her constantly, expecting to find that she had neglected to take a temperature or failed to scrub a hand. He frowned when she rose or moved about, as if waiting for her shoes to squeak. If she had "only been one of our own women!" Gradually he realized—and the realization was one of the few bright spots in his existence just then—that he had misjudged and underrated her. She prayed indeed—the little room was filled with the purity and sincerity of her prayers—but while she prayed, she watched and she worked. She had no "two hours off for rest and recreation" every afternoon, she did not state that "she could not do Miss Huntington justice unless she had at least seven hours' sleep every night"; she did not relate lengthy tales of the "very wealthy family of her last patient," who had been so "extremely considerate." Her work of healing was not a means of making money to her; it was a dedication. There were many great and noble characters among "our own nurses," and the one whom he so eagerly awaited was one of them; but there were many others who were neither—as there are in every profession—to whom he had not hesi-

tated to entrust his patients, whom he had even engaged a
second time. There was the one who woke a sufferer from
insomnia to give him a sleeping-powder, that other who lost
a hypodermic needle in a bed and "thought it didn't much
matter"; the one that gave a child with a temperature of
104° roast goose for dinner, and the other who blistered a
young girl's back with the hot-water bag from shoulder to
hip before she came out of ether. These occurrences had
once seemed to him to have rather a humorous side. Now
the greatness of his carelessness began to assume such mag-
nitude in his eyes he wondered how any one he had ever
taken care of had come through alive. Pulling himself
together, he knew how silly and morbid that was—he had
done good work, skilful work, yes, *great* work, only there
had been so much he had not understood before. Did he
understand enough now? With everything else that he
had to fight, he found that he had to contend with that
sinister thing called Fear, which he had never met before—
Fear that he himself might not be "normal"—sane, calm,
alert, watchful; Fear that no matter how "normal" he was
it would not prove enough to keep Jacqueline; Fear that he
ought not to want to keep her, if she were to suffer like
this. And then Fear, of course, began calling her sisters,
Failure and Defeat. David thought, more than once, that
they were actually on the threshold. He rose, towering,
and slammed the door in their faces. After that, Fear left
of her own accord.

He did not have to fight alone, either. For with him was
Norchais, indifferent no longer, and coming daily to see
the patient whom his pupil never left. There were Sœur
Célestine and, after the first ten days, Miss Houston, who
taught each other much; there were Marthe and Mère
Thérèse downstairs, who cooked and washed and swept,
and went to sleep at a neighbour's that the nurses might
have their beds. And finally there were monsieur le curé
and monsieur l'avocat, backed by the entire village. Old
men and women came with tears in their eyes to ask what
they might be permitted to do for *notre Désirée*. Children
brought pitiful little presents of vegetables and flowers, as
votive offerings are brought to a beloved shrine; there came

also the Marquis de Fleursy, who lived, with his widowed mother, in a château some three miles from the village, and who, before Jacqueline came, had paid his tenantry but scant attention. He brought with him Hamburg grapes and truffles, which Mère Thérèse and Marthe enjoyed extremely, and gardenias, which adorned the church altar. On the occasion of his third visit, he insisted on seeing the doctor in charge; David, somewhat reluctantly, left Jacqueline's room long enough to go down and see him, though this was after those first awful days were past. He could not help finding something very engaging and attractive about the young nobleman, who treated him with a Gallic courtesy and charm that were very pleasant.

"Tell Mademoiselle Huntington," he said, gathering up his reins to depart, "that she is not to feel concerned; there will be plenty of coal and warm clothing in the village, just as usual, and a tree at the château for the children at Christmas time. My mother has charged me to ask you if you would not bring her to us, as soon as you feel it would be safe to move her. We could perhaps make her more comfortable? And for you, monsieur, when you are able to leave her to enter Paris again—may I not have the honour of mentioning your name as a guest—or, if you are to remain indefinitely—as a member—of my club, or show you some other trifling attention?"

David watched the smart trap out of sight, and then walked thoughtfully up the stone stairs again. It was not hard to guess, from the short interview that had just taken place, that Jacqueline might, had she so chosen, have become Marquise de Fleursy. He wondered that the idea had not appealed to her—she could have remained among the people she loved, and continued to be their ministering angel, and yet she could have been surrounded by the comfort, the culture, and the love that were her due. But as he bent over again, she seemed so frail a thing that the thought of her in connection with any earthly joys seemed futile, and the hope for her recovery, which had been definitely taking shape the last twenty-four hours, faded away altogether.

"Tell me where you suffer most," he said gently.

"I don't suffer at all—that is, worth mentioning."

That was one great trouble. Jacqueline, docile and uncomplaining though she always was, helped neither them nor herself; she alone could not be made to fight. She did not seem to care whether she lived or died.

He repeated the message of the Marquis. She smiled.

"He is so kind," she said, "tell him so for me, the next time he comes." Her voice implied the natural courtesy of a gentlewoman, nothing more. Clearly there had never been any question of the Marquis.

"Are you wondering about him and me now?" she asked suddenly. David knew there was no intentional unkindness in the words; nevertheless, they stung him to the quick.

"Oh, my dear!" he exclaimed. Then, after a moment's pause, he said, trying not to show how hurt he was, "Not in the sense you mean. Can't you believe that stupid and base as I was to ever 'wonder' as far as you were concerned, I have had a sufficiently terrible lesson to teach even a man as bad as I was to be better? But I couldn't help thinking—he is so attractive, so obviously devoted to you, and it would have been—ideal—as far as you are concerned, it seems to me——"

She shivered.

"Has love—become abhorrent to you, Jacqueline?"

"Yes—that kind. It isn't love at all—it's selfishness and greed. There have been dozens of men who—wanted me—but I doubt if one of them—loved me."

"I know. But men are not all alike. This one does love you, he would have been unselfish and self-sacrificing——"

"Perhaps. But don't you see, if you lose your faith in one person, you lose it in *everybody*. I wanted to get away entirely from the kind of life I'd been leading—I couldn't bear it—not because I felt it was wrong in itself, but because its—customs and usages had—antagonized you, had come between us. Fleursy and its poverty—and this bare little house—and my peasant grandmother—were——"

"Yes, dear, I know."

"And after the way Gustav and Cyril—whom I thought were my *friends—in love with me*—treated me (he wondered how she could help saying 'after the way that you treated me') I didn't want to—to think of that sort of feeling again—in connection with anybody. I was—just aflame with feeling—*for you*—and I didn't want to feel—*at all* if it was going to bring me to . . . I wanted to *rest*. And, after I got a little rested, I wanted to *work*—to get so tired, physically, that I couldn't think or feel either. I—oh, David, don't say this isn't 'normal'——"

"I'm not going to—I hate that word, anyway. It may not have been normal, but it was perfectly natural——"

He was sitting on the edge of her bed, stroking her hair. She gave a little sigh, and turned her head, resting her cheek on his hand. He saw that she was tired, reproached himself bitterly for having let her talk so long. But after a few minutes he was stupefied to see that she had fallen asleep—into the quiet, peaceful, natural slumber that he had been praying for so long. Hour after hour went by, it grew dark. Miss Houston herself was resting. Sœur Célestine came in softly with Jacqueline's supper tray, saw what had happened, and stole silently back to the kitchen to tell Mère Thérèse. When she came back, David had slipped to the floor, his head resting beside Jacqueline's on the pillow, his hand on hers. He, too, was sound asleep.

The nun fell on her knees with a prayer of thanksgiving. The morning sun was streaming in at the little window before any of them stirred.

Up to that time, Jacqueline had accepted David's constant presence as unquestioningly as she had that of her grandmother. She had not been encouraged to talk, and she had been too ill to wish to. But the following day she began to question him, and her first query was characteristic.

"You don't know what it meant to talk to you that way yesterday—and to have you *understand*," she began. "I've led such a silent life these last years. I feel almost—almost——"

"Yes, dear?"

"As if a stone had been rolled away from a sepulchre——"

"I felt that way, too, when I saw that you *wanted* to talk

to me—and that you'd fallen asleep. Jacqueline, you are going to get well."

"Because you've made me! But I've been terribly selfish. I'm taking up all your time. I don't see when you've slept or eaten, even. I've never wanted you that you haven't been here, quite close beside me. It's wrong of me to monopolize you like this. What were you doing when you found me?"

"Hunting for you."

"No, no, I mean for a serious occupation.

"Lord, I thought that was plenty serious enough!"

"David, you know what I mean——" She was almost laughing.

"Well, I was taking some lectures with Norchais in Paris; and I have a little sister in school there who needs considerable looking after."

"Susie! That cunning youngster who went to sleep with her thumb in her mouth at your graduation? Why, how old is she?"

"She's almost sixteen; but she seems more like twelve. When you get strong enough I'm going to fetch her out to see you—you'll get a lot of fun out of her. She's an awful savage—but there's something splendid about her just the same."

"Family traits? I remember you when you were that age! Does she look like you?"

David laughed. "I believe she does," he said, as if he were pleased that this was the case.

"Well, you've been neglecting her terribly. You must go and see her tomorrow."

"I shan't go one step."

"David! Just as stubborn as ever?" They were both laughing now.

"Rather more so. Anyway, I'm not going to Paris until you're well enough to sit up at the window and wave good-bye to me out of it."

"Well—you might go out and around the village a little, at least, and come in and report to me how things are going. I'm pining for news. Or walk over to the château and see the Marquis—you know he wants you to, ever so much, and I'd like to feel that you two were friends." She paused a moment, then, with no less gaiety, but with an abrupt change of subject, she said, "Do you know what attractive ties you wear? They've made me reflect, someway, that I'm rather a fright. If you won't go into Paris yourself, will you let me send Miss Houston some day? I want a lot of *pretty* nightdresses, and some négligées—if I've got to sit up and wave to you out of a window—and violet water and scented talcum and——"

David left the room feeling as if he could weep for joy. That afternoon he told Norchais, when the latter came, that he thought the fight was over.

"No, it isn't," said the older doctor sharply. "I've seen these flashes of spirit before in persons with her temperament, and they're often followed by complete exhaustion, or worse, because there's no physical strength back of them. She has about as much vitality as an Easter lily. You've put up a wonderful battle—one that would be enough, in itself, to make you famous if all the facts were known— don't lose it now from over-confidence."

David began to comply with Jacqueline's request, and to leave her for a little while each day, finding, to his amazement, a surprising number of things to interest him in the little village. He and Mère Thérèse were already deeply attached to each other. He longed to loiter about the copper-hung kitchen, so different from the one in the little cottage "out back" from Hamstead, where he had grown up. When he praised her housekeeping, he told her about that one, showed her how his mother used to make doughnuts, initiated her into other mysteries of New England cookery. He made friends rapidly with all the neighbours, he who had never had half a dozen real friends in his life! They were enchanted to find that "Monsieur David" could milk a cow and feed a pig, and harness a horse—that he could actually give practical and valuable suggestions as to the best way of doing all these things. The village children tagged at his heels. He brought them into the house with him, and sitting by the hearthstone with two or three on his lap, and several more around him, told them stories about America which made their round eyes bulge, stuffed them with sweet chocolate sent out from Paris, sent them away, laughing, with their pockets full of coppers. He went sometimes to talk over Materia Medica with monsieur le médecin in his dusty little office, lent him, more than once, a helping hand when sickness arose. Once a week, at least, he went to smoke a pipe with monsieur l'avocat or monsieur le curé, sometimes they all had a game of cards together. He found that he liked all these men, that they all liked him. At last he walked over to the château. The Marquis welcomed him as if he had been a visiting prince. They found that they were almost exactly the same age, that they had been to many of the same places, that they had quantities of tastes in common. David was persuaded to stay to dinner. Madame la Marquise was more formal than her son, but she was handsome and gracious. She, too, urged him to come again. It was wonderful to find so much kindliness in the world. David suddenly knew that he had never been so happy in his life.

With his happiness, however, came much self-questioning, the reversal of many other theories besides those which Jacqueline's illness had overturned. He had always thought of the French as a frivolous people, with no knowledge of sanitation, and lamentably bad morals. He found them natural and gay, courteous and splendid. What *was* frivolity, after all? Was it not often a wonderful "bluff" to cover trouble? Was cleanliness something deeper than daily baths and perfect drinking water? Had he confused morality with chastity—or still greater mistake—with marriage? What were, after all, the qualities that counted most in the sight of *le bon Dieu*? He found he was going more and more often to services, that prayer came to him as naturally as breath. He would, probably, never be able to accept all the dogmas of the Church that Jacqueline loved, or to be blind to some of its errors. Nevertheless, it towered before him, a bulwark of strength to millions of souls through countless ages.

For the first time, too, the severe sincerity of the doctrine of his own Puritan forefathers revealed itself to him in its austere and dignified beauty. He saw, in his spiritual awakening, hundreds of little white churches with slender spires pointing to the sky, scattered through the valleys and hills of New England, as the tabernacles of courage and righteousness. He understood his father's simple belief, and a great longing to see him and tell him so swept over him. There was no longer any question of his being able to accept and revere the spirit of faith in whatever form he might find it.

Meanwhile, as far as Jacqueline was concerned, he feared that Norchais had been right. She grew no stronger, though her arm was out of splints, and the "clean cut" of David's knife was long since healed and all that remained of the ugly gash on her temple was a little triangular scar that her nurses covered with her soft hair. And at last Miss Houston, the practical, spoke her mind to him, as he was starting in to Paris to see Susie for the first time.

"If you want to know my opinion, Dr. Noble," she said, though, as a matter of fact, he had not told her that he did, "I don't think Miss Huntington will ever get well if she goes on this way, though there's not a thing organically the matter with her now, of course. She needs to get away from this cold, uncomfortable house and this raw disagreeable climate—the idea of trying to live without plumbing or steam heat, or *anything* civilized, especially when it's way down below freezing, and the sun doesn't shine from one week's end to another! And she needs more playing and less praying, some companions of her own age, and some pretty clothes, and a competent maid, and not a trained nurse or a nun to wait on her. I'm going back to Boston next week. I advise you to send Miss Huntington to Nice."

"With whom?"

"Oh, there are plenty of competent companions; and she can go through quite comfortably on a *wagon-lit*."

David pondered the question carefully as he motored into Paris. He found Susie overjoyed to see him. She was looking remarkably well, too, in a simple dress of red smocked silk; it was astonishing to see how much her English had improved and how rapidly she was blossoming out. She sat on his lap, ruffling his hair as he talked to her, telling her something of what had happened in the three months since he had seen her.

"Well, you did get your come-uppance, all right, didn't you?" she said, but quite tenderly. "I didn't half realize, from your notes—though you were a perfect *saint* to write me so often—I don't see how you ever managed to! Well, I must say I think you've pulled off a pretty neat job, and if I had my way I'd take a megaphone and brag about you in the Place de la Concorde, I'm so proud of you. What are you going to do next?"

"Just now I'm going out to do some shopping—want to come with me? You haven't had any Christmas present yet, for one thing—I thought you might like to help me choose it. By the way, I hope your holidays weren't too doleful?"

"Doleful? Hoo! Didn't I tell you the Graingers"—mentioning friends of his—"asked me to their house for the entire time? By the way, they know the Marquis de Fleursy—he came in several times while I was there. He's terribly impressed with you. He was nice to me too. He——"

"I wonder if she's going to make a speciality of other girls' cast-off beaus?" David smiled to himself.

"But, mercy, the French have got chaperons on the brain, haven't they? I'd never heard of such a thing before—I guess they don't grow good—I mean, well—in Hamstead. The soil wouldn't be favourable to' em. But they certainly flourish in Paris. I thought when I first heard of 'em, they were something to eat—chaperon—sounds like it might be a kind of fancy pudding, doesn't it?"

David laughed aloud. "The Marquis told me he had met you. He's a good sort. I don't think you need to worry about a chaperon as far as he's concerned."

"I'm not worrying about 'em as far as any one's concerned. It's every one else that worries the breath half out of themselves. Well, speaking of Christmas presents, I want a little pearl heart. Are you going to get something for Jacqueline, too?"

"If we can find anything good enough." He recalled with some bitterness that he had had no gift for her on Christmas day. Two servants from the château had stag-

166

gered in under the enormous basket of roses that the Marquis had sent, and even Norchais had appeared with a very stiff, round bouquet with a punched paper frill about it. He might have ordered something from Paris, but he wanted to choose it for himself. He had tried to explain, and had been suddenly tongue-tied, and awkward. He wondered if she had understood.

But it was impossible to do much wondering with Susie in tow. She was enchanted to be out with him again, and dragged him jubilantly from shop to shop. She needed, it appeared, pounds and pounds of candy for herself and all her intimate friends at school. She saw a pretty hat in a brilliant window, and insisted on going in and ordering that—a great floppy red thing, trimmed with poppies, which became her exceedingly. She stood over him with sage advice while he ordered shirts and gloves and collars to replenish his own depleted stock. At last she led him to Cartier's to buy the pearl heart, and finally to Columbin's for tea. It was not until they were saying good-bye that she spoke again of Jacqueline.

"No, I didn't forget it, but this was your day, honey. Besides, I didn't see what I wanted for her."

"Well, you're a bang-up brother, anyway, if you do slip up as a beau. Do come again—*soon*."

It was nearly eight o'clock when he reached Fleursy again. Jacqueline's room was unlighted, Miss Houston downstairs eating her supper. Sœur Célestine rose silently and went out as he entered. Jacqueline did not speak, and he went nearer to see if she were sleeping. Inadvertently, in the dark, his hand touched her cheek. It was wet with tears.

He had never known her to cry; it was strangely unlike her. The fact was the more appalling.

"Oh," he exclaimed, putting his arm around her in quick alarm, "what is the matter? I knew I ought not to go off and leave you!"

"Yes, you ought. I—didn't mean you to find me this way. But I got so lonesome and Miss Houston has been talking to me and——"

"Well, I'll talk to *her*!" said David under his breath. Then, aloud, "Have you had any supper?"

"I didn't want any."

"Well, I haven't had any either, and I've brought all kinds of things out from Paris with me—squabs, and champagne, and *petits fours* and flowers—let's have a party!" He called Sœur Célestine back and gave her hurried and merry instructions. Then while they waited for the little feast to come, he lighted the candles, propped Jacqueline up on her pillows, fetched her a pink bed-jacket, arranged violets and roses on her bed-side table. A little colour came into her cheeks. Before they had finished it had deepened, she had caught his mood, was laughing with him about Susie and the "chaperon" pudding. When Sœur Célestine came for their tray, he closed the door after her as she went out.

"Are you too tired to talk over some things with me?" he asked quietly.

"No. What?"

"I've been waiting for a long time to ask you—how much you remember—about the night I found you."

"Why, everything."

"Are you sure? I thought then you were more or less—rather more *than* less—under the influence of morphia. Since I have seen how little it affects you, I've been wondering."

He paused, his heart beating like a trip-hammer. Jacqueline did not help him.

"Would you mind telling me all that happened from the time you opened your eyes and said, 'Hello, David!' until you went under ether four hours later?"

"You thought I didn't *know*! So that's why you've never spoken of it!"

"Please, dear—I've got to be sure!"

Speaking still more quietly than he had done, she began to go over the events of the night. She seemed to remember, with perfect distinctness, everything that had passed between them. She had asked him if he had forgiven her, he had answered—she had asked whether there was a chance that she might get well, he had said—she had made a will, had allowed him to examine her, had had more morphia——

"Yes?" David found the monosyllable almost impossible to articulate.

"I asked for the Sacraments. I asked you to—marry me, if you still cared. You spoke to grand'mère and the curé and the doctor and monsieur l'avocat. He drew up a contract, performed a civil ceremony—then the curé *really* married us. I told you where my mother's wedding ring was, in my chest of drawers. Afterwards you asked me to let you put it back until I was better. We both knew I probably never would be better—you called me darling, you kissed me once—David, you are not *sorry*?"

She slid from the bed, and walked, trembling, all over, to where he stood, with arms folded, looking out of the window. He caught her up.

"Jacqueline, what are you doing?" He carried her back to the bed, covered her with hands that were shaking no less than hers, tried, unsteadily, to laugh and made a failure of it, "You mustn't start walking off like that when you haven't had your feet to the ground in months . . . *Sorry!* But you see, I thought, we all thought—you might not realize what you were doing——"

"And if I hadn't?"

"Oh, my dear! Of course, we'd never have told you! Don't you think I know that I forfeited all my right to— to even think of you, five years ago? And the others are true as steel, no one else has guessed anything except, of course, that they know we knew each other before——"

"But I *did* know. I wanted——"

"You did then. What about now?"

There was a long silence. David set his teeth and locked his hands behind him.

"Because," he went on at last, "of course a marriage like that is all right—solid as the rock of Gibraltar—there's not a court on earth that would question it, unless——"

"Unless——?"

"Unless you *wanted* it questioned. But if you do, you ought to know—I ought to tell you—that done the way it was—when you were partly unconscious, could claim that you were anyway—and never—and only—nominal—would be the easiest thing on earth to annul."

The word was out at last. He bowed his head and waited. At last Jacqueline spoke to him. "I thought, of course, I was dying, or I wouldn't have asked," she whispered, "but just the same I—I don't want it—annulled—unless—you do. I didn't know it could be—I've been worrying for fear you—that's what I was crying for when you came in. You see, it's so long, and you never mentioned it and—but if you've been satisfied and—and happy so far—if you think you can go on being satisfied and—happy . . . You've given up your home and your friends and your profession and tied yourself to a girl who may be an invalid for years, who isn't giving you anything in return——"

"You don't seem to realize," he broke in, "that it's an hourly miracle to me that you don't hate me so that you can't bear the sight of me!"

He groped his way over to the little chest, half blinded by emotion, and opened the top drawer, rummaging among the soft, scented things there until he found the tiny gold band that he sought.

"You're sure?" he asked again, dropping on his knees.

When he spoke again, his voice was entirely cheerful and steady and matter-of-fact.

"We're going to tell everybody now," he said. "They must have been doing an awful lot of wondering, mustn't they? Though they didn't suspect a secret wedding, it must have been plain as the nose on your face that we weren't a common or garden variety of patient and doctor. Tomorrow morning I'm going in to fetch Susie, and stop at the château and pick up the Marquis, and bring 'em both here to see you, and we'll have a good laugh all around. And you can try fancy stunts walking around the room, and as soon as you can wobble around as well as a year-old kid, you and I and a good maid are going to Nice. Miss Houston's perfectly right. That's where you ought to be for the present, though the idea doesn't seem to appeal to you. We'll have a good time, see if we don't! I'm not always so solemn and stupid as I've been these last three months, but you certainly did have me scared stiff, for a while! But you're coming out as fine as silk now—

invalid for life, nothing! In the spring we can go to Italy
—I never have, and I'd like to, a lot, and when it's really
warm, we'll come back here, if this is where you're happiest. Do you suppose monsieur le médecin would take
me for a partner? I'd have the time of my life practising
in Fleursy!"

He smoothed the upper sheet over the blankets, tucked
them in tightly, bent over and kissed her cheek.

"I'm going to call Sœur Célestine now to 'fix you up,'"
he said, "and go forth and spread the news. Good-night,
sweetheart."

Four hours later, before starting to bed himself, he went
in again, fearing that she might be wakeful; but she was
sleeping quietly, lying on her side, her soft hair tumbled
over the pillow, her left arm thrown out over the counter-
pane. Her wedding ring gleamed in the light of the little
night lamp that he carried. He stood looking at her for a
few minutes, his heart overflowing with ineffable thanksgiving and tenderness. Then he closed the door gently
behind him and left her.

CHAPTER VI

THE TRUCE

THE following day, after Susie and the Marquis had been
brought to see Jacqueline, and the "good laugh all around"
had taken place, David announced his intention of taking
his sister back to the boarding school, and then setting out
for Nice on the night train without returning to Fleursy.

"And as soon as I find a place fit for you to live in, and
get it fixed up according to my views of what is suitable
for you at present, Miss Houston can bring you down; I'll
have a maid—two or three of 'em—waiting for you there.
Wouldn't you rather have a villa, in the suburbs, than go
to a hotel? Of course you would! Well, I'll write you
every day how I am getting along with my house hunting,
and you can write me every day how far you can walk,
without trying any sudden spurts, of course, and we both

171

ought to find the mails fairly interesting!"

He left her, gaily, without having seen her alone for a single minute. Susie, after they had dropped the Marquis at the château, took him to task.

"You *are* the biggest fool I ever saw in my life," she said scathingly. "Jacqueline looked good enough to eat alive—she's ever, ever so much prettier than I had any idea she'd be—and you kissed her as if she was a kid with a dirty face whose nose needed wiping—what a way to say good-bye to a bride! Why, Harry——"

"Do you want me to act as if I'd sat down on a stove? Jacqueline doesn't want to be treated like—like a regular bride. She's been too unhappy, and she's been too sick. I don't want to—upset her—I want to *do* things for her."

"Oh, glory!" ejaculated Susie. "I never heard that it upset a girl to have a feller she'd been crazy over for more'n ten years who had just got around to marry her act a little affectionate! First you thought you weren't good enough for her, and you stewed around for five years over that; and then you thought she wasn't good enough for you, and you more than stewed for five years over *that*. And then you went right up in the air, and made up your mind that you was a regular Judas Iscariot and she was a sort of holy Saint Agnes, and—no, I'm not sacrilegious either, I've got some sense. Talk about sitting on stoves! Harry wasn't half so unsettled as you are. He never worried a mite about being worthy or unworthy, and neither did Hattie. They quarrelled some, and always have, but in the main they take considerable comfort out of life together. They kept company for quite a spell, and Hattie had him on edge part of the time whether he would get her, but deep down he liked her a sight better for it than he would have if she'd acted like she wanted to snap him right up for fear she'd never get another chance. And by and by they got married, and every one was pleased about it, and they went to Niagara Falls on their wedding trip. They then came home, and settled down, and after a while they had a baby. That's the way most every one in Hamstead does."

"Well, it isn't always as simple as that," said David, choking with laughter.

"No, I should judge it wasn't from some of the books I read at the Graingers' during Christmas vacation. Such goings on! Miss Simms, our dressmaker, could never keep up with 'em, and even ma, in the post-office like she was, most of the time, would have had hard work. I don't wonder chaperons got thought of—not that I can see they make much *difference*! Looks to me as if when any one *makes up their mind* to cut up, they do it, chaperons or no chaperons——"

"Well, when you have a love affair, try to strike a happy medium——"

"Hoo! I'm not figuring on getting married at all—I've told you so more'n a dozen times! The Marquis is real nice, isn't he? He said he thought likely his mother would be in to see me some day——"

David left her and took his train, feeling as if he had had a cold shower and a good rub-down after a sleepless night. True to his word, he wrote to Jacqueline every day during the next fortnight, reporting the progress of his "house hunting." He had found a furnished villa which he thought would do, so he had hired it for four months— they could keep it longer if they liked, but he thought by that time it would be too hot to stay in Nice. It overlooked the sea, it had a big garden, there was an upstairs balcony off the room that was going to be hers—she could sit there a lot, or even sleep there if she wanted to. The plumbing didn't suit him, but he was having that fixed, it would be all right soon. He had engaged two men, one for outside, one for inside, a cook, and a personal maid, named Jeanne, who seemed a very good sort indeed, for her—he thought they ought to be able to do the work, but if they couldn't it would be easy to get more. He was awfully stupid about buying linen and such things, but they'd go shopping together and get more as soon as she felt like it— he'd laid in enough to start with. He was delighted to hear she was getting along so fast—he had felt quite sure she would—would she please climb into her clothes, just to see how they felt, and take them off again in fifteen minutes? She was to kiss Mère Thérèse—and any one else she thought would like it—for him, and he was, as ever, David.

It was mid-January when Jacqueline joined him. He met her at the station with a motor ambulance, and promptly relieved Miss Houston of her charge, telling her with a grin to go and try her luck at Monte Carlo before she started away, and almost wringing her hand off as he said good-bye and thanked her for all she had done. Nevertheless, he did not seem especially broken-hearted at her departure—in fact, Jacqueline thought she had never seen him in such good spirits. When they reached the villa he picked her up and carried her over the stairs as easily as if she had been a baby and dropped her on the middle of a great mahogany bed covered with snowy, embroidered linen and a rose-coloured down puff, and stood over her, laughing a little anxiously.

"Do you like it?" he asked her, flushing like a schoolboy.

"*Like it!* Oh, David, what a perfect room!"

It was, indeed—soft rugs were scattered over a bare, polished floor, long windows, draped with snowy, frilly curtains under pink silk ones, were flung wide open, looking out to the sea, a rose-coloured couch stood beside them. On the hearth a bright fire was burning, in spite of the mildness of the day; the dressing table was covered with silver brushes and boxes and cut-glass bottles filled with toilet water. On the bedside table were a shaded reading-lamp, and two or three uncut crisp magazines. And everywhere were flowers—roses and lilies and violets in bowls and tall slim vases.

"Like it!" she said again. "*Oh, David!*"

"Well, in a day or two I'll show you the rest of the house. I think you can walk, if I put my arm around you, but if you can't, I can carry you, though you are a little fatter already—good for you! Now I'll send Jeanne to help you undress, and when you are ready, sing out—I'm coming in to have tea with you."

She was, as he had known she inevitably must be, completely exhausted, and something besides tea, though she did not see it, went into the dainty china cup which he handed her a few minutes later. She did not realize, either, when the pretty tea-service had been removed by the capable Jeanne, and he sat down beside her, that his fingers were feeling her wrist, anxiously, all the time that he seemed to be nonchalantly holding her hand. She only knew that he looked boyish and eager and altogether adorable, with his white teeth gleaming and his black head thrown back, and his slim, long, graceful body stretched out in a big willow chair, while he talked to her. . . . And then she seemed to be getting drowsy . . . and then, suddenly, she opened her eyes again—and mid-morning sunshine was flooding the room, and Jeanne was moving noiselessly about bringing in more flowers.

The first few days were very quiet. She walked as far as the glistening bathroom, revelled in the deep tub of water into which Jeanne had emptied fragrant salts; then in the afternoon, to the couch by the window, had her tea there, stepped out on the balcony, a cloak thrown over her négligé, to see the early stars come out in the dark blue sky over the dark blue sea—and then came more long, dreamless nights, more peaceful wakings to another day. But after the first week she explored the whole house. The villa was cheerful and airy and sunny, but it was simple and unpretentious. David had bought such extra furnishings as he thought would make it more comfortable and attractive, but he had spent no great amount of money. Downstairs there were two living-rooms, opening into each other, with a loggia facing the sea leading from them, a little dining-room, and the kitchen quarters. Upstairs, opening from Jacqueline's room, was a tiny one where Jeanne was installed, the bathroom, and a little alcove which David had fitted up as a chapel. Beyond, another good-sized chamber, which he said they " would fill with Susie during her Easter vacation," and his own, of which Jacqueline made fun, saying it looked exactly like the one he had had years ago in the big barn—a big desk with a clutter of books and papers, a narrow iron bed with a honeycomb spread, a chest of drawers, one straight-backed chair. He laughed.

" My bedrooms always look like that," he said. " The one I had in college did, too. It's no matter where I am— some people's do, haven't you noticed it? But the rest of the house is nice, isn't it?"

"Nice? Oh, *David*!" He loved, in those days, to hear hear her say, "Oh, David,"—"How did you happen to think of the chapel?"

"I tried to think of everything that would be likely to please you—is there anything——"

There was nothing, she said, that he hadn't thought of, that he didn't keep thinking of. Sometimes he left her, and went into Nice on further shopping excursions, began to bring her home little personal gifts—a box of candy, a new book, a bit of lace; and finding that these trifles seemed to be received with an enthusiasm quite out of proportion to their value, he ventured on more costly presents —a carved fan, a pendant of semi-precious stones, and finally appeared with a big box, from which he shook free of tissue paper, a crisp, pink, frilly dress.

"I saw it in a window, and it looked to me so much like the one that you wore at my graduation that I went in and bought it. Do you think it is pretty—do you suppose it will fit? Do try it on, and come down to dinner in it if it does—and after dinner I'm going to take you out for a little ride—oh, yes, you are plenty well enough—and there's such a moon—you can't half see it from the loggia—and it's warm as—as——"

He took her for rides—a little longer one each day—he read aloud, he played the piano with stumbling untaught fingers—in fact, there was hardly a minute all day that he was not doing something for her, and yet, as she grew stronger, David felt that in spite of his constant devotion, she needed more people about her, a wider outlook, the gayer atmosphere that some of her old friends could give her. His feelings were therefore those of the startled gratitude that usually comes with an unexpected answer to prayer, when one day, as he was coming out of a jewellery shop in Nice, he saw Freddy Lambert looking in the window. Freddy hailed him cordially, and shook him by the hand.

"Who'd ever have thought of seeing you here!" he exclaimed, "though of course, every one gravitates to Nice sooner or later. You didn't know, did you, that Rose Gray and I were married about two years ago—we're stopping at the Grand. And now you and Jacqueline, after all—I'm darned glad—always felt that someway things *ought* to come right even if that fuss wasn't explained——" he checked himself, blushing. "Excuse me—I'm always putting my foot in it. How is she?"

"Thank you; she's getting better—but she's been very ill——"

"I didn't know—I'm no end sorry! Would it be prying into things too much if I asked—how it all came about—your getting married, I mean? None of us had heard a word from her since her grandfather's death, and then, as suddenly as bombs, came little notes from a place called Fleursy, saying she had married you—they weren't much more communicative than regular announcements would have been. Shall we walk along a little way together?"

"We have a villa not far out—won't you come back to tea with us? Jacqueline would be so glad to see you, and she can tell you what there is to tell—there really isn't much——"

But Jacqueline, though courteously surprised and cordial, did not show the overwhelming delight at the sight of her old friend that David had expected. She was glad that he and Rose had married, it was a happy coincidence that they should all have come to Nice at the same time. How soon would he bring Rose to see her? How nice that there was a little Freddy—she adored babies, the baby must come to call, too. Would he have lemon, or cream, and how many lumps of sugar? Her account of her own marriage nonplussed David.

"What is there so extraordinary about it? You've heard, by this time, I suppose, what the trouble was in the beginning? No? Well, I'll tell you some other time, then, if you want to hear, but what does it matter? Don't you and Rose ever quarrel? Of course you do! But David and I made up, like everybody else, and I wasn't well, and there didn't seem to be any reason why we should wait any longer—I've been living with my French grandmother—my mother's mother, you know—for several years, so we were married at her house, yes, very quietly. I suppose I might have written more details, to Lady Thornington, anyway, but I've been rather apathetic, and besides, I've felt perhaps she hadn't been quite fair to David. But I'll write her—now. David's been studying with Norchais in Paris, so we were quite near each other, you see. David, I think Freddy would eat another cake."

David drove Freddy back to town, finished his errands, and drove back somewhat thoughtfully. On his return he found Jacqueline still on the loggia, engaged in fastening a bunch of white violets on the lace of her dress with a bar-pin he had recently given her.

"You magnificent liar!" he exclaimed, kissing her cheek, and putting his arm around her. "Do you expect to go to heaven after all that?"

"Why not?" she laughed back. "Anyway, it was all perfectly true—as far as it went."

"Oh, yes, as far as it went—and it went a darned short distance! Where did you get those flowers? More callers?"

"Yes, you'd never guess—this is a day of surprises, and mine is worth two of yours—Bobby Hutchinson came while you were gone——"

David gave a whoop of joy.

"*Bobby!* Where on earth did he drop from?"

"Paris—he had been to see Susie. She told the principal of the boarding-school that he was her uncle, and Bobby said he didn't contradict her—can't you just hear him? He said they had the time of their life together!"

"For a young lady who doesn't ever intend to get married, Susie is making quite rapid progress," said Susie's brother, dryly. "But how does he happen to be on this side of the Atlantic at all?"

"He said he felt he needed a vacation, and decided that he might as well come to see us as to go anywhere."

"Rather better, I should say. I hope you didn't tell any fancy fibs to him? It really wouldn't be worth the trouble!"

"So I should judge. He said your letters had been few, far between and brief, which was one reason he wanted to look you up—but just the same I felt as if he 'knew all the facts, in ten scenes and seven acts,' as a musical comedy I used to enjoy put it. Besides, I didn't have much chance to speak, anyway—he did most of the talking himself—

doesn't he always? I haven't seen him since he was nineteen or twenty, but he seemed to me exactly the same as he did then—shrewd and witty, and oh, so kind! He—he had a good deal to say about you."

"Any very dark disclosures?"

"On the contrary. I knew you were wonderful, of course, but not *how wonderful. Oh, David!* Why didn't you tell me about the Edgar L.—and all the rest of it?"

"Look here, what stuff has Bobby been putting into your head? He's got you worrying, making you think I want to go back"—and seeing the brimming tears in her eyes, he went on savagely, "I'll fix him, if he interferes with my patient! What do you think I care about that stuffy old hospital? I wouldn't mind if I never saw it again. I'm having the first good loaf I ever had in my life, and if you knew what that meant you'd realize that it seems pretty satisfactory to me to lie on a loggia and bask in the sun instead of messing 'round an operating room all day and half the night."

"They need you back; they *want* you——"

"Well, they can go on wanting—do 'em good. They weren't so darned enthusiastic about me a year or so ago. Just wait until I get my hands on Bobby."

"I've asked him to come to dinner tomorrow night."

So Bobby came, and, in spite of David's threats, was made very welcome by both of them, and they sat on the loggia, talking of pleasant, unimportant things, until Jacqueline's early bed time. But when she had left them, and the two men were alone again, Bobby slid down a few inches further in his chair, and began, in his usual lazy drawl.

"Well, you're a wonder, and then some. She's as graphic an advertisement to your genius as the picture of a Mellin's Food baby."

"You upset her yesterday——"

"Shucks! I set her thinking, a little, about several things. Who's pampering patients now? It's time you came back. She's getting well so fast she ought to be—mowing lawns, too. You are not going to keep up this invalid-doctor rôle for ever, are you?"

"No—we seem to have rather passed that already."

."Or this breezy, friendly, elder brother, distant-cousin, attitude?"

David got up, with something between a sob and a laugh. "Don't, Bobby," he said a little uncertainly. "Don't—you're uncanny. You guess too darned much."

"I guess you're having pretty rough sledding just now. As long as your passion was overcome with your *compassion*, so to speak——"

"You've told me once that I didn't have either in my make-up——"

"I've told you a number of lies, in a good cause, first and last. Of course, you've got 'em both, and of course you've had a hell of a time between 'em, and gritted your teeth, and said to the former, 'avaunt, clear out, git,' and you deserve a gold medal and a crown of glory, and all the rest of the usual heroic paraphernalia for having done it. But I'm hanged if I see why now you shouldn't be rewarded according to your merits."

"I'm rewarded far beyond my merits——"

"You're not—your merits are greater'n you give 'em credit for being. And Lord! Don't you think I can see how you feel? I've—I've felt that way myself, you know."

"I know," said David huskily, "but you see, I feel besides that—I forfeited my—reward five years ago. I've no right to claim it now, or even to ask for it—just because a turn of chance has happened to put it in my reach."

"Well, you did forfeit it then—but you sure have redeemed it since. I'll add another perfectly truthful statement to the ones I made that eventful day when we discussed this matter before—you may be hasty and crude and stupid, et cetera, et cetera, et cetera, but at that there isn't one woman in a thousand that gets a man that's fit to black your shoes, and Jacqueline knows it, and always has! When I told you to wait—and wait—and wait——" he added, speaking more lightly, as David still did not turn around, "I didn't mean until you were both in your grave! But you may know best. I'm certainly not going to risk trying to upset your apple cart, after you've driven it with pretty steady hand and clear eye through all kinds of heavy traffic. What I really came here for wasn't to meddle. It was to pour out a few griefs myself. . . . Helena and Roger are married at last."

David turned quickly. "Say, Bobby——"

"Yes, I knew I could count on you to feel that way about it. I didn't think I was going to be such a fool over it—but I found I wanted to get away for a while. She's awfully happy—gone to live on a flower ranch in California—they'll have bread and butter, and perhaps a little more than that, but I doubt it. I told Susie—she was greatly interested—you know she took a tremendous shine to Helena."

"Would you mind telling me what she said? Susie's comments on love-affairs are apt to be entertaining. Perhaps she regaled you with Harry and Hattie——"

"Oh, yes. But she said I was cut out for a bachelor, same as she was for an old maid."

"Just about the same, I should think."

"And—and several other things. If you can get her down here for her Easter vacation, she and I are going to paint the town as red—as her cheeks. Gosh, but she's a healthy looking kid! . . . By the way, I see you've got one of those new cars with all sorts of fancy attachments—were these included in the original price or did you pay extra for them?"

"No, everything included, and the lights work finely; but the best part of it is——" David was off. For the next half-hour automobiles, undisputed, held the stage.

"I've got to go home," exclaimed Bobby, as they both started, almost guiltily, when the clock struck midnight, for medicine had succeeded motors as a topic of conversation. "Won't you and Jacqueline come in to dine with me tomorrow night, and go to the opera with me?"

"She hasn't been anywhere yet except to church——"

Bobby threw up his hands—"Have you *asked* her?"

David laughed. "All right, *you're right!* We'll come."

So the first little dinner was followed by another, and then another, and still more. Freddy and Rose joined the circle, other friends and acquaintances were discovered in the vicinity, or just far enough off to make motoring to find them in the new car a delight. Susie telegraphed that measles had broken out in the school, and that such pupils as possessed parents who were willing might go home until the quarantine was over, and appeared, in charge of an exhausted "chaperon," as soon as the return telegram saying that her relatives, including her "uncle," would be delighted to see her. There had been two young French officers on the train. They were most kind about helping her practise her French and buying fruit and chocolate at railway stations, and explaining military tactics—explanations which they would be glad to continue and enlarge upon at some future date, as they were to be in Nice for a fortnight, if Jacqueline would ask them to call.

"Did you ask them?"

"Oh, yes, but these foreigners are so queer. Now none of the fellows at home ever dreamed of waiting for Hattie to ask them over. What *are* you all roaring at?"

The villa began to be invaded for dinner, for tea, even—by Bobby—before breakfast if he felt like it. The Mercedes vanished more than once before David knew it was gone; and when David informed Susie that she was too young to dream of going to the Mi-Carême Ball, he found he had insurrection on his hands. Jacqueline not only upheld her sister-in-law, she announced her intention of going, too.

"Just for a few dances—wouldn't you like it, David?"

"Who with?" asked David, more expressively than grammatically.

"Well, say three out of twelve with me."

He grunted, smiling in spite of himself. "The prospect seems to hold some compensations. Are you just teasing for the kid, or do you really want to go yourself?"

"Of course I want to go. Don't you think it would be fun to dance together?"

The days of négligés had long since passed. Great boxes filled with pretty dresses had been coming out from Nice steadily during these last few weeks, and Jacqueline had on one of the prettiest of them now—a crisp, embroidered pale blue linen with a round neck and elbow sleeves, that fitted her like a glove. She was standing by a wicker table, her arms lifted, arranging long sprays of pink blossoms in a clear green glass vase. She turned from her task, drying

182

her damp fingers on her handkerchief. "We might try one together now, just to see. Play something for us, Susie." She placed her hand on his shoulder, then drew back. "David, how white you are. What's the matter—are you ill,"

"Oh, *no*! You're ready?"

He had known that she would dance beautifully. Still, he had not been prepared for such absolute perfection of rhythm and unity—it seemed, as they moved, hardly possible that they were two persons. Involuntarily, as Susie stopped playing, he pulled Jacqueline closer to him instead of releasing her.

"I want more," he whispered.

"Why, of course! I told you it would be fun—perhaps you would like four at the ball, instead of three? Go on, Susie——"

There was, after that, no question about the ball, except that he exacted a promise from her that she would leave Susie in Rose's charge at midnight, and come home then, and that she would stay in bed all the next day if she were tired. If she were not, they could go to others, after that. Susie, thereafter, did her own dictating. She spent, without a murmur of disapproval from her brother, a thousand francs on a dress of scarlet tulle to wear to it, which was quite evidently as fragile as it was exquisite. Jacqueline bought her a pearl necklace. Bobby, the two young officers, and several other swains whom she had by this time added to her collection, all sent her flowers. Jacqueline was delayed with her own dressing because she and Jeanne both gave so much attention to the child. At ten o'clock David found her, still in the sketchiest of toilets, sitting on Susie's bed superintending the finishing touches.

"Oh, *David*!" she cried, as he entered. "How handsome you are—how becoming those clothes are!"

"Allow me to return the compliment—still—is that as far along as you are? Or were you intending to go to the ball that way? If not——" He took out his watch expressively.

"If you were Harry," interposed Susie, "you'd *know* how far along she was. He'd be hooking up Hattie's back long before this, while she squeezed in her waist at the sides with her fingers. She's grown fatter since the baby came, and she hasn't had any time to let things out. No wonder you can't keep track of Jacqueline, half way down the hall from her! If you and she and a baby all slept in one room that wasn't large enough to hold anything but a big bed and a little bureau, same as Harry and Hattie do——"

Jacqueline sprang up, regardless of scanty draperies, and threw her arm around Susie's neck, stopping her mouth with a kiss.

"You run along down to Bobby," she said a little breathlessly, "and don't tell him too many intimate Hamstead histories. I'm not very fat, you see, and with Jeanne here on purpose to help, it seems rather foolish to make David do up hooks, doesn't it? But if he will come to my room in twenty minutes—I promise not to be any longer than that—I'd like to have him tell me how he likes my dress before the rest of you see it. I only hope it'll be half so pretty and becoming as yours, my dear."

David paced up and down the little corridor, his heart pounding, the blood surging in his head. What had become of the self-control he was so sure of? Once he had sent Jacqueline away from him, because he knew that he was only an undisciplined boy, that she would not be safe with him because he had none. This time he had ventured to keep her near him because he thought he had so much. Was he wrong, after all? Was it only the memory of that brief dance the other day, the prospect of longer ones this evening, that made him throb all over until he ached? Or was it Susie's thoughtless speech that sent insistent, white-hot questions through his brain—if he were like Harry—well, why *not*? What was there to prevent—nothing, nothing in God's world—except the tardy and repentant humility of his own estimate of himself, his worth, his deserving; the fear of shattering Jacqueline's new-found faith, and confidence, and joy in life by any act—yes, even any word—that would seem to her still supersensitive and easily startled senses ungentle or unchivalrous—the thought of the phrase she herself had used, "until you love her
184

well enough to serve and not——"

The door opened, and Jeanne came out. "*Madame vous attend, monsieur*," she said quietly, and went down the stairs with Jacqueline's cloak over her arm. David nodded, and passed her without speaking.

He had sent Jacqueline a bouquet of white orchids and lilies of the valley, and, as he entered the room, she was standing in front of her long mirror, lifting them from their tissue-paper wrappings. A robe of silver and white brocade fell in unbroken line from her shoulders to the ground; a scarf of white tulle, which she had thrown over her bare shoulders, had caught on a jewelled pin in her hair, and partially covered her head as well. David thought, suddenly, of the fabric of which the great dress-maker had told him, saw that the misty gauze enveloped her like a veil——

"Oh, you lovely thing!" he exclaimed, almost involuntarily. "Jacqueline—my dear——"

"Is it really all right?"

"*All right!*"

"I mean—you don't think it is—too low, or anything, do you?"

There was a little catch of wistfulness, almost of anxiety, in her voice.

He flushed. "No, darling, of course I don't. What ornaments are you going to wear?"

"All my jewellery of any value is in England. It does need something—beautiful, doesn't it? Rubies and diamonds, for instance."

There was no premeditation in the words. But as soon as she had spoken them she flushed too, and tried to catch them back. If she had hurt him, however, David gave no sign of it.

"You'll need your jewellery, now that you are going out so much again—I can easily run over to London and get it for you. But meanwhile—wait a minute."

He left her, hurriedly, and came back the next moment with a velvet box in his hand.

"I bought this for you some time ago," he said, hesitating a little, "the day I met Freddy, in fact. I have been waiting for the right time to ask you if you would wear it —and the time seems to have come." He handed her the box, gravely, and watched her, almost breathlessly, while she opened it. Inside lay a necklace—a necklace of rubies and diamonds, worth a queen's ransom, sparkling and glittering and glowing on the soft satin. Instinctively Jacqueline saw what this represented, though David, perhaps, had hardly been conscious of it—the sacrifice that the ring had meant multiplied a thousand times, not brought, as that had been, from a victor to a captive, but as a subject to a sovereign—almost as a worshipper to a sacred shrine. She came closer to him, trembling with emotion, half-blinded with tears.

"Aren't you going to put it on yourself?" she asked— "the way—you did the ring?"

CHAPTER VII

VICTORY

DAVID's room was dark, and, groping his way to his desk, he lighted the reading lamp, and flung himself into the chair. It was one o'clock in the morning. Jacqueline, flushed and lovely and laughing, but true to her agreement, had left the ball promptly at twelve—"just like Cinderella," she said merrily, "only my glory is all *real*," and had come home with him and gone to bed, insisting she was "not the least bit tired"; Bobby had not yet brought Susie home, and, from indications when David departed, he felt that it might be some time before he did. The house was silent, almost hushed. . . .

The desk was littered with a collection hardly less miscellaneous than that which had lain on the one in Hamstead, many years before. David pushed aside a few letters, some receipted bills, and several medical journals and pamphlets, and opened a volume of many closely printed pages, with somewhat sinister illustrations, bearing on its back the forbidding title, "Aseptic Surgery as Applied to the Major Operations." He read for some time, at first with deep interest—for the book was a new one, which

186

Bobby had just called to his attention, and written by one of the "big men"—and making notes as he read. But after a time his attention wavered, and he tossed it aside to pick up something more suited to the hour and his mood. He took the first thing that came to his hand. It was a book of Jacqueline's which he had been reading aloud to her, and had carried into his room by mistake, and which opened of its own accord, at a page of verses. Something in the first two lines arrested his attention. Instead of laying the volume down again, he read them through.

> "For lo! thy law is passed
> That this my love should manifestly be:
> To serve and honour thee.
> And so I do; and my delight is full
> Accepted as the servant of thy rule."

> "Lady, since I first conceived
> Thy pleasurable aspect in my heart,
> My life has been apart
> In shining brightness and the place of truth,
> Which, till that time, good sooth,
> Groped among shadows in a darkened place;
> Where many hours and days
> It hardly ever had remembered good.
> But now my servitude
> Is thine, and I am full of joy and rest—
> A man from a wild beast
> Thou madest me, since for thy love I lived."

He closed the book, and laid it from him, picking up another, and began to turn the leaves, with trembling, irresolute fingers; then, suddenly, it dropped, unheeded on the floor, and bowing his head on his hands, he wept like a little child.

. . . .

He was startled by a slight rustle, and looked up quickly.

Jacqueline was standing beside him. She had on a soft white dressing-gown that hung loose from the shoulders like the one she had worn so many years before. Her neck and arms were bare. Her hair, still damp about the temples from her bath, hung like a veil of bronze around her. A delicate perfume enveloped her in its fragrant mist.

"What is it?" he cried, mastering himself quickly—"You did get overtired—you're not sleeping—Oh, I'm so sorry!"

"No, no," she said, detaining him as he tried to rise, "I never felt better in my life. But history repeats itself. I felt just as I used to when I ran away and came to your little room in the barn—which as I've said before, wasn't very different from this—I couldn't seem to wait another minute to find out what you were doing, to talk to you——"

She bent over the desk and glanced at the titles of the books and papers, straightening out the chaos as she did so.

"Is this the way you spend your nights?" she asked gravely. "I take up all your days—and you miss it as much as that?"

"Oh, no," he protested, "I don't miss it at all. Sometimes, when I don't feel sleepy, I read a little, that's all."

She did not answer at once, continuing to straighten the mass before her.

"All this makes me realize," she said at last, when order was completely restored, "that it is almost time we went home. We've had a lovely holiday, and we've given Susie one. But we must send her back to school pretty soon. Bobby's half-serious, and half-earnest, and still so badly hurt over Helena that I'm glad we've been able to help him over this hard place. But just the same, she's growing up so fast now—she's changed so almost unbelievably in just a few months—that I think he ought to wait now until she's grown up a good deal *more* before he sees much of her again. And when she's back in Paris, we'll go to Italy in Mercedes—and then—we must go home. I'm well—gloriously well—again. We're—just throwing part of the most beautiful time of our lives away if we keep on pretending I'm not."

"Home!" echoed David, stupidly. "You mean to Fleursy? Wait until you are a little stronger, dear—you *are* well, but you haven't much endurance yet, and you work so hard there."

"No," she said slowly, "I wasn't thinking of Fleursy. Of course, I want to go back there for a week or so, to make sure that everything is all right, and say good-bye to grand'mère—and I hope we'll always be able to go there often. But, when I said home, I meant Boston."

He sprang to his feet in spite of her this time "What do you mean?" he asked, his voice shaking.

She dropped her eyes, and stood silent for a moment. then raised them to his face, and looked straight into his.

"David," she said softly, "can you—look back at me— the way I'm looking at you—and tell me that you don't want to get back to work—to Boston, and the Edgar L.— and everything that stands—for your career?"

He hesitated, but the unwavering truthfulness of a life time was too strong for him.

"Yes," he said at last, "I can. I am done with the Edgar L.—and Boston—and all that they stood for in my career. I am done with the career itself—the career I meant to have. But——"

"Yes?" asked Jacqueline.

"For a while," he went on, hesitating, "I honestly didn't care if I never went back to America at all. I was so thankful to find you, to be with you again, to know that you didn't hate me, that nothing else mattered. But I wasn't just ambitious in my work. I loved it, too I suppose I shall always love it. The only difference that way is that I don't love it *best* any more. And I feel now. some way, as if I'd do better in it than I ever did before—as if I wouldn't be merely a ' clever mechanician ' as Bobby called me—quite rightly. Because you've taught me so many things. these last months. my dear. that I didn't know before. About success."

"Yes."

"It's—it's service. There's no trade that isn't—a trust."

"Yes, David."

"It doesn't matter much where or how. I mean, for one person it's one kind, in one place For another, it's another kind, in another place. I've known, of course, for a long time, that Dr. Ross was a ' successful man. that he had a wonderful ' career.' That was perfectly obvious Any one could see that. It's you that have taught me the things— that aren't so obvious, but that really matter more. For I

189

didn't realize until I went to stay in Fleursy that my—mother—was a ' successful ' woman—that she'd had a wonderful ' career ' too. And it's—it's marvellous for a man who—hasn't loved his mother—who's felt that he'd missed something great and sweet and precious—to suddenly learn that she was—great."

" Yes," said Jacqueline, a third time.

" And now—I seem to have a lot of new power stored up —with all this new knowledge. Power—that ought to be *used*—not folded in a napkin like the talent in the Bible! But I don't want to use it in Boston. That, of course, is where Bobby ought to use his—where he can be most successful because he can serve most there—and Bobby has served—is serving all the time! He calls himself a ' stupid bungler.' It's I that have been that always!"

" No, never—never stupid, never a bungler. Just—mistaken, sometimes, or a little blind."

" Well. perhaps I'm blind and mistaken now—I—I haven't as much self-confidence as I used to have. But the way I want to serve—the place I want to go . . . Oh, you wouldn't be willing! It wouldn't be fair to you!"

" But I *am* willing! I want to do what you want. I don't know where the place is, but that's where I'll be happiest. *David! Is it Hamstead?*"

" What made you think so?" he asked breathlessly.

" Because—because that's what I've been longing for, too! Only I supposed *you* wouldn't be willing! If I had died, you'd have built a hospital there—well, why shouldn't you build it if I'm *alive*—and let me help? And we'll make it everything that it *can* be made—not just what a ' clever mechanician ' would have made the Edgar L., but what your genius—and my love—can do for your work—and our home . . ."

" And," she went on, kindling, after a moment's pause, " it isn't just—just the hospital! I think we owe your father at least as much as we do my grandmother, don't you? That we must try hard, these next years, to make him think how truly we're his children, how much we love him. I want to see Sam and Leon, too, and Harry and Hattie and the baby." She stopped, laughing, at the memory of the anecdotes that the last names brought back to her. "I want to see Sheldon and old Miss Manning. I want to open the Big House, to keep it open always, to feel that we aren't just 'summer people' but that we really *belong*, and make other people feel it too! I want to see if we can *help* Hamstead—just as we helped Fleursy—to see how much we can do for it. And that isn't all! Think how much Hamstead can help—has helped us!

"Are there any places in the world," she continued, her voice trembling a little, "that produce finer men and women than those little villages in the Connecticut Valley? Why, David, I'd rather have married a man that was born on a tiny farm 'out back' than one who was born in a king's palace! I think there's something—the spirit of their ancestors, who settled the country, still surviving, or perhaps the country itself—that makes them what they are —that's made—that's made *you* what *you* are! We were both so wrong, so mistaken, when we were children, to underestimate it. Can't you shut your eyes now, and see the river and the mountains glowing in the sunshine, or white with snow, or shining under a harvest moon? Don't you want to go down the lane with the willows with me again? Don't you—want to go over the road to Wallace-town?"

She swayed toward him slightly. He caught her hand in his.

"Jacqueline," he said hoarsely, "don't—unless you really know what you're saying—can't you see—Oh, my darling, I have tried—just to serve—but I—I *want you*——"

"Do you know," she said, her eyes still holding his, "that in all these months that is the first time you've told me so? That you've never called me by my second name? That, until tonight, when you put my necklace on, you've never kissed me—really kissed me—since the night—you found me?"

"I beseech you——" he began, but she went on steadily. "Do you know, that you've never let me tell you, either, any of the things I've wanted to say? How freely I forgave you, long ago, if there should ever have been any question of forgiveness between us—everything that happened—five years ago? How well I see now—though it nearly killed me to lose you then—that we both had too much to learn to be happy together at that time? I think, now, we've—both learned it, don't you? You would have sacrificed your whole life to me, if I would have let you—and still you doubted whether I would pardon a trivial fault in return. You'd have gone on, for ever, like this . . . I couldn't wait any longer, David—I had to come and tell you how much I love you!"

"Jacqueline," he cried, "you must stop! It's only your boundless generosity, your everlasting mercy, that makes you talk like this. If I had been crucified for what I did, it would have been far less than I deserved!"

"And haven't you," she asked, "been crucified—more than once? The night you learned from Bobby—that I was not to blame? The night you—found me? And—to-night? Oh, my darling, you've been wonderful—but I've pitied you so!

"Did you really think," she said, as he turned his head away from her, without answering, "that I was so supremely selfish, even if I had not loved you with all my heart and soul—as to accept all that you were willing to give—and give you nothing in return?" She waited a full minute before he stirred. Then he dropped on his knees before her, laying his hot face against her soft, cool dress, and covering her hands with kisses.

"You dear saint——"

"No, no—not *that*——"

"What then?"

"Get up and look at me, and you will know——"

"My darling—*Désirée*——"

"It's—it's more than—that——"

He took her in his arms, the full glory of what she was trying to make him say breaking on him like a flood of golden light. He pressed his lips against hers, drawing her closer still.

"My wife," he whispered; "is that it?"

But this time he did not need an answer.

THE END